Praise for James Patterson's previous novels:

'Unputdownable. It will sell millions' *The Times*

'Packed with white-knuckled twists' *Daily Mail*

'Relish the inventive twists of the plot'
The Sunday Times

'A novel which makes for sleepless nights'
Daily Express

'Breakneck pacing and loop-the-loop plotting'
Publishers Weekly

'A magic hat-trick with the million-dollar-promo
thriller . . . Big warm feelings, usually foreign to
thrillers, coax laughter during times of high tension.
Reads like a dream' *Kirkus Reviews*

'A fast-paced, electric story that is utterly believable'
Booklist

'Ticks like a time bomb – full of threat and terror'
Los Angeles Times

'Abs͏͏͏ ͏͏͏ ͏͏ ͏͏ Bookseller

JAMES
PATTERSON
&
MICHAEL
LEDWIDGE

STEP ON A CRACK

headline

Copyright © 2007 James Patterson

The right of James Patterson to be identified as the Author of
the Work has been asserted by him in accordance with the
Copyright, Designs and Patents Act 1988.

First published in Great Britain in 2007 by
HEADLINE PUBLISHING GROUP

First published in paperback in Great Britain in 2008 by
HEADLINE PUBLISHING GROUP

12

Apart from any use permitted under UK copyright law,
this publication may only be reproduced, stored, or transmitted,
in any form, or by any means, with prior permission in writing of the
publishers or, in the case of reprographic production, in accordance
with the terms of licences issued by the Copyright Licensing Agency

All characters in this publication are fictitious and any resemblance
to real persons, living or dead, is purely coincidental.

ISBN 978 0 7553 3041 6

Typeset in Palatino Light by Palimpsest Book Production Limited,
Grangemouth, Stirlingshire

Printed and bound in Great Britain by Clays Ltd, St Ives plc

Headline's policy is to use papers that are natural, renewable and
recyclable products and made from wood grown in sustainable
forests. The logging and manufacturing processes are expected to
conform to the environmental regulations of the country of origin.

HEADLINE PUBLISHING GROUP
An Hachette Livre UK Company
338 Euston Road
London NW1 3BH

www.headline.co.uk
www.hachettelivre.co.uk

For Richie, Deirdre, and Sheilah.
And MaryEllen, Carole, and Teresa.

From Michael

———————————————

Dedicated to W and J and their four children
C, M, A, and N.
The book is also dedicated to the
Palm Beach Day Academy.

Also in appreciation of Manhattan College.

From James

'Step on a crack,
Break your mother's back.'

'Step on a crack, and you'll soon be eaten
By the bears that congregate at street corners,
Waiting for their lunch to walk by.'

—City sayings

THE LAST SUPPER

One

The back of the table captain's cream-colored evening jacket had just turned away when Stephen Hopkins leaned across the secluded corner booth and kissed his wife. Caroline closed her eyes, tasting the cold champagne he'd just sipped, then felt a tug as Stephen's hand caught one of the silk spaghetti straps of her Chanel gown.

'These puppies aren't exactly secured in this frock, if you haven't noticed,' she said as she came up for air. 'Keep playing around and we're going to have a serious wardrobe malfunction. How's my lipstick?'

'Delicious,' Stephen said, smiling like a bleeping movie star. Then he touched her thigh.

'You're past *fifty*,' Caroline said. 'Not fifteen.'

Having this much fun with your husband, Caroline thought, playfully twisting Stephen's hand away, had to be illegal. That their annual 'Christmas in New York' date got better every year was beyond her, but there you had it. Dinner here at L'Arène, probably the most elegant, most seductive French restaurant in New York City; a horse-and-buggy ride through Central Park; and then back to the Pierre's presidential suite. It had been their Christmas gift to themselves for the past four years. And every year it turned out to be more romantic than the last, more and more exquisite.

As if on cue, snow began falling outside the copper-trimmed windows of the restaurant, big silver flakes that hung in glittering cones from Madison Avenue's old-fashioned black-iron lampposts.

'If you could have anything this Christmas, what would it be?' Caroline asked suddenly.

Stephen raised his gold-tinged glass of Laurent-Perrier Grand Siècle Brut trying to come up with something funny.

'I wish . . . I wish . . .'

A stilling sadness extinguished the humor from his face as he stared into his flute.

'I wish this were hot chocolate.'

Caroline felt dizzy as her mouth opened and her breath left.

Many years ago, she and Stephen had been homesick scholarship freshmen at Harvard, without enough money to make it home for Christmas. One morning they'd been the only two breakfast diners in cavernous

Annenberg Hall, and Stephen had sat down at her table. 'Just for a little warmth,' he'd said.

Soon they learned they were both planning to be poli-sci majors, and they hit it off immediately. In the Yard outside, in front of redbrick Hollis Hall, Caroline impulsively dropped to the ground and made a snow angel. Their faces almost touched when Stephen helped her up. Then she took a quick sip of the hot chocolate she'd smuggled out of the dining hall – so as not to kiss this boy she'd just met and somehow already cared about.

Caroline could still see Stephen as he had been, smiling in the bright, nickeled winter light. That lovely boy standing before her in Harvard Yard, clueless to the fact that he would marry her. Give her a beautiful daughter. Go on to become the president of the United States.

The question he'd asked as she'd lowered her cocoa mug thirty years before reverberated poignantly now in her ears, like crystal struck by shining silver: 'Does yours taste like champagne, too?'

Hot chocolate to champagne, Caroline thought, lifting her bubbling flute. Now champagne to hot chocolate. Two and a half decades of marriage come full circle.

What a life they'd had, she thought, savoring the moment. Lucky and worthwhile and . . .

'Excuse me, Mr President,' a voice whispered. 'I'm sorry. *Excuse me.*'

A pasty-looking blond man in a metallic-gray double-breasted suit stood ten feet in front of their booth. He was waving a menu and a pen. Henri, the maître d', arrived immediately. He assisted Steve Beplar, the Hopkinses' Secret Service agent, in trying to escort the intruder discreetly out of sight.

'Oh, I'm so sorry,' the man said to the Secret Service agent in a defeated voice. 'I just thought the president could sign my menu.'

'It's okay, Steve,' Stephen Hopkins said with a quick wave. He shrugged at his wife in apology.

Fame, Caroline thought, placing her champagne glass down on the immaculate linen. *Ain't it a bitch?*

'Could you make that out to my wife? Carla.' The pale man spoke over the Secret Service agent's wide shoulder.

'Carla's my wife!' the man said a little too loudly. 'Oh my God! I just said that, didn't I? I have the insane luck to run into the greatest president of the last century, and what do I do? Jesus, look, I'm blushing now. I have to say, you guys look terrific tonight. Especially you, Mrs Hopkins.'

'Merry Christmas to you, sir,' Stephen Hopkins said, smiling back as graciously as he could manage.

'Hope it was no bother,' the man said, the sheen of his suit flashing as he backed away, bowing.

'Bother?' Stephen Hopkins said, grinning at his wife after the man had departed. 'Now how could Carla's husband think that demolishing the most romantic moment of our lives was a bother?'

They were still laughing when a beaming waiter materialized out of the shadows, placed down their plates, and vanished. Caroline smiled at the avant-garde architecture of her terrine of foie gras as her husband topped off her champagne.

It's almost too beautiful to eat, Caroline thought, lifting her knife and fork. *Almost.*

The first bite was so ethereal that it took a few seconds for her to place the taste.

By then it was too late.

What felt like high-pressure superheated air instantly inflated Caroline Hopkins's lungs, throat, and face. Her eyeballs felt like they were going to pop by the time her scrolled silver fork fell from her lips and clattered against china.

'Oh my God, Caroline,' she heard Stephen say as he looked at her in horror. 'Steve! Help! Something's wrong with Caroline! She can't breathe.'

Two

*P*lease God, no. Don't let this happen. Don't!* Stephen Hopkins thought as he staggered to his feet. He was just opening his mouth to cry out again when Steve Beplar snatched the edge of the dining table and flung it out of the way.

Crystal and china exploded against the varnished hardwood floor as Agent Susan Wu, the next closest of their four-person security detail, pulled Mrs Hopkins from the booth seat. The female agent immediately probed Caroline's mouth with her finger to dislodge any food. Then she got behind her, a fist already under her rib cage as she began the Heimlich maneuver.

It was as if an ice-cold hand had reached into Stephen's chest. He watched helplessly as his wife's face turned from red to almost blackish purple.

'Stop. Wait!' he said. 'She's not choking. It's her allergy! She's allergic to peanuts. Her emergency adrenaline! The little pen thing she carries. Where's her bag?'

'It's in the car out front!' Agent Wu said. She bolted across the dining room and returned a moment later at a run. She had Caroline's bag!

Stephen Hopkins upended his wife's handbag onto the satin of the booth seat. 'It's not here!' he said, sending makeup and perfume flying.

Steve Beplar barked into his sleeve mike; then he scooped up the former First Lady in his arms as if she were a tired toddler.

'Time to get to a hospital, sir,' he said, moving toward the exit as everyone else in the restaurant stared in horror.

Moments later, in the rear of a speeding Police Interceptor Crown Victoria, Stephen Hopkins cradled his wife's head in his lap. Breath whistled weakly from her throat as if it were coming through a cocktail straw. He ached for his wife, watching her eyes tighten in severe pain.

A doctor and a gurney were already waiting out on the sidewalk when the sedan came to a curb-hopping stop out in front of the St Vincent's Midtown Hospital emergency room entrance on 52nd Street.

'You think it's an allergic reaction?' one of the doctors asked, taking Caroline's pulse as two attendants rushed her through the sliding glass doors on a stretcher.

'She's highly allergic to peanuts. Ever since she was a kid,' Stephen said, jogging at Caroline's other side. 'We told the kitchen at L'Arène. There must have been some mix-up.'

'She's in shock, sir,' the doctor said. He blocked the former president as Caroline was pushed through a HOSPITAL PERSONNEL ONLY side door. 'We're going to have to try to stabilize her. We'll do everything—'

Stephen Hopkins suddenly shoved the stunned doctor out of the way. 'I'm not leaving her side,' he said. 'Let's go. That's *an order.*'

They were already attaching an IV drip to Caroline's arm and an oxygen mask to her face when he entered the trauma room. He winced as they sliced her beautiful gown to the navel so they could attach the leads of the heart monitor.

The machine bleated out an awful, continuous beep when they flicked it on. Then a flat black line appeared on the scrolling red graph readout. A nurse immediately started CPR.

'Clear,' the doctor yelled, and put the electrified paddles to Caroline's chest.

Stephen watched Caroline's chest surge upward with a pulse, and then a new, gentle *bloop-bloop* started on the monitor. A sharp, glorious scratch spiked upward on the spooling readout. Then another.

One for every miraculous beat of Caroline Hopkins's heart.

Tears of gratitude had formed in Stephen's eyes – when the awful *beeeeeeeeeeep* returned.

The doctor tried several more times with the defibrillator, but the screeching monitor wouldn't change its grating one-note tune. The last thing the former president witnessed was another act of mercy by his loyal Secret Service.

Teary-eyed, Steve Beplar reached over and yanked the plug out of the yellow tile wall, halting the machine's evil shriek.

'I'm so sorry, sir. She's gone.'

Three

The pale, blond autograph seeker from L'Arène told the pathetic sonofabitch of a cabdriver to pull over on Ninth Avenue, a block north of St Vincent's Hospital. He stuffed a ten into the grimy divider slot and elbowed open the greasy door latch to avoid touching it. There were good reasons he was known as *the Neat Man*.

A Channel 12 EyeScene news van screeched to a halt beside him as he made it to the corner. He stopped on his heels when he saw uniformed NYPD holding back a growing crowd of reporters and cameramen at the entrance to the hospital's emergency room.

No, he thought. It couldn't be! Were the fun and games already over?

He was crossing 52nd Street when he spotted a distraught-looking female EMT slumping out of the crowd.

'Miss?' he said, stepping up to her. 'Could you tell me? Is this where they've brought First Lady Caroline?'

The full-figured Hispanic woman nodded her head,

and then she suddenly moaned. Tears began to stream down her cheeks. A quivering hand went to her mouth.

'She just *died*,' she said. 'Caroline Hopkins just died.'

The Neat Man felt dizzy for a second. Like the wind had been knocked right out of him. He blinked rapidly as he shook his head, stunned and elated.

'No,' he said. 'Are you sure?'

The overwrought paramedic sobbed as she suddenly embraced him. '*Ay Dios mío!* She was a saint. All the work she did for poor people and AIDS. One time, she came to my mother's project in the Bronx, and we shook her hand like she was the Queen of England. Her Service America campaign was one of the reasons I became a paramedic. How could she be dead?'

'Lord knows,' the Neat Man said soothingly. 'But she's in His hands now, isn't she?'

He could practically feel the billions of germs the woman was carrying. He shuddered, thinking of the indescribable filth a New York City paramedic came into contact with every day of her pitiful existence. A Hell's Kitchen hospital worker for that matter!

'God, what am I doing?' the medic said, releasing him. 'The news. The shock of it. I guess it tore me up. I was thinking about going to get some candles or flowers or something. It's just so unreal. I . . . I'm Yolanda, by the way.'

'Yolanda? Yeah. I'm . . . uh . . . leaving,' the Neat Man said, brushing past her into the street.

He had his cell phone in his hand by the time he made it to the east side of Ninth Avenue. He could hear loudly clattering plates and chefs yelling in French when his call was picked up at L'Arène.

'It's done, Julio,' he said. 'She's dead. Now get the hell out of there. You killed Caroline Hopkins. Congratulations.'

The Neat Man was about to shake his head in wonder at his good luck, but then stopped himself. Luck had absolutely nothing to do with it.

Three years to plan, he thought wistfully as he rounded the corner of 49th Street and headed east. Now they had just three days to pull off the rest of this job.

Minutes later, he was in the back of another taxi, heading north up Eighth. He took a couple of alcohol wipes out of his wallet and scoured his hands and face. He smoothed his lapels and crossed his hands in his lap as he sped through the bright lights, escaping the unclean city.

I'll tell you what's really so unreal, Yolanda baby, the Neat Man thought as the cab swerved around Columbus Circle and made its way up Broadway.

First Lady Caroline's death is just the beginning!

PART ONE

THE PERFECT TEN

Chapter One

I'll tell you this – even on the so-called mean streets of New York, where the only thing harder to get than a taxi in the rain is attention, we were managing to turn heads that grim, gray December afternoon.

If anything could tug at the coiled-steel heart-strings of the Big Apple's residents, I guess the sight of my mobilized Bennett clan – Chrissy, three; Shawna, four; Trent, five; twins Fiona and Bridget, seven; Eddie, eight; Ricky, nine; Jane, ten; Brian, eleven; and Juliana, twelve – all dressed in their Sunday best and walking in size order behind me, could do the trick.

I suppose I should have felt some privilege in being granted the knowledge that the milk of human kindness hasn't completely dried up in our jaded metropolis.

But at the time, the gentle nods and warm smiles we received from every Maclaren stroller-pushing Yummie, construction worker, and hot dog vendor from the subway exit next to Bloomingdale's all the way to First Avenue were completely lost on me.

I had a lot my mind.

The only New Yorker who *didn't* seem like he wanted to go on a cheek-pinching bender was the old man in the hospital gown who cupped his cigarette and wheeled his IV cart out of the way to let us into our destination – the main entrance of the terminal wing of the New York Hospital Cancer Center.

I guess he had a lot on his mind, too.

I don't know where New York Hospital recruits its staff for the terminal cancer wing, but my guess is somebody in Human Resources hacks into St Peter's mainframe and swipes the saint list. The constancy of their compassion and the absolute decency with which they treated me and my family were truly awe-inspiring.

But as I passed forever-smiling Kevin at reception and angelic Sally Hitchens, the head of the Nursing Department, it took everything I had to raise my head and manage a weak nod back at them.

To say I wasn't feeling very social would have been putting it mildly.

'Oh, look, Tom,' a middle-aged woman, clearly a *visitor*, said to her husband at the elevator. 'A teacher brought some students in to sing Christmas carols. Isn't that so nice? Merry Christmas, children!'

We get that a lot. I'm of Irish-American extraction, but my kids – all adopted – run the gamut. Trent and Shawna are African-American; Ricky and Julia, Hispanic; and Jane is Korean. My youngest's favorite show is *The Magic School Bus.* When we brought home the DVD, she exclaimed, 'Daddy, it's a show about our family!'

Give me a fuzzy red wig and I'm a six-foot-two, two-hundred-pound Ms Frizzle. I certainly don't look like what I am – a senior detective with the NYPD Homicide Division, a troubleshooter, negotiator, whatever's needed by whoever needs it.

'Do you boys and girls know "It Came Upon the Midnight Clear"?' the woman who had latched on to us persisted. I was just about to sharply point out her ignorance when Brian, my oldest son, glanced at the smoke coming out of my ears and piped in.

'Oh, no, ma'am. I'm sorry. We don't. But we know "Jingle Bells."'

All the way up to dreaded *Five*, my ten kids sang 'Jingle Bells' with gusto, and as we piled out of the elevator, I could see a happy tear in the woman's eye. She wasn't here on vacation either, I realized, and my son had salvaged the situation better than a United

Nations diplomat, certainly better than I ever could have.

I wanted to kiss his forehead, but eleven-year-old boys have killed over less, so I just gave him a manly pat on the back as we turned down a silent white corridor.

Chrissy, with her arm around Shawna, her 'best little pal' as she calls her, was into the second verse of 'Rudolph the Red-Nosed Reindeer' as we passed the nurses' station. The little ones could have been life-size Precious Moments figurines in their dresses and pigtailed hair, thanks to the extreme makeover work of their older sisters, Juliana and Jane.

My kids are great. Amazing, really. Like everyone else lately, they had gone so far above and beyond that it was hard to believe sometimes.

I guess it just pissed me off that they had to.

At the end of the second hallway we turned, a woman, wearing a flowered dress over her ninety-pound frame and a Yankees cap over her hairless head, was sitting in a wheelchair at the open door of 513.

'MOM!' the kids yelled, and the thunder of twenty feet suddenly shattered the relative silence of the hospital hall.

Chapter Two

There was hardly enough of my wife left to get twenty arms around, but the kids managed it somehow. There were twenty-two arms when I got there. My wife was on morphine, codeine, and Percocet, but the only time I saw her completely pain-free was that first moment when we arrived, when she had all her ducklings pressed around her.

'Michael,' Maeve whispered to me. 'Thank you. *Thank you.* They look so wonderful.'

'So do you,' I whispered back. 'You didn't get out of that bed by yourself again, did you?'

Every day when we came to see her, she was dressed for company, her intravenous pain pack hidden away, a smile on her face.

'If you didn't want glamour, Mr Bennett,' my wife said, fighting the weariness in her glazed eyes, 'I guess you should have married someone else.'

It was the morning of the previous New Year's Day when Maeve had complained about some stomach pain. We'd thought it was just some holiday indigestion, but when it hadn't gone away in two weeks, her doctor wanted to do a laparoscopy just to be on the safe side. They found growths on both ovaries, and the biopsy came back with the worst news of all. Malignant. A week later, a second biopsy of the lymph nodes they took out with her uterus reported even worse news. The cancer had spread, and it wasn't going to stop.

'Let me help you up this time, Maeve,' I whispered as she started to push herself up out of the chair.

'You *want* to get seriously hurt?' she said, glaring at me. 'Mr *Tough Guy* Detective!'

Maeve fought for her life and dignity like a banshee. She took on cancer the way the outclassed Jake LaMotta took on Sugar Ray Robinson in the fifties, with an epic ferocity not to be believed.

She was a nurse herself and used every contact and every ounce of wisdom and experience she'd gained. She underwent so many chemo and radiation treatments, it put a life-threatening strain on her heart. But even after the radical attempts, after everything there was to be done had been done, the CAT scan revealed growing tumors in both lungs, her liver, and her pancreas.

A quote from LaMotta rang in my ears as I watched

Maeve stand on her wobbling toothpick legs to prop herself up behind her wheelchair. 'You never knocked me down, Ray,' he supposedly said after Robinson TKO'd him. *'You never knocked me down.'*

Chapter Three

Maeve sat down on the bed and lifted a white chart from beside her.

'I got something for you, guys,' she said softly. 'Since it looks like I'm going to be stuck here in this ridiculous place for a while longer, I decided I needed to come up with a list of chores for you.'

Some of the older kids groaned. 'Mom!'

'I know, I know. Chores. Who needs them?' Maeve said. 'But here's my thinking. If you all work together, you can keep the apartment running for me until I get back. Okay, team? Then here we go. *Julia*, you're on lifeguard duty for baths for the youngin's, and you're also responsible for getting them dressed in the morning.

'*Brian*, you're my cruise director, okay? Board games, video games, Duck, Duck, Goose. Anything you can think of that's *not the TV*. I need you to keep all the young men as occupied as possible.

'*Jane*, you're on homework patrol. Get the house

genius, *Eddie,* to help you. *Ricky,* I hereby dub you the Bennett house personal lunch chef. Remember, peanut butter and jelly for everyone except Eddie and Shawna – they get baloney.

'Let's see. *Fiona* and *Bridget.* Table setting and clearing. You could alternate, figure it out . . .'

'What about me?' Trent squeaked. 'What's my job? I don't have a job yet.'

'You're on shoe patrol, *Trent* Bennett,' Maeve said. 'All I ever hear from these complainers is "Where's my shoes? Where's my shoes?" Your job is to gather up all ten pairs and get them next to everybody's bed. Don't forget your own.'

'I won't,' Trent said, nodding with five-year-old intensity.

'*Shawna* and *Chrissy.* I have a job for you girls, too.'

'Yay,' Chrissy said, and did a little ballerina twirl. She'd gotten the *Barbie of Swan Lake* DVD for her birthday a month before, and every emotion now came with an impromptu interpretive dance.

'You know Socky's dish in the kitchen?' Maeve said.

Socky was a fickle white-and-gray cat that Maeve had pulled out of the garbage alongside our West End Avenue apartment house. My wife obviously has a thing for the misfortunate and strays. The fact that she married me proved that a long time ago.

Shawna nodded solemnly. At four, she was the quietest and most obedient and easygoing of all my kids. Maeve and I used to laugh at the nature versus nurture debate. All ten of our kids came from the womb prepackaged with his or her own personality. A parent could enhance and certainly damage, but change? Make a quiet kid gabby or a social butterfly more cerebral? Uh-uh. Not gonna happen.

'Well, it's your job to make sure Socky always has water to drink in her dish. Oh, and listen up, gang,' Maeve said, sliding down a little on the bed. At that point, just sitting too long in one spot hurt her.

'I want to go over a couple of other things before I forget. In this family, we always celebrate each other's birthdays. I don't care if you're four or fourteen, or forty and scattered around the world. We gotta stick by each other, okay? And meals – as long as you live under the same roof, you have at least one meal a day together. I don't care if it's a dreaded hot dog in front of the dastardly TV as long as you're all there. I'm always there for you, right? Well, you have to be like me even if I'm *not* there. You got me? *Trent*, are you listening?'

'Hot dogs in front of the TV,' Trent said, grinning. 'I love hot dogs and TV.'

We all laughed.

'And I love you,' Maeve said. I could see her eyelids beginning to droop. 'You've made me so proud. You too, Michael, my brave detective.'

Maeve was facing the grave with a dignity I was unaware human beings were capable of, *and she was proud of us*? Of me? What felt like an entire main of frigid water suddenly burst down the length of my spine. I wanted to start wailing, to put my fist through something – the window, the TV, the dirty lead skylight out in the lounge. Instead, I stepped forward through the crowd of my children, took off my wife's cap, and kissed her gently on the forehead.

'Okay, guys. Mom needs her rest,' I said, fiercely struggling to keep the crack that was in my heart out of my voice. 'Time to go. Let's move it, troop.'

Chapter Four

It was three forty-five when the Neat Man stepped off Fifth Avenue, climbed the stone stairs, and walked into St Patrick's Cathedral.

He snorted at the good folk kneeling in heavy silence and prayer. Sure, he thought, the Big Guy upstairs had to be real impressed with all this piety coming from the nerve center of the modern world's Gomorrah.

A prim, dough-faced old gal had beaten him to the first seat in the pew beside the nearest confessional along the cathedral's south wall. What the hell kind of sins did she have to admit? he wondered, sitting down beside her. *Forgive me, Father, I bought the cheap chocolate chips for the grandkids' cookies.*

A fortyish priest with salon-trimmed hair showed up a minute later. Father Patrick Mackey did a poor job of hiding his double-take when he spotted the Neat Man's icy smile.

It took a little longer for the baggy-necked old lady

to get out of the pew than to make her confession. Then the Neat Man almost knocked her down as he slid in after her through the confessional door.

'Yes, my son,' said the priest behind the screen.

'Northeast corner of Fifty-first and Madison,' the Neat Man said. 'Twenty minutes, Fodder. Be there, or else there will be consequences.'

It was more like thirty minutes later when Father Mackey opened the passenger door of the Neat Man's idling van. He had exchanged his priest duds for a bright blue ski jacket and jeans. He pulled a cardboard tube from beneath the jacket's puffy folds.

'You got it!' the Neat Man said. 'Well done, Fodder. You're a good assistant.'

The priest nodded as he craned his neck back toward the church. 'We should drive,' he said.

Ten minutes later, they parked in an empty lot beside an abandoned heliport. Out through the windshield, the East River looked like a field of trampled mud stretching before them. The Neat Man stifled a joke as he popped the lid off the cylinder the priest had brought. You could practically taste the PCBs in the air, he thought.

The prints inside were old and cracked, yellowed at the edges like parchment. The Neat Man stopped his tracing finger at the center of the second print.

There it was! It wasn't just a rumor. It was real. And he had it.

The final detail for his masterpiece.

'And no one knows you have these?' the Neat Man said.

'No one,' the priest said, and chuckled. 'Doesn't the paranoia of the Church boggle the mind? The institution I work for is a puzzle palace.'

The Neat Man clucked his tongue, unable to take his eyes off the architectural drawing. But finally, he lifted a silenced Colt Woodsman out from underneath the seat of the van. The double tap of the .22 was subtle to the ear, but it was as if a grenade had gone off inside Father Mackey's head. 'Go straight to hell,' the Neat Man said.

Then he did a frantic scan of his face in the rearview and threw his head back in horror. Specks of blood freckled his forehead above his right eye. It was only after he'd scoured the hateful spots with Wet-Naps and upended a bottle of rubbing alcohol onto his face that his breathing returned to normal.

Then the Neat Man whistled tunelessly as he rolled up the prints and put them back into their cylinder.

A masterpiece, he thought once again, *in the making.*

Chapter Five

The kids were a blur of activity once we got back home that evening. From every room of our apartment, instead of television and electronic gunfire, came the satisfying sound of busy Bennetts.

Water splashed as Julia prepped Shawna and Chrissy's bath. Brian sat at the dining-room table with a deck of cards, patiently teaching Trent and Eddie how to play Twenty-one.

'Bam.' I could hear Ricky, like an Emeril Mini-Me, say from the kitchen as he squeezed jelly onto each slice of Wonder bread. 'Bam . . . bam.'

Jane had the flash cards out on the floor of her room and was preparing Fiona and Bridget for the 2014 SAT.

I didn't hear a complaint, a whine, or even a silly question out of anyone.

Add *brilliant* to the list of my wife's attributes. She must have known how much the kids were hurting, how disoriented and useless they felt, so she had given them something to do to fill that void, to feel useful.

I only wished I could come up with something to make myself feel the same way.

As most parents will tell you, bedtime is the roughest time of day. Everyone, not excluding parents, is tired and cranky, and restlessness can degrade quickly to frustration, yelling, threats, and punishments. I didn't know how Maeve did it every night – some magical, innate sense of measure and calm, I had assumed. It was one of the things that I was most worried about having to take on.

But by eight o'clock that night, from the sound coming out of the apartment, you would have thought we had all left on a Christmas vacation.

I almost expected to see the window open and bedsheets tied together when I went into the little girls' room – but all I saw were Chrissy, Shawna, Fiona, and Bridget with their sheets tucked to their chins, and Julia closing an Olivia book.

'Good night, Chrissy,' I said, kissing her on her forehead. 'Much love from your dad.'

I was heartened by my clutch Dad performance as I went on my rounds.

The boys were all in bed as well. 'Good night, Trent,' I said, giving him a kiss on his brow. 'You did one great job today. How about coming to work with me tomorrow?'

Trent's tiny forehead crinkled as he thought about it.

'Is it anybody's birthday at work?' he said after a little while. 'Any of the other detectives?'

'No,' I said.

'I'll just go to school then,' Trent said, closing his eyes. 'It's Lucy Shapiro's birthday tomorrow, and birthdays mean chocolate cupcakes.'

'Good night, guys,' I said as I stepped toward the door. 'I couldn't do this without you.'

'We know, Dad,' Brian called from the top bunk. 'Don't worry about it. We got your back.'

Chapter Six

I pulled the final door closed and stood for a moment in the hall outside the boys' room. On a *normal* night, in about a half-hour, when I'd come home from my precinct, the living room would be flashing blue light from Maeve watching television, or a warm, steady yellow light from her sitting on our sectional reading a book, waiting for me to arrive.

As I stared from that corridor at the blackened doorway of my living room, I realized I was experiencing for the first time what darkness truly was.

I went into the living room and flicked on the lamp beside the couch. Then I sat in the silence, passing my eyes slowly across all the memories.

The wallpaper we'd painstakingly put up. All the family photographs Maeve had shot and framed. Christmas trips to the Bronx Botanical Garden. And pumpkin-picking upstate. She'd made shadow boxes of vacations we'd taken, with seashells and sand from our two-years-ago trip down to Myrtle Beach, pinecones and leaves from the week we spent in the Poconos the August before.

How could she have had the energy for that? I wondered. How could she have had the time?

Because my wife was something special, was the answer to that one.

And I wasn't the only one who thought so. In fact, I didn't know anyone who didn't adore Maeve.

After we'd adopted Julia, Maeve quit the hospital in order to spend more time with her, and she took a job taking care of an elderly man on West End Avenue. Mr Kessler was ninety-five, from an old-money railroad family, and he was bitter and angry at the modern world and everything in it. But week after week, Maeve wore him down with small kindnesses and compassion. She would regularly wheel him out to sit in the sun at Riverside Park, make him remember he was alive, even if he didn't want to.

By the end, he had become a different person, let go of his bitterness, even made amends with his estranged daughter.

After he died, we found out that the old man had bequeathed to Maeve his apartment, the one our family lives in now.

And instead of the antiques and Persian rugs a lot of our neighbors seem to be into, Maeve filled our house with children. Four months after we got the apartment, we adopted Brian. Six months after that came Jane. And on . . . and on . . .

Saint was a pretty trite term, I knew, but as I sat there alone, gazing at all my wife's accomplishments, that was the word that kept popping into my mind.

The life of a saint, I thought bitterly.

All the way down to the martyrdom.

My heart literally skipped when the doorbell rang.

The outside world could go scratch, I thought as it rang again.

I figured that it was an errant guest of the Underhills, our frequent-cocktail-party-throwing neighbors across the hall – when it rang a third time.

I finally stood, annoyed.

Big mistake, dude, I thought as I yanked back the doorknob. You just woke up the Grinch.

Chapter Seven

Judging from the wrinkled jeans and dusty navy peacoat of the young blond woman on the other side of my door, I decided she probably wasn't headed to a Manhattan-style cocktail party.

But with a dirty knapsack that bulged over her back and a duffel bag clutched in her gloveless hands, she definitely seemed to be heading somewhere.

'Mr Bennett?' she said, dropping her bag and extending a small, well-formed hand. 'Mr Michael Bennett?'

Her Irish accent was as warm as her hand was cold.

'It's me, Mary Catherine,' she said. 'I made it.'

From her accent, I *suspected* she must be some relative of my wife's. I tried to place Mary Catherine's face from the small contingent of Maeve's side who had attended our wedding. But all I could remember was an elderly granduncle, some distant cousins, and a trio of middle-aged bachelors. What the heck was this about?

'Made it?' I repeated warily.

'I'm the au pair,' Mary Catherine said. 'Nona said she spoke with you.'

Au pair? Nona? I thought. Then I remembered that Nona was Maeve's mother's name. My wife had always been insistently vague about her past, growing up in Donegal. I had a feeling her people were a little eccentric.

'I'm sorry, um, Mary, is it?' I said. 'Ah, I don't think I know exactly what you're talking about.'

Mary Catherine's mouth opened as if she was about to say something. Then it closed. Her porcelain features blushed crimson as she picked up her bag.

'Sorry I wasted your time, sir,' she said quickly and a tad sadly. 'There must have been some mistake on my part. I'm sorry.'

Her duffel bag slipped out of her hand as she approached the elevator. I stepped out of the doorway to give her a hand, then noticed my mail on the floor. It had been piling up a little, and my helpful neighbors, the Underhills, had dumped it beneath the alcove's table we share in order to make way for their antique wooden nutcracker collection.

I noticed a small, odd-looking letter sticking out from the pile's center.

'Wait,' I said. 'Hold up a second, Mary Catherine. Just a sec.'

I tore open the letter. It was handwritten in a tiny, all but illegible script, but I was able to make out the *Dear Michael*, a couple of *Mary Catherines*, and the *God Bless You In Your Time of Need, Love Nona* closing.

I still didn't know what the hell it all meant, though.

I wasn't even 100 percent aware my mother-in-law was still alive until that moment. One thing I was sure of, though, was that it was too late and I was too tired to try to figure it all out right now.

'Oh,' I said to the girl as the elevator door rumbled open. 'You're Mary Catherine, the au pair.'

Naked hope twinkled in her bright blue eyes. But where the heck was I going to put her? Our inn was filled to capacity. Then I remembered the maid's room on the top floor; it had come with the apartment and was currently being used for storage.

'C'mon,' I said, grabbing her bag and walking her into the elevator. 'I'll show you where you're staying.'

It took me a good twenty minutes to get the crib, baby toys, some old car seats, and Chrissy's Barbie and Shawna's Three Princesses bikes out of the small room.

By the time I went down to the apartment and came back with some sheets, Mary Catherine had the mattress unrolled on the steel-frame twin bed and was putting her stuff neatly into the drawers of the dresser we'd used for a changing table.

I studied her for a moment. She was in her late twenties. Though she wasn't very tall, there seemed to be an energetic heartiness to her. Spunky, I thought, which was good, considering the job she was applying for.

'Nona didn't happen to mention how big my family is, did she?'

'A brood, she said. "Quite a brood," I believe was the phrase she used.'

'How many is "quite a brood" where you come from?' I asked.

Mary Catherine's eyebrows raised.

'Five?'

I shook my head, put out my thumb, and jerked it upward.

'Seven?'

I watched a ripple of panic cross Mary Catherine's face when I motioned for her to shoot higher.

'Not ten?' she said.

I nodded.

'They're all toilet-trained, thank God. And they're great kids. But if you want to walk away now or tomorrow or next week, I won't blame you.'

'Ten?' Mary Catherine said again.

'A one and a zero,' I said with a smile. 'Oh, and if you're going to work for us, you have to call me Mike. Or idiot, if you want. But please don't call me Mr Bennett.'

'Okay, Mike,' Mary Catherine said.

As I left, I noticed that the panic seemed to have stuck in her face.

'Ten,' I repeated under my breath.

The perfect ten.

Chapter Eight

Downstairs, I couldn't sleep a wink after I slid in between the cold sheets of my bed. I remembered that tomorrow was Caroline Hopkins's funeral, and that was yet another sad fact to consider tonight.

I lay in the dark, listening to the winter wind howl around the corner of my building. Somewhere, on Broadway probably, a distant car alarm started up, went all the way through its excruciating phases of electronic agony only to start up again.

For about an hour, I steadfastly refused to feel sorry for myself. I wasn't the one whose body had mutinied. I wasn't the one who had devoted my life to helping others for thirty-eight years – and for that trouble wouldn't be seeing thirty-nine.

Then I started to cry. It came on slowly, achingly, like the first cracks of ice on a pond you've wandered too far onto. After a minute, my steely composure was shattered into a thousand pieces, and I was lost.

Originally, I had just gone along with my wife's idea

to adopt. After we found out we couldn... would have done whatever Maeve wanted. so much and just wanted to make her happy way I could.

But after we got Jane, I was a little reluctant to go on. Three kids in New York? Even owning an apartment was expensive, and it wasn't like I was Mr Moneybags.

Maeve showed me that we had room in our home, and in our hearts, for one more. After Fiona and Bridget, I'd roll my eyes whenever Maeve would mention another foster case or needy child she'd heard about and say, 'What's another pound on an elephant?'

But how can an elephant live without a heart? I thought as I lay there with tears streaming down my cheeks.

There was no way I was going to be able to do this. The older kids were becoming teenagers, and the younger ones . . . Jesus Christ, how could I be in charge of their lives and their happiness and their future all by myself?

Then I heard my door crack open.

'Peep-peep,' someone small said.

It was Chrissy. Every morning, she'd come into our room with her empty cereal bowl pretending to be a different baby animal in need of feeding. A kitten, a puppy, a baby penguin, a baby armadillo one time.

She padded up to the edge of the bed.

'Peep-peep can't sleep,' she said.

I wiped my tears on the pillow.

'Big Peep can't either,' I said.

She hadn't slept in our bed since she was two, and I was about to get up to tuck her back in her own bed, but then I pulled open the covers.

'Get in the nest, Peep, quick!'

As Chrissy dove in beside me, I realized how I'd gotten it dead wrong as usual. My kids weren't a burden. They were the only thing holding me together.

Chrissy was asleep in about two minutes. After she dug the tiny icicles of her feet snugly into my kidneys, I realized sleepily that maybe you couldn't call this happy. But it was the first time in weeks I'd seen the ballpark.

Chapter Nine

What an interesting day this was going to be. Eventful, historic as a son of a bitch.

The silver chimes of St Patrick's morning bells were still hanging in the chilled air over Fifth Avenue when the Neat Man arrived outside the cathedral's massive entrance doors. He sipped his venti drip and shook his head at the crowd of loonies who already lined the sidewalk four-deep behind the police barricades.

Caroline Hopkins's funeral wouldn't start for another forty minutes, and already the turnout was as thick as the mounds of donated flowers that buried the base of the block-long church. Caroline had been a popular First Lady to be sure, but more important to many of these imbeciles, she'd been born and raised in New York City. She was one of their own. Yeah, right. Like the mayor of New York was one of the people.

The Neat Man took another shot of caffeine and continued to check out the scene. Up on the front steps of St Paddy's, he watched a red-faced FDNY bagpiper struggling to hold down a plaid skirt over his tighty whities in the frigid wind.

In the vestibule, just inside the open three-story bronze doors, a marine drill sergeant inspected the Army, Navy, Air Force, and Marine honor guard. He snapped the bottom of the marine's dress-blue jacket and slapped the blade of his hand across the sailor's immaculate shoulder, knocking away an imaginary speck of dirt.

Then the limousines started arriving.

Mayor Andrew Thurman got there first, which made sense, the Neat Man thought. The mayor claimed to be a close friend of the Hopkinses.

Politically active movie-star couple Marilyn and Kenneth Rubenstein arrived next. The proenvironmentalist actors had done touchy-feely commercials with Caroline to put a stop to Alaskan wilderness oil drilling, or some such horseshit. In the meantime, both of their teenage kids were having major trouble with drugs and alcohol up in Westchester.

When someone in the crowd across Fifth whistled, two-time Oscar winner Kenneth Rubenstein turned with his million-dollar smile and waved with both hands as if he were about to receive a third award. The Neat Man grinned as he watched Rubenstein's raven-haired wife, Marilyn, elbow him hard in the ribs. *Cinema verité*, he thought.

On the movie stars' heels came real-estate mogul Xavier Brown and his wife, a Chanel-clad fashion diva named Celeste. The power couple were also *close* friends of the First Lady. Hell, who wasn't?

The next to de-limo was New York Giants quarterback Todd Snow. His Super Bowl ring glittered as he put his arm around his attractive model wife. The athlete had done charity work with Caroline Hopkins as well.

The Neat Man gazed with satisfaction at the tinted-window freight train of limousines forming to the north up Fifth Avenue. *Hail, hail, the gang's all here. Well, almost.*

Finally, he looked up at the gigantic rose window and majestic three-hundred-foot stone towers at the front of the cathedral. With the ego-per-square-inch ratio this thing was developing, he thought, stamping his shoes on the flagstones to warm his feet, it would be surprising if there'd still be room for the casket.

Chapter Ten

John Rooney made a face like the Grinch as his limousine finally stopped in front of the churning crowds at St Patrick's. As Hollywood's current lead box-office-grossing actor, he'd come to appreciate the loyal fans who turned out for events of any kind. Most of them were just regular folks who wanted to show their support and appreciation. And he'd certainly take them over the paparazzi leeches. Any day, anywhere.

But now as he looked out at the rapacious faces and the raised picture phones, he was a little wary. Standing room only at a funeral, even at a high-profile ceremony, was a little too close to creepy.

Fortunately for him, the church side of Fifth Avenue was VIP only. Rooney exited onto the street behind Big Dan, his security guy. There was already a line of press – legitimate newspeople for the most part – stacked along both sides of the stairs and entrance.

With effort, he managed not to turn when someone

from the crowd across Fifth yelled, 'WUZ UP, DORK?' the catchphrase from his latest comedy hit.

But he couldn't quite resist the inviting looks on the faces of the press column along both sides of the cathedral entrance. Adrenaline burst into his bloodstream as a firefight of camera flash packs blistered his eyes. He looked up at the gray sky and scratched his head.

Then Rooney unleashed the day's first high-kilowatt smile.

'I don't know if this is such a great idea, guys,' he said casually. 'Anyone hear if there's lightning in today's forecast?'

He quickly scanned the ranks of mostly grinning newsies, then stopped the next joke in his throat as he spotted offended alarm on the face of some pretty brunette standing near the entrance. She was right, of course. What an attention slut he was. Grandstanding at a funeral.

Rooney made his face go somber, and then he entered the church.

He could see people in the back pews turning and nudging one another as he gave his invitation to the red-coated security guard.

Yep, it's me. I'm here, Rooney thought, irritated. That was one aspect of fame that had gotten old real fast.

In a real-world setting, a restaurant or an airport, having people gawk at you was simply uncomfortable. It was as if people wanted something from him, but what? He didn't know, and he suspected they didn't either. People thought stars wore sunglasses to disguise themselves, but really it was to avoid eye contact.

Rooney turned back toward the church entrance as he heard cameras *pop* and *click* like an angry swarm of metal crickets.

Well, look who's here!

Linda London, twenty-year-old reality TV socialite, had arrived at the same time as Mercedes Freer, twenty-year-old bubblegum pop diva. That the two ladies were sharing the same slab of sidewalk was news enough, Rooney knew. But what was really creating a frenzy was the fact that they were both wearing the same micromini black-widow outfit and veil.

To make things a little more interesting, seventies rock legend Charlie Conlan climbed out of *his* stretch and walked up the church's stairs a few feet from the potential catfight. The tall, hopelessly cool icon had to be close to sixty now, but he still looked real good. He shook Rooney's hand in the vestibule.

Charlie had written and performed three magical songs for a children's movie Rooney had starred in the year before. They'd gone on a brief promotional tour together. The whole time, Conlan had never stopped smiling; tipped every waiter, doorman, and limo driver they came across; and signed autographs for any and all. Even the paparazzi seemed to like him.

'Friggin' circus, huh?' Charlie said in his patented gravelly voice. 'You one of the clowns, Johnny?'

'If I am, then you're the ringmaster,' said Rooney, laughing as the cameras went off again.

Another loud cheer rose from the crowd. Out on the street, Eugena Humphrey was exiting her trademark pink Lincoln Town Car limousine.

'Now, now, people,' the charismatic 'Queen of LA' talk-show host chided the crowd. 'This is a funeral, not the Emmys. Let's have a little respect, *please*.'

Amazingly, the crowd quieted right down.

'Eugena rules,' someone said, and that seemed to be the God's honest truth.

Chapter Eleven

*N*ew York Times reporter Cathy Calvin didn't know
where to look for the day's next startling image.
She turned as the First Lady's hearse appeared over
the northern rise of an emptied Fifth Avenue. It was
led by a nine-strong V formation of NYPD parade-
speed Harleys, their mufflers popping smartly in the
cold hush of the world-famous street.

It was as if a contingent of the cathedral's statues
had come to life when the honor guard broke rank
in the vestibule and marched slowly out onto the
sidewalk.

The guard arrived at the curb the moment the
hearse did.

Flashbulbs popped as they ceremoniously slid out the
American-flag-draped casket from the long black car.

Two Secret Service men in dark suits appeared from
the crowd and completed the line of pallbearers as
the former First Lady's body was effortlessly raised to
shoulder height.

The soldiers and agents stopped at the top of the stairs, just behind the former president and his daughter, as a low, violent rumbling began to the south.

A moment later, a group of five F-15s appeared low in the slot of downtown sky. As they swooped over 42nd Street, the most western aircraft suddenly broke rank and arced upward and upward as the remaining planes roared over the cathedral in the 'missing man' formation.

The pallbearers waited until the last echo of the jet engines' thunder had dissipated from Fifth Avenue's stone-and-steel canyon, and then began to enter the church carrying Caroline Hopkins.

The high skirl of the lone bagpiper didn't start until the former president passed over the church's threshold. It was as if the whole city was observing an impromptu moment of silence as the familiar strains of 'Amazing Grace' began.

Cathy Calvin looked out over the crowd, and the *Times* reporter knew she had the lead she would never write. People were taking off their hats, had their hands over their hearts, and were singing along with the hymn. Everywhere, jaded New Yorkers were weeping openly.

But that wasn't the biggest shock to her.

No, the big surprise was when Cathy Calvin, seen-it-all reporter, put her hand up to her own cheek and realized she was crying too.

Chapter Twelve

S end-off like that almost brought tears to your eyes, the Neat Man thought as he stared through binoculars from his swivel chair in the back of his black van.

Gaw-damn, he thought, and was grinning so hard it was starting to hurt his cheeks.

Tears of joy.

The van was parked near 51st and Fifth Avenue, kitty-corner to the grand cathedral, and for the last hour, through the one-way tinted window at the van's rear, he'd been watching the nonstop parade of arriving celebs and dignitaries.

It was one thing to predict something, the Neat Man thought as the church's entrance doors closed behind President Hopkins and his entourage of inspired toadies.

Quite another to watch your each and every prediction come incredibly true.

He lowered the binocs to rip a baby wipe from the top of the plastic canister at his feet. His red hands stung wonderfully when he started scouring them. He usually carried a supply of soothing Jergens hand lotion to counteract the chafing, but he'd forgotten it in all the excitement.

About the only thing I missed, he thought, smiling as he dropped the used wipey onto the mound at his feet and raised the binoculars again.

He scanned the perimeter of the church's wide block, lingering at each security post with his high-resolution Steiner 15x80 field glasses.

There was a line of Manhattan Task Force beat cops scattered about the front of the church with the press, and an NYPD Emergency Service Unit truck blocking the side streets at each corner.

The baseball-hat-wearing ESU police commandos had intimidating Colt Commando submachine guns strapped across their chests, but there were coffee cups in their hands, and cigarettes. Instead of being vigil-ant, they were standing around goofing on one another, telling lies about what they would do with all the overtime they were raking in.

Question: Were they that stupid? the Neat Man thought. Answer: Yes, they were.

His cell phone went off when the bagpiper's screech

started winding down. The Neat Man lowered the binoculars and raised the phone to his ear.

The excitement of what was about to go down hissed along his nerve endings.

'All clear, Jack,' the Neat Man said. 'It's a go. Now make us proud.'

Chapter Thirteen

I n the nave of the cathedral, 'Jack' bit the antenna of his just-closed cell phone nervously as he gazed out at the dozens of Secret Service agents and private security and cops stationed around the church.

Would this scheme actually work? he thought for the thousandth, no, make that the hundred thousandth time. Well, no time like the present to find out. He holstered the phone and headed for the 51st Street exit.

Seconds later, he hustled down the marble stairs and unhooked the latch that was holding open the two-foot-thick wooden door. A female uniformed NYPD cop smoking a cigarette in the threshold glanced at him. She looked irritated.

'In or out?' Jack said with a smile. Though he was on the short side, he was capable of turning on the charm when he wanted. 'Service is starting. We got to close 'em up.'

In the predawn security meeting, law enforcement

personnel had been told to give the church security force deference in all matters concerning the ceremony.

'Out, I guess,' the cop said.

Good choice, flatfoot, Jack thought, pulling the heavy doors shut and snapping the key off in the lock. *Choose life.*

He hurried up the stairs and around the ambulatory along the back of the altar.

It was packed – standing room only – with white-frocked priests.

The organ started and the casket appeared from under the choir loft just as he arrived at the south transept.

Jack jogged down the stairs to the 50th Street side entrance and closed and locked the thick door there, too. He refrained from breaking the key in the lock because they'd need this exit in about a minute.

Next order of business. Jack took a deep breath.

Half of Hollywood, Wall Street, and Washington was now boxed inside the cathedral.

Quickly, he went back along the ambulatory. Beyond one of the massive columns there was a leather bank rope. It blocked off a small, narrow marble stairwell at the rear of the altar. He stepped over the rope and descended.

At the bottom of the marble stairs was an ornate green copper door. The sign above it read: CRYPT OF THE ARCHBISHOPS OF NEW YORK.

Jack stepped in quickly and yanked the door closed. He moved inside the crypt, then tightly shut the door behind him. In the dimness, he could make out the stone sarcophaguses of the interred archbishops arrayed in a semicircle around the rough-hewn stone walls of the chamber.

'It's me, idiots,' he said in a low voice after another second. 'Hit the light.'

There was a *click*, and the wall sconces came on.

Behind the stone caskets were a dozen men. Most were wearing T-shirts and sweatpants. They were big, muscular, and not very friendly-looking.

There were rips of Velcro as the men strapped on bulletproof Kevlar vests. Smith & Wesson nine-millimeter handguns in underarm holsters went on next. The black fingerless gloves they put on were known as 'sappers' and had cushioned lead shot over the knuckles.

Then the mysterious cadre pulled brown-hooded Franciscan monk robes over the Kevlar vests. Into the pockets of these were placed what looked like remote controls but were actually the latest in electric shock weaponry.

They slipped big-bored riot guns up the billowing sleeves of their robes. Half of the guns were loaded with rubber bullets; the other half with canisters of extremely caustic CS tear gas.

Last, the men pulled black ski masks over their faces. It was as if they were made of shadow when they flipped up the hoods.

Jack smiled approvingly as he threw on his own vest, robe, and black ski mask, then pulled up his hood.

'Lock, load, and strap your nuts on, ladies,' Jack said, smiling as he slowly pulled back the heavy door of the crypt. 'It's time to put the *fun* back into funeral.'

Chapter Fourteen

Movie star and comedian John Rooney felt the breath rush out of him as the honor guard finally arrived at the front of the church with the flag-draped coffin.

Throughout the procession up the center aisle, they had stopped for a long, motionless moment after each step, the organ thundering from above. It was as if the casket weighed so much they needed to pause in order to carry it, Rooney thought sadly.

As the pallbearers laid down the coffin, Rooney remembered his own father's burial at Arlington National Cemetery. Say what you want about the military, he thought, choking up. Flat out, no one knew better how to honor the dead.

He turned to his right when he saw the line of cowled, brown-robed monks appear. They walked with the same solemnity of the honor guard as they approached the altar. He could see another line of them walking down the aisle to his left.

In the dimness of the church, you couldn't see faces beneath the hoods. He knew there was going to be a lot of ritual and ceremony today, but this was a new one on him. If the military knew how to honor the dead, leave it to the Catholics to put the fear of God into the living.

The organ was reaching a crescendo when the monks spaced themselves out and stopped suddenly in the side aisles.

Rooney jumped when he heard a series of muffled blasts under the rumble of the organ. Then smoke, white and enveloping, came billowing from all sides.

What had been the austere VIP section looked like a mosh pit as the people in there panicked, clawing at one another to get out of the pews.

Rooney thought he saw one of the monks setting off a shotgun into the crowd.

No, he thought, blinking hard in disbelief. He must have banged his head. That couldn't be right.

He opened his eyes as a uniformed cop stumbled up the center aisle with blood pouring out of his nose and ears.

Beside Rooney, his bodyguard, Big Dan, had a handkerchief to his mouth as he cleared the .380 from his belt holster. It looked like Dan was trying to decide which direction to point it when one of the monks appeared like an apparition from the smoke and jabbed the bodyguard in the neck with a square of black plastic. There was an ominous clacking sound, and Big Dan dropped his weapon and was down on the seat, shaking like some huge spirit-struck worshipper.

Then the organ died!

Fear slapped through John Rooney. With the music gone, he could hear the screaming, the panicked shrieks of thousands soaring off the high stone vaults.

Someone had just taken over St Patrick's!

Chapter Fifteen

I had no idea what was going on yet, which was my usual state lately, since Maeve had gotten sick. I was still groggy when I took a quick head count and pulled our van away from the hunter-green awning of my building. It was eight forty-one, and I had exactly four minutes to get us to Holy Name on Amsterdam. Or there was going to be at least one kid from every grade in detention.

From the top of my building, you could probably 'roof' my kids' school on 97th with a Spalding ball, but anyone who's familiar with morning rush hour in Manhattan will tell you that if you planned on going two blocks in four minutes you were taking your chances.

I knew I could have let them walk. Julia and Brian and the older kids had proved themselves more than capable of looking out for the pip-squeaks. But I wanted to spend as much time as possible with them right now, wanted them to know they weren't on their own.

That and the fact that recently I had a terrible need to have them with me at all times.

In fact, the only thing that had stopped me from writing out ten bogus sick notes to share my day off with them was Holy Name's principal, Sister Sheilah. My butt already had enough memories of the principal's bench to last it a lifetime.

I got them to the school's corner on Amsterdam Avenue with seconds to spare. I hopped out and threw open the door of our family vehicle, a twelve-passenger Ford Super Duty van I had bought at a police auction. Minivans were for 2.2-kid-toting suburban soccer moms. My NYC Bennett Nation required heavy troop transport.

'Run!' I yelled as I pulled out children with both hands and deposited them on the sidewalk.

Shawna just made it in as Sister Sheilah was taking the hook off the oak door to shut and lock it. I could see the withered old nun scanning the street for me, her stern look cocked and ready to fire.

My tires barked as I dropped the Super D's tranny into drive, punched the gas, and fled the scene.

Chapter Sixteen

I couldn't believe my nose when I finally got back to the apartment. It smelled like coffee. Good coffee. Strong coffee.

And that other smell. I didn't want to jinx it, but I had a deep hunch that something was baking.

Mary Catherine was just pulling out a tray of muffins when I entered the kitchen. *Blueberry muffins.* I like blueberry muffins the way Homer Simpson likes doughnuts. A young lady like her couldn't possibly have six muffins for breakfast, could she? Would she share one with me?

And the kitchen. It was sparkling. Every surface gleaming, every cereal bowl put away. Where was the *Clean Sweep* team?

'Mary Catherine?'

'Mr Bennett,' Mary Catherine said, blowing a wisp of blond hair out of her face as she put the muffins on top of the stove. 'Where is everyone? I thought I was Snow White entering the dwarves' cottage when I came down this morning. Lots of little beds, but no sign of anyone.'

'The dwarves are at school,' I said.

Mary Catherine gave me a questioning look, similar to the one I'd just seen on Sister Sheilah.

'What time do they leave?' she asked.

'Around eight,' I said, unable to take my eyes off the steaming muffins on the stove.

'Then I start at seven, Mr Bennett. Not nine. There's no sense in me coming all this way to help out if you won't let me.'

'I apologize. And the name is Mike, remember?' I said. 'Are those . . .'

'For after breakfast. How do you like your eggs?' she said. 'Mike.'

After breakfast? I thought. I'd assumed they *were* breakfast. Maybe this au pair thing would work out.

'Over easy?' I said.

'Bacon or sausage?' she said.

No *maybe* about it, I thought with a smile and a shake of my head.

I was contemplating that win-win decision when I felt my cell phone vibrate. I looked at the caller ID. My boss. I closed my eyes and mentally willed his number off the screen. So much for my telepathic powers, I thought, feeling the phone jump in my hand like a freshly caught trout.

I was sorry it wasn't a real fish.

I would have thrown it back.

Chapter Seventeen

I shook my head again as I finally unfolded my phone and brought it up to my ear.

Calls at home from my boss, on my day off, meant one sure thing, I knew.

An express delivery of ill tidings was about to land in my lap.

'Bennett,' I said.

'Thank God,' my boss, Harry Grissom, said. Harry is the lieutenant detective in charge of my unit, the Manhattan North Homicide Squad. Being able to say you're the go-to guy on the elite Manhattan North Homicide will get you a lot of respectful nods at most cop parties. Right then, though, I was more than willing to trade in every last one of them for a couple of fried eggs. And a nice fat blueberry muffin.

'You heard what just happened?' my boss said.

'Where? What?' I said, already thinking the worst. There must have been a distinct note of urgency in my voice because Mary Catherine turned from the sink. Post 9/11, for a lot of New Yorkers – New York cops, firemen, and EMTs especially – the next terror hit wasn't a question of if but when.

'What the hell's happened? What's going on?' I asked.

'Slow down, Mike,' Harry said. 'No explosions. Not yet at least. All I was told was that about ten minutes ago, at St Patrick's Cathedral, shots were fired. First Lady Caroline's funeral was going on at the time, so it doesn't sound too good.'

What felt like a door breach hit me full in the stomach. Shots fired at a state funeral? Inside St Patrick's? A short while ago? This morning?

'Terrorists?' I said. 'From where?'

'I don't think we know yet,' my boss said. 'I do know that Manhattan South borough commander Will Matthews is on the scene, and he wants you down there ASAP.'

In what capacity? I wondered. I had been on the NYPD's Hostage Negotiation Team before making the switch to Homicide.

And wasn't I too fried already with my family crisis to take on a much larger one?

When it rains cats, it pours kittens too, I thought. Story of my life. I hoped this was just a run-of-the-mill barricade incident. Or better yet, maybe the borough commander needed me for a simple single murder. I could do barricades and murders. It was the 'weapons of mass destruction' thing that made the hairs on the back of my neck stand up.

'Does he need me for negotiating?' I asked my boss. 'Or was there a homicide at the cathedral? Help me out here, Harry.'

'I was too busy getting screamed at to get a chance to ask,' my boss said. 'I don't think it's because they ran out of altar boys, though. Just get your ass down there and find out everything you can. Then let me know what the hell is going on.'

'On my way,' I said, and hung up.

I went into my bedroom and threw on jeans, a sweat-shirt, and my NYPD Windbreaker. The *Homicide* one.

I splashed cold water on my face and retrieved my service Glock from the closet safe.

Mary Catherine was waiting in the front hall with my travel coffee mug and a brown bag of muffins. Even with my mind and adrenaline racing, I noticed that Socky, who hates everyone except Maeve, Chrissy, and Shawna, was rubbing his whiskers on her ankles. Talk about hitting the ground running.

I was struggling to come up with appropriate words of thanks and pertinent household-running instruc-tions, when she just opened the front door and said, 'Go, Mike.'

PART TWO

SINNERS

Chapter Eighteen

A low whistle escaped through my teeth as I pulled my department-issue blue Impala up to the barricade thrown across Fifth Avenue at 52nd Street. I hadn't seen so many cops out in front of the landmark church since the St Patrick's Day Parade.

Only instead of goofy tam-o'-shanters, shamrocks, and smiles, they were wearing black steel ballistic helmets, automatic weapons, and deadly serious frowns.

I showed my shield to a sergeant by one of the blue-and-white sawhorses. She directed me to the mobile command center, a long white bus parked across the street from the cathedral. The sergeant told me to park in front of the Sanitation Department dump trucks that blocked up Fifth next to the 51st Street barricade.

Two barricades, I thought. Mobile command centers. This was no single homicide for sure. This was a disaster in the making.

As I got out of my car, a jackhammer throbbing sounded, and I looked up as a police helicopter swung out from behind Rockefeller Center and hovered low over the cathedral. Dust and coffee cups and newspaper pages spiraled up in the rotor wash as a sniper in the helicopter's open door scanned the stained glass and stone spires over the barrel of a rifle.

I took my eyes off the helicopter when I almost walked into a famous, controversial radio host who, for some reason, was holding court on the street in front of the inner barricade. 'What in the hell did those friggin' priests do this time?' I heard him say as I passed.

As I entered the staging area between the grilles of the parked dump trucks, I stopped and stared in disbelief. A half-dozen Emergency Service Unit cops were crossing the avenue with their heads down. They stopped and pressed their bulletproof backs against the side of the long black hearse parked at the curb.

How could this be happening at Caroline Hopkins's funeral?

Chapter Nineteen

Though only five seven, with his broken nose and violently frank way of looking at everybody, except *maybe* his mother, borough commander Will Matthews was about as pugnacious-looking an Irish cop as you could still find on the force. He looked like he'd just gone fourteen and a half bare-knuckle rounds when I found him standing on the sidewalk smack in front of the command center bus.

'Bennett,' he said. 'Glad you could join us. Here's the deal. The mayor, the former president, the cardinal, several movie, music, and sports stars . . . *who else*? Eugena Humphrey and about three thousand other VIPs are being held hostage inside by a dozen or more heavily armed masked men. You follow me so far?'

It was hard to register what Will Matthews had just said to me. The mayor and the former president alone would have been mind-boggling, but all the rest?

The borough commander stared at me belligerently,

waiting for me to pick my jaw up off the sidewalk before he continued his rant.

'We *don't know* if the gunmen are terrorists. Preliminary reports from the law enforcement personnel who were just released from inside the church indicate that the lead hijacker, at least, is non-Arab. He spoke to the crowd and, I quote, "sounds white," unquote.

'These unidentified masked men took out thirty-one cops and about two dozen federal agents, including the former president's Secret Service detail, with *nonlethal weapons.* Tear gas and rubber bullets and Tasers.

'There's more. Twenty minutes ago, they opened the Fiftieth Street entrance doors and bum-rushed all of the cops and security personnel. There were a lot of broken noses and black eyes, but they could have gunned them down just as easy as let them go. So I guess we can be grateful for small mercies.'

I struggled to keep the shock and confusion off my face. It wasn't that easy. The security must have been incredible, and it was taken out? Using nonlethal weapons?

'How can I help?' I asked.

'Excellent first question. Ned Mason, our top nego-tiator, is on his way. But he has a place upstate, in

Orange County or some other ridiculous place. Newburgh, I think. I know you're not in Hostage Negotiation anymore, but I needed our best option in case these guys call before he gets here.

'*Also*, as I recall, you've got a lot of media airtime under your belt. So I might need you to run interference with the locust swarm of press this thing is bringing. Steve Reno's got the tactical lead. You can consult with him when he comes down off that bird, okay? Sit tight. Think about what to say to the press.'

I was following orders, 'sitting tight,' staring across at the huge, stately church, beginning to try to figure out what kind of person or persons would pull this – when I heard a terrible commotion by the 50th Street barricade. Something bad was happening. *Now!*

Instinctually, I went for my gun as a shirtless blond man and a heavily made-up redheaded woman sprinted out from behind the barricade. What the hell? They made it across cleared-out Fifth Avenue and were running up the cathedral's stairs when three ESU officers came out from behind the hearse – and tackled them.

The redhead's wig flew off, revealing a crew cut. The blond kid was still smiling, and I saw that his drug-addled pupils were as big as dinner plates.

'One love! Transgender love!' the blond yelled as

the cops carried him and the kicking transvestite right past the press at 51st Street.

I released a tense breath. Nothing to worry about. No suicide bombers. Just another performance of bizarre street theater courtesy of New York City.

I saw Commander Will Matthews staring open-mouthed on the sidewalk beside me as I holstered my Glock. He took off his hat and rubbed at his stubbled head.

'You wouldn't have a cigarette on you by any chance?' he said.

I shook my head. 'Don't smoke,' I said.

'Neither do I,' Will Matthews said, stepping away. 'I thought I'd start.'

Chapter Twenty

The FBI arrived in style about ten minutes later.

Four black-on-black Chevy Suburbans were let through the 49th Street barricade, and a fully armed tactical team poured out of the vehicles. Tall and gracefully quick, the black-uniformed commandos resembled a team of professional athletes. I wondered if they were part of the FBI's famed Hostage Rescue Team. The current situation certainly called for it.

A middle-aged man with hair the color of his charcoal suit came up and shook my hand.

'Mike Bennett?' he said amicably. 'Paul Martelli. Crisis Negotiation Unit. The special agent in charge sent us up from Twenty-six Fed to give you guys a hand if we can.'

The FBI's CNU was at the cutting edge in hostage negotiation. Martelli, its head, was famous in negotiation circles. A book he'd written was pretty much the bible on the subject.

I usually bristle at the presence of Feds, but I had

to admit, I was relieved that Martelli was here. I'd done some stand-offs in my three years in Hostage Negotiation, but nothing like this. Especially right now, given the sad state of my own emotions over Maeve and the kids. This situation was obviously off the chart in terms of importance and profile. Hell, I'd take all the help I could get.

'I see you guys got the communication and press angles taken care of,' Martelli said, looking around casually at the command center and the barricades. 'Mike, who's the primary negotiator?'

Even talking about trivial stuff, Martelli exuded tranquil confidence that was contagious. I could see why he was at the top of the game.

'Me for now,' I said. 'They have me holding the fort until our top guy gets here. Then I switch to secondary. ESU lieutenant Steve Reno has the tactical lead. Commander Will Matthews, our team commander, has the final word.'

All crisis incidents required a strict chain of command. The negotiator can't make decisions. He has to ask higher authorities before acting on hostage-takers' demands. This buys time as well as engenders a bond between the hostage-taker and the negotiator. Also, there has to be someone there to make the final decision – to keep negotiating or to go tactical.

Negotiators tend to want to keep talking. Tactical guys, to start shooting.

'Most important thing now,' Martelli said with a half-smile, 'is to show patience. We have to burn some time. Time for us to set up. Let SWAT gather tactical intelligence. And time for whoever's inside to cool off. Time dissipates pressure.'

I think I read that in a book, actually – Paul Martelli's book.

Chapter Twenty-One

The two of us turned as a cop in a flapping NYPD Windbreaker roared in through the 49th Street cordon on a dusty black Suzuki 750.

'Any contact?' Ned Mason barked at me in greeting as he got off his bike.

I'd worked with Mason briefly before I had left the Negotiation Team. The intense sandy-haired cop was a triathlete and a health nut. A lot of people dismissed him as arrogant and obnoxious, but I knew him to be one of those quirky loner cops who succeeds more by meticulousness and the solitary power of his strong will than teamwork.

'Not yet,' I said.

I started to brief Mason, but an NYPD Communications Division sergeant popped his head out the door of the bus holding a cell phone above his head.

'It's them!' he said.

Commander Will Matthews joined us as we all rushed inside the bus.

'Write down everything I tell you to,' Mason said to me brusquely. 'Don't miss a word.'

I could see by Mason's cocky attitude that he hadn't changed a bit.

'Call came in to nine-one-one. We routed it to here,' a communications tech cop said, offering up the phone. 'Who gets this? Which one of you guys?'

Mason snatched the phone out of his hand as Will Matthews and Martelli and myself pulled on headsets so we could listen in.

'Whoever you are,' Mason said into the phone, 'listen closely. Listen to me.'

Mason's voice was powerful, his tone stark and very serious.

'This is the United States Army. What you have done has gone beyond the bounds of governmental negotiation. The president of the United States has signed an executive order, and all normal channels have now been closed. In five minutes' time, starting now, you will either release the hostages or you will be killed. The only guarantee I will give you is this: If you lay down your weapons right now and let everyone out, you walk away with your lives. This is your one and *only* chance to respond. Tell me now. Are these the last five minutes of your life?'

Mason was making a very bold move, I knew. He

was using a controversial strategy, originated by Army Intelligence to end a stand-off by basically scaring the living shit out of the hostage-taker. He'd just gone 'all in' on the very first poker hand. If pressure was gasoline, Mason had just dropped a five-thousand-pound daisy cutter.

'If this *asshole*,' a voice replied with equal starkness after a short pause, 'isn't *off* the line in five *seconds*, the former president joins his wife in the afterlife. *Five . . .*'

I almost felt sorry for Mason when I saw the deep frown cross his face. It had been a risky bluff, one that had completely blown up on him. And it didn't look like he had a backup plan.

'Four,' the voice said.

Commander Will Matthews stepped forward.

'Mason!' he said.

'Three.'

Mason was clutching the phone; he didn't seem to be breathing.

And nobody else was doing anything either.

'Two.'

I had been a good negotiator, but I hadn't done it in three years, and this was a precarious time to dip my toes back into the pool.

But Ned Mason had just crashed and burned, and

like it or not, rusty or not, as secondary negotiator, it was my job to step in.

'One.'

I stepped across the bus and pulled the phone out of Mason's hand.

Chapter Twenty-Two

'Hi,' I said calmly. 'My name's Mike. Sorry about the screwup. The person who spoke to you wasn't authorized. Disregard everything he said. I'm the negotiator. We will not attack the cathedral. In fact we don't want anyone to get hurt. Again, I'm sorry for what just happened. Who am I speaking with, please?'

'On account of the fact that I just jacked this cathedral and everyone in it,' the voice said, 'why don't you call me Jack?'

'Okay, Jack,' I said. 'Thanks for talking to me.'

'No problemo,' Jack said. 'Do me a favor, Mike, would you? You tell that soldier-of-fortune dickhead who was just on that before he goes Raid on Entebbe on our asses, I got news for him. We have *every* window and door and wall in this place rigged up to a whole lotta C-4 on a multipoint motion-detector laser trigger. He better not breach.

'In fact, he better not let a pigeon shit in a three-mile radius of St Paddy's, or everybody on this block is going to be blown to thy will be done kingdom come. In fact, I'd seriously consider moving that NYPD helicopter off the roof if I were you. And I'd do it PDQ.'

I found Commander Will Matthews with my eyes and made a cutting motion toward the roof of the bus. Will Matthews spoke to one of his cop entourage, a radio crackled, and a couple of seconds later the rotor thump of the helicopter began to fall away.

'Okay, Jack. I got my boss to move the helicopter back. Now, is everybody okay in there? I know we have some older folks who might need medical attention. There were reports of some gunfire. Has anybody been shot?'

'Not yet,' Jack said.

I ignored the provocative response for the time being. Once I bonded a little more, I would try to curtail the threats, get him to speak more reasonably, more calmly.

'You guys need food or water or anything?' I asked.

'We're good for now,' Jack said. 'At this point, I just want to lay two things on you that you need to start wrapping your mind around. You're going to give us what we want, and we're going to get away with this. *Say it*, Mike.'

'We're going to give you what you want, and you're going to get away with this,' I said without hesitation.

Until we had more of an advantage, I needed to get him to accept me as quickly as possible. See me as someone who was willing to give him what he wanted anyway.

'Good boy,' Jack said. 'I know it's a little hard to compute, sitting where you're sitting, Mike. A little hard to believe. So I just wanted to reach out and plant the seed there. Because it's gonna happen. No matter how hard you try to resist. No matter how much you tough guys huff and puff. *We're going to get away with this.*'

'My job is to make sure we all come out of this in one piece. Including you, Jack. I want you to believe that.'

'Aww, Mike, what a sweet thing to say. Oh, and don't forget. *It's already over, okay?* We win. Smell you later,' the hijacker said – and the line went dead on me.

Chapter Twenty-Three

'What's your take on these guys, Mike?' Mason suddenly found his voice again.

I was about to try to answer, but being the closest to the command center window, I was the first to see the movement at the front of the cathedral.

'Wait a second,' I said. 'The doors are opening. *The front door!* Something's going down.'

The crackle of frantic radio calls ricocheted through the cop-filled trailer like one of my kids' dime-store bouncy balls.

At first I could only make out the dimness of the church's interior. Then a man in a torn blue dress shirt appeared in the doorway. He was blinking in the pale sunlight as he stepped onto the flagstone plaza.

Who was this? What was happening?

'I have him,' I heard one of the snipers call over the police band.

'Hold fire!' Will Matthews called back.

A woman in a broken-heeled shoe hobbled out behind the man in the blue shirt.

'*What the* . . .' Will Matthews said as a thin stream, then a flood of people started pouring out onto the cathedral's front steps.

Hundreds, maybe a thousand people were suddenly swarming out onto Fifth Avenue.

Were the hijackers letting everyone go? The other cops around me seemed as confused as I was.

We stared, silently watching the churchgoers scramble down the front steps. It was an unfathomable mob scene. Uniformed task-force cops waded in immediately and guided the people south past the 49th Street barricade.

'Get every detective down here. Robbery, Special Victims, everyone! I want those released hostages identified and interviewed,' Commander Will Matthews barked at one of the assistant chiefs.

Then the doors of the cathedral began to close again. What was happening now?

Martelli patted me on the back.

'Nice work, Mike,' he said. 'Textbook negotiating. You just saved thousands of lives.'

I appreciated the compliment, but I didn't think what had just happened had much to do with me.

Maybe the strong-arm tactic Mason used had worked after all. Or they'd lost their nerve.

The whole thing was so utterly *bizarre*.

'Is it over?' Will Matthews asked. 'Is that possible?'

There was a communal flinch around the room when the phone I was holding suddenly rang.

'My guess,' I said, 'would be no.'

Chapter Twenty-Four

'M ike,' said Jack. 'How's it hanging out there, buddy? People make it to safety okay? Nobody trampled to death, I hope.'

'No, Jack,' I said. 'Everybody seems to be okay. Thanks for being reasonable.'

'I'm trying, Mike. Giving it my all. I thought I better clear up any misperceptions, though . . . now that we've tossed back the *small* fish, I'd like to talk about the *whales* we're still holding on to.'

I glanced out the window and scanned the people who had been released. My God! He was right. Where was former president Hopkins? The mayor of New York? Eugena Humphrey? The A-list people were still inside. *How many of them?*

'To make it easier on everybody, we're holding thirty-four hostages,' Jack said as if reading my mind. 'Celebrities, of course, some *tycoons,* couple of politicians. Get me a fax number, and I'll send you a list.

Along with our requirements. Here's where things can either get real simple or real complicated, Mike. The choice is entirely up to you guys.'

Things were starting to come into tighter focus now, I realized. It was a stunning kidnapping! The most amazing one ever attempted; nothing even came close to it.

'We're holding all the chips, Mike. So far, no one's been hurt. But if you guys want to take this personally and try to sneak in here and take us out, there's gonna be a bloodbath like this country's never seen. I mean, all that Mom and Pop Flyover have left is *their celebrities*. It's the only friggin' thing we export anymore. Movie stars and pop music, right? Give us what we want, Mike, and this ugly scene will go away. Face it. You're outdone here.'

It was kind of incredible, but I felt relief. Criminals were horrible, kidnappers especially. But at least we weren't dealing with terrorists, a mindless force out to kill as many people as possible. You had a shot at taking down people who wanted to come out of a situation alive.

'We want to resolve this thing as much as you do, Jack,' I said.

'That's actually good to hear, Mike,' Jack said. 'Music

to my ears. Because I'm giving you and these fat cats the opportunity to haul your asses out of trouble the good old-fashioned American way. I'm going to let you buy your way out.'

Chapter Twenty-Five

Jack disconnected the second after I gave him the fax number that was handed to me by the communications sergeant. Paul Martelli took off his headphones and crossed the room. He sat down next to me. 'You're doing good, Mike. Cool heads prevail.'

'What's your take on this guy, Paul?' I asked him. 'First reaction, whatever.'

'Well, he's obviously not mentally disturbed,' Martelli said. 'And he sounds confident. Think about it from his side, his point of view. He's in there surrounded by every cop in the tristate area, and he's being a wiseass, cracking jokes. I get the feeling that he knows *something* we haven't figured out yet. I just don't know what it is. What does "Jack" know that we don't?'

I nodded. I had that same feeling; I just hadn't put it into words. And I had no idea what Jack knew.

'We're probably looking at a hard-core, extremely professional criminal,' Martelli went on. 'Plus, some of his references sounded like he knows military tactics.'

'The thing he said about explosives on the windows and doors. You think it's legit?'

'Looking at the way he's handled himself so far, I'd say yeah, we have to consider that it's a real threat. If we breach the building, he blows it up.'

I looked around for Ned Mason. He'd found a seat in the farthest corner of the room. With his failure still hanging heavy in the air, he looked like he was trying to make himself invisible.

'Ned. Tell me,' I said, 'why do you think they let all those people go when they could have held on to them? Make any sense to you?'

Mason looked up, maybe surprised that anyone was still talking to him.

'Well, let's see,' he said, standing and rejoining the group. 'Logistics, for one thing. If you don't need those extra hostages, why keep them around? They could get sick or hurt, and it would be your fault. Or worse, they could resist. Dispersing a crowd is one thing. Controlling one over a long period of time would be tricky. Plus, it follows a pattern that I'm seeing. They ejected the law enforcement people immediately because they knew they might try to fight back.'

Martelli nodded and said, 'Also, maybe they thought

letting out most of the people would look good for the cameras. You know, let the real people go. Only hold on to the rich. Like a Robin Hood thing. They're playing to the crowd.'

'Bastards have the angles covered so far, don't they?' Mason said. 'The locale, Midtown Manhattan. How they punched holes through the security. They must have been planning this for months. Maybe years. One monster hit.'

Our coffee cups jumped as my fist hit the counter. *That was it.* What had been bothering me. I couldn't believe it. The conclusion I'd come to sent a chill through me.

'This whole takedown was choreographed, right? No detail was overlooked. But how the hell can you plan to take over a state funeral without a body? Somehow, they killed Caroline Hopkins.'

Chapter Twenty-Six

Gazing through the frosted crystalline web of a giant snowflake on the fourth-floor picture window of Saks Fifth Avenue, the Neat Man chuckled down at the street.

Look at all the little assholes scurry, he thought. Replace the piped-in fa-la-la-la-la Christmas crap with some old-timey piano music, and you'd have a live-action version of the Keystone Kops down on Fifth.

Christ, this felt good, he thought. He held a mildly shaking hand out in front of his smiling face. He wouldn't deny it anymore. He lived for this.

He scrolled through his ready store of violent fantasies. His all-time favorite was the one where he was standing in the middle of Grand Central Station during rush hour. All of a sudden he would remove something from his jacket. Sometimes it was a Samurai sword. Sometimes a chainsaw. In his favorite, it was a flamethrower. Talk about shock and awe.

But the real thing was so much better than fantasy, he decided, peering down at the 'authorities' and 'crisis experts' trying to get up to speed in a hurry.

Now he had real power over real people.

The music suddenly stopped in the perfumed air of the department store. Now what?

'Due to a police emergency, Saks Fifth Avenue is closing. Please make your way to the nearest exit and please remain calm. You are in no danger.'

The Neat Man couldn't hold back a smile.

Now they were playing his song.

He'd refined his dark urges, hadn't he? Transformed them, made them work in his favor.

He was a master.

He removed a Wet-Nap from his pocket. His hands were still shaking a bit as he tore it open, but by the time he was done with his face, he was steady as a rock.

Then he called home – talked to his wife and kids. 'I'm fine, Helen. I'm in no danger.'

Chapter Twenty-Seven

Stephen Hopkins sat by himself in a pew in a small chapel behind the main altar. His head was buried in his hands. He was almost glad Caroline wasn't around to see what had happened on account of her death. She was such a good soul, it would have hurt her deeply, and it wouldn't have been an act with Caroline.

There were maybe thirty hostages scattered in the pews around him. He recognized a lot of the faces, well-known folks for the most part, the generous ones whom Caroline had gotten to do charity work and other good deeds.

He looked up at the three masked gunmen standing at the front of the chapel. The bastards were always alert. He'd been around a lot of soldiers, and that's what they reminded him of. Soldiers? Was that what they were? Former military?

Did that make the motivation political? When the takeover started, his first thought was that it had to be Middle Eastern terrorists – but it was obvious these men were Americans. What the hell did they want? How could they be so brazen? So unafraid of death?

A short, muscular hijacker stepped into the center aisle and cleared his throat rather theatrically.

'Hi, everybody. I'm *Jack*. You can call my big bad buddy over there *Little John*. Our sincerest apologies for detaining you like this. Anyone who needs to use a bathroom, just raise your hand, and you'll be escorted. There's food and water. Again, just raise your hand. Feel free to lie down in the pews or on the floor there in the back. If you cooperate, things will go smoothly. If you don't, well, the consequences will be very unpleasant. The choice is yours.'

Who was this little twerp to lecture them like they were schoolchildren being held in detention? Stephen Hopkins stood up at the same time as the mayor of New York. The mayor sat back down.

'What's this all about?' Hopkins said angrily. 'What do you want with us? Why do you dishonor my wife?'

'Mr President,' the hijacker said, smiling as he walked down the aisle. 'That tone of voice will not do. I'm going out of my way to be polite. I sincerely urge you to do the same.'

Stephen Hopkins's knuckles went white as he gripped the back of the pew in front of him. He wasn't used to being spoken to like this by anyone. Not in a long, long time.

'Oh, I'm sorry,' he said. 'You want decorum. Then would the gentleman *in the ski mask* deign to let the assembly know why he's holding them hostage?'

A few hostages in the pews laughed nervously and sat up a little straighter.

The lead hijacker looked around at the group. He laughed too. Then he leaned in and grabbed the former president by his full head of white hair.

'Why, why, why?' he said into his ear. 'That was always your weakest side, Stevie-boy. You always had to intellectualize everything.'

'You son of a bitch,' Hopkins yelled, partly because of the pain. It felt like his hair was tearing out of his scalp. This small man, Jack, was very strong.

'Now you're calling my mother a bitch?' Jack said. 'Maybe you've gotten your ass kissed so much you forget that it can get kicked too. Disrespect me again, asshole, and I'll kick your guts out and make you eat 'em.'

Jack yanked the former president out into the aisle. Finally he let go of his hair, and Hopkins sank to the floor.

The hijacker let out a deep breath and smiled at the other hostages.

'See that? There goes my temper,' Jack said. 'Now you've seen my one weakness.'

After a long, thoughtful moment, he made a thumbing motion at the former president.

'Mr President, you know what? You've been through enough today,' he said. 'Why don't you go home? You're dismissed! Get him the hell out of my church.'

Two of the hijackers grabbed the former president roughly by his elbows and started shoving him quickly into the main part of the church, toward the front doors.

'Tell you the truth, though, Hopkins,' Jack called at the former president's back. 'After meeting you, I'm actually *glad* I voted for Nader. Both times.'

Chapter Twenty-Eight

John Rooney, *LA Times*-proclaimed 'film comic of the decade,' was praying. Seriously lapsed or not, he was baptized a Christian, and he was sitting as still as he could in his pew, silently saying the Lord's Prayer to beat the band.

He stopped in midprayer when something small and sharp struck him in the side of the neck. When he looked down, he saw that there was a little wad of folded paper on the pew beside him. What the heck was this?

The paper ball was made from a page ripped out of a hymnal. In black ink, someone had written OPEN ME right over the musical notes.

Rooney palmed the note as he looked up at the hijackers guarding them. The biggest one – Little John, was it? – sat on the altar as if it were the hood of a car, and he yawned so wide that Rooney could see his back molars.

Rooney opened the note in his lap.

ROONEY – I'M IN THE ROW BEHIND YOU. *SLOWLY* SCOOTCH OVER INTO THE CENTER OF YOUR PEW SO WE CAN TALK. WHAT-EVER YOU DO, DON'T LET THE SCUM IN FRONT SEE YOU! – CHARLIE CONLAN

Rooney shoved the note into his pocket, at least until he could get rid of it. Over the course of the next few minutes, he slid over the polished ash wood of the pew.

When he was about halfway, a gravelly voice behind him whispered, 'Jesus, Johnny. I said slowly, not glacially.'

'Sorry,' Rooney whispered back.

'You saw what they did to Hopkins?' Conlan said.

Rooney nodded grimly. 'What do you think they want with the rest of us?' he said.

'Nothing good,' Conlan said. 'I guarantee you. Thing that scares me is how surrounded by cops this church is. Only thing between these guys getting shot or going to jail for life is us.'

'What can we do about it, though?' Rooney said.

'Fight back,' Conlan said. 'Todd Snow's a row behind me. He's talking to the tycoon Xavier Brown, behind him. With you – it's four.'

'To do what?' Rooney asked. 'You saw what they did to Hopkins when he just opened his mouth.'

'We wait for now. Be patient. Pick our spot. Four of us can take one or two of these guys. We go from there. *John, we may not have a choice.*'

Chapter Twenty-Nine

The elation that *New York Times* reporter Cathy Calvin had felt at being released from the cathedral was quickly being burned away by her annoyance at having to wait in line with everybody else to be interviewed by the police. The NYPD had all the detainees corralled outside of Saks Fifth Avenue, and they weren't letting anyone go until they'd been debriefed by one of four detectives sitting at a row of folding tables set up on the sidewalk.

Calvin noticed for the first time the news-van microwave towers beyond the blue-and-white saw-horses. They rose above the crowd like the masts of some invading armada.

Wait a second. What was she thinking? And complaining about? *She was where everyone else was trying to get. Inside the ropes!*

Calvin quickly calculated the strategic advantage of her position. She'd been in the cathedral before, during, and after the takeover. She was an eyewitness to the siege, which would make it her exclusive.

Then she spotted Carmella, the lingerie super-model, three people back in line. Not super-A-list, but a good start.

'Carmella? Hi. Cathy Calvin from the *Times*. You okay? Where were you when it happened? What did you see in there?'

'I vas near da front on da left,' the six-foot-two blonde said in her best Austrian-American accent. 'Poor Caroline's casket had jus' come past our pew. Zen Eberhard, my security man, vas shot right in his crotch with a tear-gas canister. Now I can't find Eberhard anywhere. I keep texting his cell, but he von't answer. Have you seen him?'

Cathy Calvin looked at the towering model curiously. Maybe she was in shock. Hopefully that was it.

'Um. I don't think so,' Cathy said. 'Rumor has it that not all of the hostages have been released. You know anything about that? What have you heard?'

'*Hel-lo,*' the blonde said. 'Have you seen John Rooney? How about Laura Winston, or zat little slut Mercedes? Zey are still inside. Zee mayor is still inside. Deez hijackers have no taste. Vy else keep such losers and let me go?'

Vy else, indeed? Cathy Calvin thought, nodding as

she carefully backed away from the model. This psycho woman was actually complaining that she wasn't still inside. Even if the VIP room was under siege, she wanted in. Yeah, celebrities were normal. They were just like you and me.

Calvin turned away as a hush rolled through the crowd. She peered with the rest of the craning heads toward the cathedral.

Over the hood of a Sanitation Department dump truck, she could see the top of one of the cathedral's main doors coming open again. *Now what?* She ran forward, hustling to get as close as she could to the hot breaking news.

And then, for the second or third time already this morning, the *Times* reporter couldn't believe what she was seeing.

'Oh my God,' she whispered out loud.

Chapter Thirty

I was still in the command center bus, discussing negotiation strategy with Martelli and Mason, when the cathedral doors went flying open for the second time.

It felt like someone had dumped a tray of ice down the back of my shirt when I saw who it was coming out.

Jesus. What were they up to now?

A stunned-looking Stephen Hopkins came stumbling onto the flagstone plaza, and then the doors quickly closed behind him. They'd released Hopkins? But why?

Another completely unexpected move from the hijackers, I thought with a queasy feeling. It was great that they had released the former president, but the way in which they were doing things was all over the place, impossible to predict. Was that the idea? I doubted it.

A spontaneous thunderous cheer ripped from

both the police and the crowd of civilians beyond the barricades.

'Move in,' I heard Commander Will Matthews say. 'Pick the president up. I repeat. *Move in and get him out of there. Now!*'

The words were hardly out of the borough commander's mouth before half a dozen ESU cops nearly gang-tackled the former president and rushed him around the sanitation truck barricade at 50th Street.

I stood, just staring at the cathedral through the trailer window. The spooky gothic arches, the pale granite walls, the dark stained glass, and now Stephen Hopkins released unharmed.

How was I supposed to come up with a way to solve this thing? I thought of Maeve and my kids. I'm not usually one to make excuses, but didn't I have enough on my plate? I needed another crisis?

Paul Martelli's hand found my shoulder. 'You're doing the best with a horrible situation, Mike,' he said as if reading my mind. 'It's the losers inside who are responsible for this quagmire. Not us. Don't forget that.'

'Hey, did you hear the one about the multiagency manhunt for the rabbit in the forest?' Ned Mason said from the corner of the trailer.

I looked up at him. I guess it was joke time.

'No,' I said politely.

'They sent the CIA in first, right?' Mason said. 'CIA comes back, says their operatives report there is no rabbit and no forest. Then they send in the Friggin' Blithering Idiots, and all of a sudden, the forest is on fire and they report that the rabbit had pyrotechnic tendencies and that they saw him with a Zippo. Know what happened when they sent the NYPD into the trees?'

'No, but I'm sure you'll tell me,' I said with a weary attempt at a smile.

Mason just kept talking. He was even scarier than I remembered him being.

'Two detectives go in and come back out five minutes later, pulling a handcuffed bear with a huge black eye who keeps saying, "All right, all right. I'm a rabbit."'

Martelli looked at Mason as I rolled my eyes.

'That joke wasn't half bad,' Martelli said. 'It was all bad.'

Chapter Thirty-One

E ugena Humphrey sat motionless and numb, staring at the flickering candles in front of the altar. She was trying to put the last hour into some kind of worthwhile perspective.

The Los Angeles-based talk-show host knew that in order to get through any horrifying ordeal the first thing you needed to do was to calm your own emotions. The row of votive candles along the south wall of the chapel had caught her attention almost immediately. There was something reassuring, some comforting element in the way the tiny white flames burned behind the gold-and-red glass.

I can get through this, she thought to herself. An enormous number of rescuers had to be clustered outside the church right now. And the press. Something this high-profile would be resolved, for the simple reason that it had to be.

Eugena swallowed hard, and let out a breath.

Things would be resolved.

When she'd first entered the cathedral for the funeral, she'd thought that its high stone and marble walls were too cold, too stark. But after a few moments of looking upon the votives and feeling the deep silence of this place, she realized it expressed the same spiritual warmness she remembered from the Baptist church her mother took her to every Sunday back in West Virginia.

'My God,' a woman whispered next to her. 'My God. How will this horror end?'

It was Laura Winston, the New York fashion magazine institution. Poor Laura was *still* trembling. Her gray-blue eyes bulged as if they were about to pop free of her surgically tightened face. Eugena remembered an attempt to get the trendsetter on her show. She'd obtained Laura's personal number and had called Laura herself in order to discuss her idea – the most fashionable woman in the world's advice for a real-world budget.

And she still remembered the high, cackling laugh that had erupted from her earpiece. 'Oh, who put you up to this?' Winston had said. 'It's Calvin, isn't it? Tell Calvin I'll do Eugena when he goes to work at the Gap.'

What was worse was when, three months later, Winston actually did appear on daytime talk in a segment called 'Haute Couture Meets Main Street.' But it was with Oprah, Eugena's biggest competitor.

Poor woman was a puddle now, though, wasn't she? Eugena thought with compassion.

She'd been vicious, but *that was then.*

Eugena reached across the space of the pew that separated them.

This was now.

Her soft black hand found the fashionista's bony white one, and she squeezed gently until Winston looked into her eyes. Eugena put her arm around the distraught woman as she started to hyperventilate.

'Now, now. We're in a church and in His hands,' Eugena said soothingly. She could hear the strength and faith in her own voice and was proud of herself.

She really could get through this. They all could. Somehow, some way.

'Everything's going to be all right,' she said. 'You're fine, Laura. This too shall pass.'

'Yes. But will any of us still be alive?'

Chapter Thirty-Two

Laura Winston had dried most of her tears with a chic red silk scarf she'd removed from her jacket pocket and was quietly thanking Eugena for her kindness when there was a loud commotion up toward the altar.

Somebody was standing up!

From the tangle of blond hair and black mini, Laura could tell it was the haute-trash pop singer Mercedes Freer.

Marble rang as she clicked in her six-inch stilettos toward the rear of the chapel.

'Sit the hell down!' one of the hijackers yelled at her immediately, and very loudly.

'Could I fucking talk to someone, please? I need to talk to your boss, if you don't fucking mind,' the diva said, her foul language echoing off the walls of the church. 'Just let me talk to somebody in charge!'

Laura and Eugena craned their necks to watch the spectacle along with the rest of the hostages. What the hell was this crazy woman up to?

The lead hijacker arrived on the scene a moment later.

'What is it?' Jack said. '*Talk* to me. I'm a fan, after all. How can I help?'

Mercedes plucked first one, then the other of her diamond earrings off and offered them to Jack.

'These are Cartier,' she said in a loud whisper. 'I paid, or whatever, a quarter of a million dollars for them. Now, I'm supposed to be on Leno tonight, and he tapes at six, *LA time,* and I'm already running late. You know what I'm saying? I'm not political or religious, nothing like that. My label arranged for me to sing "Ave Maria" and jet out. Please take 'em. They're real, and they're yours. They're not enough, I'll get my manager on the phone. Say the word. Let's make a deal, sugar.'

Eugena winced at the white girl's attempted inner-city speak. After booking her on the show a year ago, Eugena remembered reading in her bio that she'd been born in white-bread New Canaan, Connecticut. Eugena thought about all the elocution books she herself had gotten out of the library to get the sound of poor *out* of her voice. What a sorry state this upside-down world had come to.

The hijacker held up the earrings as if appraising them. Then he flicked them one after the other right into the girl's face.

'How about instead,' he said slowly, 'you sit your slutty ass down?'

Mercedes's face darkened. Then she snapped her fingers in the hijacker's face. 'Slutty what?' she said angrily. 'Who do you think you're talkin' to, shorty?'

The hijacker immediately pulled out a spray canister from his pocket. He grabbed the singer by her hair and emptied it into her face. Mercedes's skin looked like it was blistering as she screamed through the pepper spray.

As she fell to her knees, Jack calmly dragged her across the marble center aisle by her hair, right to the door of a confessional on the north wall. He opened it, threw the girl in with force, then slammed it shut.

'Little hot shit for the hot shit,' he said to the wide-eyed hostages. 'Anybody else want to discuss their travel plans?'

Jack tapped his foot in the silence.

'Guess not,' he said finally. 'Well, listen up, kids. We need to start an individual interview process, so I'm going to have to go ahead and ask everyone to line up in front of the first door to the right at the back of the chapel. *Now!*'

Eugena stood and turned meekly around along with the rest of the hostages. As she came out into the aisle, she could hear Mercedes whimpering inside the confessional.

She almost felt sorry for the girl, but what good did it do to antagonize these men? What did she think was going to happen? What was she thinking? She probably actually thought he would let her go, Eugena decided. When was the last time a human being had said no to the spoiled-brat music star?

As Eugena got in the queue behind the others, she decided that out of everyone in here, *she* was the one to speak to their captors. No one had a better chance of success than she did. For better or worse, it had always been that way.

She glanced at the golden, glowing rows of flickering candles. Maybe that was the reason she'd been put here, Eugena thought.

To try to talk her way out of this.

Chapter Thirty-Three

C harlie Conlan waited in line for his 'interview' in front of one of the purple-draped confessionals along the south walkway.

Sounded a little melodramatic if you asked him, more cheesy scare tactics like the masks and robes. It seemed like the hijackers were trying to play off the gothic mood of the place, get people afraid, keep 'em off balance at all times. Fairly intelligent tactics, actually.

Conlan knew most over-the-hill rock legends like him were pretty soft. But few had his background. What growing up poor on the downtown streets of Detroit had failed to teach him, an extended stay at the Hanoi Hilton for most of '69 had filled in pretty well.

Conlan steeled himself as the dark-wood door finally opened and a woman, Marilyn Rubenstein, emerged from her 'interview.' He saw that the young actress looked shaken as she came closer to him. Her blond hair was plastered to her scalp with sweat, and her glazed-over eyes looked as if she had just been forced to witness something grossly wrong.

She caught Conlan gaping at her as the guards led her past. 'Do what they say,' she advised in a whisper.

'*Next*,' the hijacker at the door called in a bored voice. 'That means *you*, hotshot.'

Conlan hesitated; then he stepped across the marble entryway and into the room.

It wasn't a confessional, Conlan realized immediately. It was a little security room. Some folding chairs, a table. A coffee machine and a row of charging walkie-talkies on a metal desk along one wall.

Sitting at the metal table in the middle of the room was the lead hijacker, Jack. He motioned to the empty metal chair on the opposite side of the table.

'Please, Mr Conlan, have a seat. I'm a big fan, by the way.'

Conlan sat. 'Thank you.'

On the table between them were two items. A pair of handcuffs in a clear plastic bag, and a roll of duct tape. Conlan eyed the items, trying to keep the fear in his belly from rising. *Don't show 'em anything, Charlie. Everything close to the vest.*

Jack lifted a clipboard from his lap. His pen clicked. 'Okay, Mr Charlie Conlan,' he said. 'In order to facilitate things here, I'm going to have to ask you for the names and numbers of your financial people. Any kind of pin or access codes that are needed to get to your funds, passwords, that sort of thing, would be most helpful.'

Conlan forced himself to smile as he made eye contact with Jack.

'So all this is about money?' he said.

The hijacker tapped the pen against the top of the clipboard and frowned.

'I don't have the time for idle chitchat, Mr Conlan,' Jack said. 'Are you going to cooperate or not? Last chance.'

Conlan decided he needed to push the envelope some. See exactly what they were dealing with here.

'Let me think about that for a second,' he said, rubbing his chin with his fingertips. 'Agghh. Ummmm. Fuck, no?'

Jack slowly took the cuffs out of the plastic bag, and then he stood. He walked behind Conlan and quickly, expertly cuffed his wrists behind his back.

Conlan clenched his jaw as he waited for the first blow to come. He'd had teeth pulled out with pliers. He hoped the little Napoleonic bastard had brought his lunch.

But the first blow didn't come.

Instead there was a quick rustle – and the plastic bag was plopped over Conlan's head.

Tape shrieked, and then a nooselike pressure encased Charlie Conlan's neck, closing the bag with an airtight seal. Sweat immediately began flooding out of his pores. The plastic clung to his skin like grease, rattled in his mouth and nostrils as he took a panicked breath.

'Little hot in there, isn't it, hardass?' Jack said through the membrane of plastic near Conlan's ear.

Conlan gagged. His throat was burning up. *Oh God, Christ, no. Not like this.*

Jack sat down, yawned, and crossed his legs as Conlan convulsed. After an eternity, Jack checked his watch.

'You want to sign up for my cash-for-oxygen program?' he asked. 'Up to you.'

Plastic crackled in Conlan's ears as he nodded vigorously.

Jack reached across the table, and air, sweet air, rushed in around his gloved finger as he poked a small hole in the bag.

'I thought the Beatles were an influence of yours, Charlie,' Jack said, smiling as he drummed his fingers on the table. 'C'mon. Don't you remember? "The best things in life are free"?'

Conlan gasped and wheezed with his head down against the table. The clipboard was slid beside his chin. A pen landed on top of it.

Two thoughts pounded through Conlan's brain with the returning oxygen. The first was a prayer. The second a curse.

My God.

We're completely fucked.

Chapter Thirty-Four

I had just gotten off the phone with Maeve, and I was thinking, *I needed to hear her voice even more than she needed to hear from me.*

Just then, Steve Reno sauntered into the command trailer carrying a cardboard box of sandwiches and coffee. He gave me one of the coffees along with a handshake.

I remembered Steve from several standoffs. Like most of the top cops in the NYPD, the tall, long-haired, muscular tactical officer was kind of an anomaly. No one was more patient and compassionate on the outside of a barricaded door – and no one was quicker when it had to be kicked in. Steve Reno was definitely a mystery man. Three wives so far, five kids, lived in SoHo but drove a pickup truck with a Semper Fi sticker on the rear window.

Behind him were two FBI commandos in black SWAT fatigues. The shorter of the two could have been a plumber, or a schoolteacher, except for the bright green eyes that scanned the trailer and me with the efficient sweep of a copying machine light bar.

'Mike, this is Dave Oakley from HRT,' Steve told me. 'The greatest tactical team supervisor alive.'

'Let's just keep it that way, huh, Steve? No mess-ups today,' the commando said with a gruff, humorless laugh as I shook his callused hand. 'What's the story with our new best friends inside?'

I filled him in as best I could. The only change in the commando's expression was a compression of his lips when I mentioned the explosives. He nodded quietly when I was done.

'We got our work cut out for us today,' Reno said finally. 'We already spoke to Secret Service. President Hopkins told them the remaining hostages are being held in the Lady Chapel at the far rear of the church. He said that in addition to being extremely calm, the kidnappers aren't taking an iota of shit from any of the captives. They seemed trained, well disciplined. They're not terrorists. They're American, apparently. New one to me.'

'New one to all of us,' I said as the door opened again behind Reno.

Another baseball-hat-wearing ESU cop came in with an elderly man in a tweed cap. The old man was carrying a large cardboard cylinder. What the hell was this all about?

'I'm Mike Nardy, the cathedral's caretaker,' he said, popping open the cylinder's lid. 'The rectory told me to bring these here.'

I helped him unroll the blueprints. The paper was old, yellowed at the edges, but the detailing of the cathedral was extensive. I used a couple of chattering radios to hold it open as Reno, Oakley, and Commander Will Matthews leaned over to look.

The overhead view of St Patrick's Cathedral looked like a cross. The main Fifth Avenue entrance was at the bottom of the long piece, and the 50th and 51st Street entryways at the sides of the shorter one. The Lady Chapel, like a small extension at the top of the long part of the cross, had no way in or out.

'I got snipers in Saks on Forty-ninth and in 620 Fifth behind us,' said Oakley. 'I'll have to get one on Madison at the rear to watch the Lady Chapel. Too bad these damn stained-glass windows are about as clear as a brick wall. Mr Nardy, it's hard to tell from these schematics. Is there a clear line of sight from the rose window here in the front to the Lady Chapel in the rear?'

'In part,' the serious old man said with a curious squint of his face. 'Though there are columns along the back of the altar and a fifty-seven-foot baldachin – that's a bronze gazebo-type structure – over the altar.'

'The cathedral's a block long. What's that, five hundred feet?' Oakley said to his second-in-command. 'We do our reconnaissance. Fiber-optic camera through one of those windows, maybe. Get heat signatures of the weapons to pick out the bad guys. Time's right, we rappel down the front edifice, blow the rose window and all the chapel windows simultaneously.'

'I know I must be going a little deaf,' the caretaker, Nardy, said to Oakley. 'Because for a second there I thought you said you were going to destroy the great rose window of St Patrick's Cathedral.'

'You don't have to concern yourself with police business, Mr Nardy, is it?' Oakley said. 'Lives are on the line. We'll do what we have to do.'

'That rose window is a hundred and fifty years old, sir,' the caretaker said, folding his stick-thin arms. 'It's irreplaceable, as are the windows of the Lady Chapel and every other of the cathedral's last artifacts and statues. You wouldn't be so quick to blow a hole in the side of the Statue of Liberty, would you? Well, this church is this city's Statue of Faith, so you better come up with some other plan. You'll destroy it over my dead body.'

'Remove Mr Nardy, somebody, please,' Oakley said, annoyed.

'You better listen to me!' Nardy said forcefully as the ESU cop escorted him back outside. 'I'll go right to the press.'

That's all we needed, wasn't it? I thought. Another challenge, another messy obstacle. This thing wasn't hard enough without having our hands tied behind our backs.

Oakley turned his black baseball hat around on his head. He looked like a catcher who'd missed the throw to second on a steal as he exhaled loudly into his cupped hands.

'Jesus, would you look at this clambake?' Oakley said. 'The granite walls are what? Two feet thick? The doors are foot-thick bronze. I don't think we've ever tried to breach either a door *that big*, or one made of *bronze*.

'Even the *precious* windows have stone tracery. There's no adjoining buildings we can try to tunnel our way in from. This place is a fortress. St Pat's is probably the best place in this city to hold off an army. And we have to infiltrate it without blowing it up or leaving a scratch. Would somebody please remind me why I took this job?'

'The fat sneaker contracts and the book deals,' I said. 'Just like the rest of us.'

It was a lame joke, but under the circumstances

I didn't need to be Billy Crystal to provide an outlet for the mounting stress. Everyone, including the stoic Oakley, got a pretty good laugh.

It was either that or cry.

Chapter Thirty-Five

Ten minutes later, we were outside in the frosty air, staring up at the magnificent church. As we stepped around the side of one of the dump trucks, Oakley spoke into his hands-free radio and ordered his snipers to get an angle on the irreplaceable windows of the Lady Chapel.

The gray light cast shadows into the church's second-story windows and its arched entryway. The front of the cathedral resembled a large face, I thought: wide, dark eyes and a very large mouth, gaping open as if in outrage and shock.

I stopped dead still and almost went for my Glock again when the bells started sounding. I thought it was another move by the hijackers – until I glanced at my watch and saw that it was twelve.

The bells, set on some timer no doubt, were sounding out the Angelus, reminding the bustling heathens of Midtown to pray for some specific devotion I couldn't remember. If failing to induce a communal saying of the Rosary, the tolling of the bells at least silenced the crowd of cops and press and onlookers.

Each long peal rang out loudly and forebodingly off the surrounding skyscrapers' stone and aluminum and glass.

I scanned the crowd as an idea occurred to me.

I spotted the caretaker, Nardy, talking to a young woman across the 50th Street barricade.

'Mr Nardy, where are the bells located?' I said as I jogged up to him, interrupting his conversation with the woman.

He stared at me before answering. 'In the north spire,' he said with a grimace.

I looked at the ornate thirty-story cone of stone. About a hundred feet up, I noticed green slats that seemed like faded copper shutters.

'Is there access to the bells from inside?' I asked Nardy.

The caretaker nodded. 'There's an old winding set of wooden maintenance stairs from a time when the bells were rung by hand.'

It seemed risky, but if we could get up there somehow – maybe we could quietly pry loose some of the copper slats and get in.

'Can the inside of the north spire be seen from down in the church?' I asked.

'Why?' asked the woman Nardy had been talking to. 'Do you plan to blow it up, too? Detective . . . ?'

Chapter Thirty-Six

I noticed the *New York Times* press pass on the lapel of her cloth coat for the first time. So much for my keen detectively powers of observation.

'Bennett,' I said.

'Bennett, yes. You're Manhattan North, right? I've heard of you. How's Will Matthews doing?'

Like most cops, I couldn't quite buy the whole 'the people have a right to know' argument the press likes to toss around. I might, if all that journalistic nobility didn't have a price tag attached to it. They *sold* newspapers last time I checked.

I gave the young newsie my best pissed-off-cop face. Though it was easily as fierce as Commander Will Matthews's, she didn't seem fazed by it in the least, the little snot.

'Why don't you ask him yourself?' I finally said.

'I would. But he has caller ID. So, what's the story, Detective? Does nobody know nuttin'?' she said, her cultured voice dropping into passable New Yorkese. 'Or is nobody tawkin'?'

'Why don't you choose the answer you like the most?' I advised, turning away.

'Hmmm. Speaking of choices, I wonder if my editor will like BIGGEST SECURITY BLUNDER IN WORLD HISTORY for the headline? Or maybe, NYPD DROPS BALL THEN STONEWALLS?' the *Times* reporter said. 'That's kinda catchy. What do you think, Detective Bennett? Too *New York Post*?'

I winced, remembering what Will Matthews had said. He wouldn't like it if I were the one to single-handedly bring more bad press for the NYPD.

'Listen, Ms Calvin,' I said, turning. 'Let's not get off on the wrong foot here. I'll talk to you, of course, but strictly off the record. Agreed?'

The reporter nodded quickly.

'You basically know as much as we do at this point. We're in contact with the kidnappers, but they have yet to give us their demands. As soon as we know, and I get permission, I'll give you all the information I can, all right? But we are in crisis mode right now. If the psychos inside have a radio or a TV and get tipped off about what we're going to do, then people will die. Very important people.'

When I turned, I saw Ned Mason waving frantic-ally at me from the door of the trailer.

'We all have to come together on this,' I yelled over my shoulder as I began to run.

Chapter Thirty-Seven

Mason handed me the ringing cell phone just as I made it to the doorway.

'Mike here,' I said.

'Mike. Hey, buddy,' Jack said. 'What's up with letting the phone keep ringing like that? You falling asleep on me? If I didn't know what a sweet guy you were, I might get the impression you were busy plotting against me or something.'

'Thanks for releasing the president,' I said sincerely.

'Ah, don't mention it,' Jack said. 'It was the least I could do. Say, listen, the reason I'm calling is, I've got those demands together, and I was thinking of maybe e-mailing them to you. That all right? I'm usually a snail-mail kind of guy, to tell you the truth, but you know how much of a zoo the post office is around the holidays.'

The pseudocasual way Jack was speaking to me was starting to grate on my nerves. My negotiation training was mostly based on calming dangerous people who were actually distraught, people who had snapped, had gone over the edge.

But Jack was nothing but a cocky wiseass . . . killer?

In the parlance of the NYPD, with apologies to mixed-breed dogs, criminals – human beings who have forgone their humanity – are referred to as 'mutts.' As I stood there with the phone in my hand, I reminded myself that that was all Jack was. A smart mutt, a sophisticated mutt maybe, but a mutt all the same.

I checked my anger by visualizing cuffing him, dragging him by the scruff of his neck past the people he was terrorizing. It was going to happen, I knew. Just a matter of time, I thought as I was handed an e-mail address by a tech cop.

'All right, Jack,' I said. 'Here's our address.'

'Okay,' Jack said after I gave him the specifics on the NYPD web site. 'We'll send the stuff over in a minute or two. I'll give you a little while to absorb things and then call you back. How does that sound?'

'Sounds good,' I said.

'Oh, and Mike?' Jack said.

'What's that?' I said.

'I'm really appreciating all the cooperation. We all do. Things keep running this smooth, it's going to turn out to be a real holly, jolly Christmas,' Jack said, and hung up.

Chapter Thirty-Eight

'Here it is,' one of the youngish cops in front of a laptop at the back of the trailer called in a high-pitched choirboy's voice. 'The demands are coming in.'

I raced to the rear.

I couldn't believe what I was seeing as I looked at the screen. I was expecting a number, but what appeared looked like a long, fairly sophisticated spreadsheet.

Down the left-hand margin were the full names of the thirty-three hostages.

Next to each name was a ransom between two and four million dollars, followed by contacts: the names of the hostages' lawyers, agents, business managers, spouses, and all of their respective phone numbers.

At the bottom of the sheet was a bank routeing number and specific, very clear instructions on how to wire the money via the Internet into the account.

I absolutely couldn't believe this bullshit. The hijackers, instead of negotiating with us directly, were going straight to the source – namely the wealthy hostages themselves.

ESU lieutenant Steve Reno cracked his knuckles loudly behind me. 'First they take us out of action,' he said angrily. 'Now they make us their errand boys.'

Steve was right. These hijackers were acting like we didn't exist. They were acting the way a kidnapper in a concealed location would – not like ten to a dozen guys surrounded by a battalion of heavily armed law enforcement, NYPD, and FBI.

'Let's get some people in here to start calling those numbers and get this thing organized,' Commander Will Matthews said. 'And give that account number to the Bureau. See if maybe they can get a lead for us.'

I closed my eyes and tapped the cell phone against my head in order to jolt something loose. Nothing was coming, so I checked my watch. Mistake. Only four hours had passed. Based on how completely exhausted I felt, I would have guessed it was four weeks.

Somebody handed me a coffee. There were cartoon reindeer and a smiling Santa on the paper cup. For a moment, I thought of how nice it would be when I finally got home. Christmas music playing softly as Maeve directed our ten elves in decorating the tree.

Then I remembered there was no tree.

And no Maeve.

I put the cup of coffee down and picked up one of the printouts of the demands, my fingers shaking slightly as they went down the list of contact numbers.

The great and glorious NYPD – acting as messengers.

Chapter Thirty-Nine

John Rooney lifted his chin off his hands when something hard poked into his ribs. He glanced over and saw Little John, holding out his billy club.

'Hey, prima donna,' Little John said. 'I'm getting bored. Time for you to get up on that altar and give us a little holiday entertainment. Whattaya say, guy?'

'I'm really not in the mood,' Rooney said, dropping his head back down.

Rooney's teeth clicked together loudly when Little John gave him a love tap on the chin with the end of the club.

'Here's your motivation,' Little John said. 'Get up there and make me laugh like a hyena. Or I'll shatter your Oscar-nominated skull open.'

My God, Rooney thought as he arrived up on the altar and stared out at the other hostages. Some of them were still crying. Just about every face was filled with wide-eyed terror.

Talk about a hard crowd to work. Plus, he hadn't

done stand-up since he'd broken into film eight years ago. And even then, all his jokes had been rehearsed ad nauseam in front of the bathroom mirror of his studio apartment in Hell's Kitchen.

Little John, sitting in the back row, made a *c'mon* gesture with his baton.

What the hell could be funny about any of this? But what choice did he have?

'Hey, everybody,' Rooney tried. 'Thanks for coming this morning. Heeere's Johnny!'

He heard somebody, a woman, give a real laugh. Who was that? It was Eugena Humphrey. Good for her!

Then Rooney felt something in him flick like a circuit-breaker.

'Eugena, hey, how YOU doin', honey chile?' he said, mimicking the opening tagline from her morning show. She really started cracking up now, along with a few more people. Charlie Conlan was grinning broadly.

Rooney faked checking his watch.

'Talk about a long frickin' Mass,' he said.

There were more laughs.

'You know what I really hate?' Rooney said, stalking back and forth now in front of the altar. 'Don't you just hate it when you go to a friend's funeral and you get *kidnapped*?'

Rooney chuckled along with the cackles, maximizing the pause for effect. He was rolling pretty good now. He could feel it all through his nervous system.

'I mean, there you are, all dressed up, a little sad about the person gone – but a little happy that it's not you, then wham! Wouldn't you know it? The monks at the altar whip out sawn-off shotguns and grenades.'

Almost everybody was laughing now. Even a few of the hijackers in the back were cracking up. The laughter rolled like a wave off the stone walls.

Rooney started doing a Gregorian chant and then imitated whipping out a gun. He made a terrified face and ran and hid behind the altar. 'Here, take my diamond earrings so I can jet,' he said, imitating Mercedes Freer to a tee. Then he rolled around on the marble floor, holding his face and whining like a hurt chihuahua.

When he glanced at the crowd, he could see smiles everywhere. At least his routine was relaxing everyone a little. At the back of the chapel, he spotted Little John doubled over, holding his sides.

Keep laughing, asshole, Rooney thought, getting up off his knees. *I got a million of 'em. Wait'll you hear the one about the kidnapper getting the electric chair.*

Chapter Forty

From the back of the chapel, former rock-and-roller Charlie Conlan pretended to laugh at John Rooney's shtick as he studied the hijackers one by one.

There were six of the jackals along the rear rail of the chapel. The big one, Little John, was there, but the leader, Jack, along with another five or six others, seemed to be away somewhere else in the church.

As the rest of the hostages continued to laugh at Rooney, Conlan did his best to recall some of his army training. He counted the grenades on the kidnappers' chests, eyed the guns they carried, the batons, the bulge at the waist of their robes where bulletproof vests seemed to end.

He slid a couple of feet to the left in his pew, nothing too obvious, nothing to draw any attention.

'Todd,' he whispered.

'What's up?' the New York Giants football star murmured near his ear.

'Is Brown with us?' The real-estate tycoon was a big man, in his fifties, who looked to be in pretty good shape.

'He's psyched,' the athlete said. 'He talked to Rubenstein. Rubenstein's going to try to get the mayor on board.'

Conlan was glad the quarterback was with them. Out of all of them, the six-four, two-hundred-thirty-pound athlete had the best shot at physically over-powering one of the hijackers.

'That's progress,' Conlan said to Snow out of the corner of his mouth. 'With Rooney, that makes at least five of us. The more, the better our chances.'

'What's our move?' the quarterback asked.

'This is between me and you for now. You know how they frisked us? Took away our cell phones and wallets?' Conlan said.

He paused as Rooney told another joke.

'They missed the twenty-two in my boot,' Conlan whispered.

There, he'd said it, he thought. He didn't have a gun, but survival meant keeping up people's spirits, keeping them hopeful and motivated to act when the time was right.

Conlan glanced up at the altar when he heard more applause. Rooney was taking a bow now. The show was over.

'We've got a shot,' the quarterback said through the clapping. 'Say the word. We go. We roll.'

Chapter Forty-One

The Neat Man winced as he probed a gloved hand behind the pay phone in the kiosk on the northwest corner of 51st and Madison. The sour reek of stale urine rising from the phone's pedestal teared his eyes as he groped around blindly. *Where the hell was the device?*

Of all the places to set up a rendezvous, he thought as his fingers finally, mercifully found the plastic-coated wire behind the steel box.

Yet another bullet point in their plan, he noted as he clipped a phone company dial set across the pair of hidden colored wires. Three weeks before, his boys had actually snaked a pair of phone lines through a street duct in the rectory basement, into the corner phone company manhole, and, from the manhole, up the pay phone duct here to the street. Anticipating that all cell phone and landline transmissions in and out of the church would be monitored, they had created their own undocumented line.

The Neat Man checked his watch as he lifted the dial set to his ear.

At exactly 6:00 p.m. there was a crackle as one of the hijackers inside St Patrick's attached a simple nine-volt battery to the opposite end of the line, powering it. Instead of going high tech, they had outwitted the dopes by going low tech. He had every angle covered, right through to the dramatic climax and escape, which, he had to admit, was a real doozy.

The Neat Man whistled softly – 'O Come, All Ye Faithful,' a holiday favorite of his.

'You there, Jack?'

'Where else would I be? How's it looking from your end?' Jack answered.

'When you sent out that first wave,' the Neat Man said with a smile, 'they didn't know whether to shit or go blind. Ditto with Hopkins. They're still shaking their heads in disbelief.'

'That's what I like to hear,' Jack said.

'How'd the interviews with all our rich friends go?'

'Real informative,' Jack said. 'Question now is, will law enforcement stay stunned and stumped for the amount of time we need to get this done?'

'From what I've seen so far,' the Neat Man said with a laugh, 'they'll be scratching their heads 'til *next* Christmas.'

'Pardon me for not chuckling along with you there, buddy,' Jack said coldly. 'For some reason things don't seem so funny on the side of the wall everyone's pointing guns at.'

'We all have our part to play, Jack,' the Neat Man said. His partner in crime was a born worrier. Not his most attractive quality.

'Yeah, well, if I was you, I'd make extra sure I didn't screw up,' Jack said with menace before disconnecting their private line.

Chapter Forty-Two

T he next time I glanced up from the notes I was
making on the negotiation with Jack, the
command center's small window to the outside had
somehow become dark. The time had flown. Paul
Martelli was busy talking on the phone beside me. Ned
Mason was on the phone, too. A dozen or more other
cops were working laptops, including Steve Reno.

I stood up and palmed the low ceiling as I stretched
pretty close to my full six two.

The demands had been sent to the FBI's New York
headquarters downtown, at 26 Federal Plaza. The
Bureau's White Collar Crime Squad was crunching the
numbers. The grand total of the ransom was nearly
eighty million dollars.

It was a massive sum for one person to pay, but if
you broke it down to the two and a half million or so
for each hostage, it wasn't that outrageous.

In fact, it was incredible how *willing* to pay these
people seemed to be.

Celebrity spouses and family members were giving me the numbers of their financial people almost before I had a chance to explain who I was. More than one Hollywood talent agency I spoke to didn't hesitate to put up the firm's money for their lucrative clients. Three investment banks were working overtime organizing all the wire transfers.

One Beverly Hills lawyer actually asked for the hijackers' number – to see if he could negotiate directly. *Uh, Jack – Marv Begelman from California wants to talk with you.*

It irked me, but I had to agree with what Jack had said before giving the demands. The fat cats were more than willing to buy their way out of trouble.

As I stepped outside the bus for some much-needed air, the first thing that hit me was the buzz-saw chattering of diesel generators. A half dozen portable crime scene light carts had been set up, and they illuminated the cathedral as if this were Times Square. For a second, the scene reminded me of another annoying NYC phenomenon: location shoots for movies – idling trailers, blocked-off streets, bright lights anywhere you looked.

Time to hit the catering van, I thought. See if I could keep some food down.

As I walked east along 50th, I could see that the

sides of the cathedral were lit up too. There should have been families strolling hand in hand down this block around now. Rosy-cheeked visitors from across the country and the world, sipping hot cocoa and smiling as they caught the candle glow from the famous stained-glass windows.

On the northwest corner of the Saks Fifth Avenue roof, I spotted a motionless FBI sniper.

The whole thing was totally insane.

What was even crazier was that these maniacs thought they were going to get away with it.

How? Every inch of the cathedral was being scoped out by snipers. Air traffic had been diverted, so even an unlikely helicopter escape couldn't work. As Oakley, the HRT supervisor, had mentioned, the hundred-and-fifty-year-old church was built right on top of Manhattan bedrock. So there was no basement, no way to get out from underground.

I tried to convince myself that the hijackers hadn't thought the grand finale through, that Jack had put their escape plan in the cross-that-bridge-when-we-come-to-it file.

But as I stood out on that cold, deserted street, all evidence pointed to the alternative. The boldness of their action, the confidence that we would do exactly as they said. It was looking more and more like the hijackers knew something about their exodus that we didn't.

I was rubbing my hands for warmth when my cell phone rang.

I snatched the line to Jack, stiffening for the next ninety-mile-an-hour curveball that was more than likely heading straight for my forehead.

Then I realized it wasn't the police cell ringing but my own personal one. I rolled my eyes when I saw that the number on my caller ID was my grandfather Seamus.

As if I didn't have enough on my mind.

Chapter Forty-Three

'Seamus, I'm busy. What is it?' I greeted my grandfather. Not the warmest of salutations, maybe, but I wasn't filled with Christmas cheer right at that moment. Besides, conversation to my grandfather, even at seventy-four years old, is a form of combat. If you don't put yourself on the offensive immediately, he will eat you alive.

'Well, a fine good evening to you as well, young Micheál,' Seamus said. I knew I was in for it when my Hibernian forebear reverted to the Gaelic form of my name. My grandfather didn't just kiss the Blarney Stone, family legend had it. He bit off a chunk and swallowed it. *Daily.*

'And an especially fine way of conversing with the man currently taking care of your flock of goslings,' he finished.

Flock of goslings, I thought, rolling my eyes. My grandfather could make Malachy or Frank McCourt eat his tweed cap. He was the biggest, most blustery stage Irishman alive. He'd come to this country in the forties at the age of twelve. Sixty-some years had passed since he'd set foot on the 'old sod,' as he called it, but if you didn't know him better, at any given moment you'd think he'd just put up the donkey after cutting turf from the bog.

He was constantly coming in to check on his great-grandkids, though. Underneath the mile-thick crust of blarney, thank God, actually lay a heart of pure gold.

'Where's Mary Catherine?' I said.

'Is that her name, now? We weren't formally introduced. Why didn't you tell me you were adopting another child?'

I knew it. The lethal innuendo just beneath the surface. If you looked closely, you could see that Seamus's tongue was really the blade of a slicing machine.

'That's a good one, old man,' I said. 'You must have been saving it up all afternoon. Mary Catherine happens to be the au pair.'

'*Au pair.* Is that whatcher callin'm these days?' my grandfather said. 'Be careful, young Micheál. Eileen, your grandmother, caught me talking to an *au pair* once on a street corner one Sunday in Dublin. She broke three of me ribs with a hurling stick.'

'Dublin?' I said. 'That's funny. I thought Grandma Eileen was from Queens.'

As he began to stammer out an explanation, I told him about the letter from Maeve's mother and Mary Catherine's mysterious arrival the night before.

'You're the authority on all things Irish,' I said. 'What do you make of it?'

'I don't like it,' he said. 'This young girl could be after something. Keep track of the silverware.'

'Gee, thanks for the heads-up, you suspicious old coot,' I finally said. 'And speaking of the goslings, I don't know when I'll have a chance to get out of here, but you tell them to get their homework out of the way and to start their jobs. Their *duties*. They'll know what you're talking about.'

'Does it have to do with that chart on the icebox in the kitchen?' my grandfather asked.

'Yes,' I said. 'It does indeed.'

'Whose idea was that? You or Maeve?' my grandfather said suspiciously.

'Maeve,' I said. 'She thought it would be good to give them something positive to do. Get their minds off everything else. Besides, they're actually helping out. It's amazing what ten pairs of hands, even little ones, can get done.'

'It's not a good idea,' my grandfather finally said

brightly. 'It's a great one. No wonder Maeve came up with it.'

'You done now?' I said, half laughing. He loved Maeve as much as any of us.

'Any last insults before I hang up?' I said, conceding him the last word to get the call over with.

'A few,' Seamus said. 'But I'll be seeing you later. I might as well save them up.'

Chapter Forty-Four

This was the kind of outlandish nightmare scene during which you were continually thinking, *This can't possibly be happening. I'll wake up soon and it'll be over.*

The 'danger zone' was occupied by police only and was off-limits to the press. The next outer ring belonged to the media and was dominated by TV trucks with giant antennae extended. The scene in the 'staging area' was all crisscrossing cables, reporters at their computers, dozens of TV monitors. Periodically we would convene a press conference and feed the newsies.

The portable generators for the lights were still roaring in the cold when I started walking back toward the bus. I found Commander Will Matthews inside. All the hostage advocates had been contacted, he informed me, and the situation was now officially in a holding pattern.

'Now for the excruciating part,' Will Matthews said. 'It's time to sit and wait this thing out.'

'Hey, Mike,' Martelli said as he stood. Though he'd been at this siege situation from the beginning, he didn't look it.

'Nothing personal, but you seem beat. Why don't you get out of here for a little while? These jokers say they won't call back for hours, and when they do, we – and more important, those hostages inside – are going to need you calm and collected.'

'He's right. Grab a bite. We need you on ice,' said Commander Will Matthews. 'That's an order, Mike.'

All the talk, and the thoughts of Maeve on my stroll, made me want to see her. The New York Hospital Cancer Center was only twenty blocks uptown, I thought. It wouldn't take very long to swing by there.

I'm going to head to a cancer center to blow off steam, I realized.

I left my cell number with Martelli and stowed my badge before I stepped out from the checkpoints. Countless reporters, producers, correspondents, and technicians were camped out around both sides of blocked-off Fifth Avenue with the giddy camaraderie of deadheads with tickets to Jerry Garcia's back-from-the-grave concert.

I had to wake up a burly cameraman who was sleeping in a folding chair in front of my blue Imp. I jumped inside the car and hit the road.

I made two stops actually. The first was at a great, crazy place called Burger Joint in the lobby of the Le Méridien hotel on 57th. Minutes later, I left there with a greasy brown paper bag under my arm. The second stop was at Amy's Bread on Ninth, where I left with another bag.

I put on my light and siren as I made a left onto Park Avenue. Poinsettias and white lights fringed the center median as far as the eye could see to the north. Massive wreaths were hung above the revolving doors of the gleaming glass office towers, as well as from the polished brass doors of the luxury apartment houses I passed farther uptown.

As I drove, I couldn't help staring at the high, stately old buildings lit up through the billowing silver of the avenue steam stacks, the gleaming wood-paneled walls beneath the opulent awnings.

As I waited on the light at 61st, a top-hatted doorman escorted a pale, devastatingly beautiful brunette in an ankle-length white mink and a little girl in red plaid into the plush rear leather of a waiting Mercedes.

The holiday beauty I saw everywhere I looked made my chest literally ache with guilt. I'd been so shot to pieces lately, I hadn't even gotten a tree.

No wonder so many people went and killed themselves around the holidays, I thought as I screeched around the CL55 and the corner. Christmas was geared to make you explode with contentment, to burn with the passing year's tremendous love and good fortune.

To be anything short of excited seemed, well, impolite.

To be depressed at this time of year, I thought, gunning my car east down a cold, black side street, to be actually sick with sadness, felt like an unforgivable sin.

Chapter Forty-Five

My sweet Maeve had her eyes closed as I stepped through her open hospital room door.

But her nose was definitely still in working order because she smiled when I put the smuggled packages on her drab-colored tray.

'No,' she said in her cracked voice. 'You didn't?' I lifted her plastic water cup and made her drink some. Her eyes teared with pain as she sat up. So did mine.

'I smell cheeseburgers,' she said with a dead seriousness. 'If this is a dream and you wake me up, I won't be responsible, Mike.'

'You're not dreaming, angel,' I said into her ear as I climbed in carefully beside her. 'Do you want the double onion or the double onion?'

Though Maeve only ate half of the burger and only about a quarter of the blondie, her cheeks flushed with healthy color as she pushed back the waxed paper.

'Remember our midnight junk-a-thons?' she said.

I smiled. When we started going out, we both

worked four-to-twelves. At first, we used to hit a bar, but that tired quickly, and soon we found ourselves visiting the local video store and an all-night super-market, heading straight for the frozen-food aisle. Chicken wings, pizza, mozzarella sticks – *health food.* The rule was anything you wanted, as long as you could cook it in a microwave and eat it in front of an old movie.

God, they were great times, though. Sometimes we'd stay up after we ate, just talking, not wanting it to end, until birds started tweeting outside the bedroom window.

'Remember all the work I used to bring you?' I said.

Maeve had been in the trauma ward at Jacobi Medical Center in the Bronx just around the corner from the four-nine, my rookie precinct.

The whole time during my tour, I would practically kidnap people off the streets and bring them into the emergency room just to get a chance to see her.

'Remember when that huge, homeless, toothless man you brought in hugged you?' Maeve said with a hard laugh. 'What did he say? "You ain't like those other jive turkeys, man. You care."'

'No,' I said, laughing with her now. 'He said, "Man, you're the nicest damn honky I ever met."'

Her eyes closed, and then she stopped laughing.

Just like that. She must have taken something before I came in, and now she was fading fast into sleep.

I squeezed Maeve's hand gently. Then I rose from the bed as quietly as I could. I cleaned up our mess and tucked her sheet around her shoulders, and then I knelt beside her.

For more than ten minutes, I watched my wife's chest rise and fall. It was strange because for the first time I didn't feel angry at the world or at God. I just loved her and always would. I wiped my tears on my sleeves before I leaned in beside her.

'Remember when you changed me forever,' I whispered in Maeve's ear.

Chapter Forty-Six

I checked in with Paul Martelli on my cell as I pulled out from the hospital.

'Still nothing,' he told me. 'Take your time. The hijackers are sitting tight. I've got your cell number.'

'Ned Mason still there?' I asked.

'He's around here somewhere. We have you covered, Mike.'

I followed Martelli's advice. I made a U-turn and then a left onto 66th Street, heading west to give a quick check on my kids.

It had started snowing lightly when I was in the hospital with Maeve, and the dusting on the brown-stone walls and tunnels of the Central Park traverse I passed through looked like soft shakes of confectioner's sugar on gingerbread.

This damn city, I thought, shaking my head, was determined to break my heart into a million pieces with its incessant Currier & Ives holiday season quaintness.

Where was a good mugging-in-progress when you needed one?

When I flicked on the FM radio under the police one, the song 'Silver Bells' was playing. I was dangerously close to emptying my Glock into the dashboard when the soft, dulcet *Ring-a-ling, hear them ring* stanza began.

'Highway to Hell' by AC/DC was just starting when I flicked violently to the nearest rock station. That was more like it. My new theme song! I cranked the volume as high as it would go for the rest of the ride home.

I could hear my kids through my closed apartment door when I stepped off the elevator into the vestibule. Never a good sign, I thought as I turned the knob.

In the foyer, Juliana was sitting on the floor with her back to me, giggling into the phone. I patted her on the head lovingly before I disconnected the cord from the hall jack.

'Bed,' I said.

My second stop was the girls' room, where a Mercedes Freer song was blasting. With her back to me, Jane was leading Chrissy and Shawna in an inspired dance routine. Though I could have scooped up the lot of them in a bear hug they were so cute, I vaguely remembered Maeve's dictum on the inappropriateness of Mercedes Freer.

Three crystal-shattering shrieks sounded when I flicked off the radio, followed by an explosion of giggles and blushing when the girls realized I had been watching them dance.

'Well, well. I didn't know Mercedes Freer was having a concert here at our house. I'm sure the Underhills next door are quite pleased. I take it you all forgot to get your chores done as well?'

Jane looked cross for a moment, as if she was about to counter with some excuse, but then dropped her head.

'Sorry, Dad,' she said.

'Now that was the right answer, Jane,' I said. 'No wonder you get such good grades. Come along. Looks like I have a few more arrests to make.'

Next stop was the living room, where Ricky, Eddie and Trent were beached out in front of the blaring TV. They were watching the nonstop news coverage of the church takeover on CNN. The network already had its slogan in place – 'Cathedral Countdown.' Again, I distinctly remembered that the channels allowed were restricted to ESPN, Food Network, occasionally TLC and Cartoon Network, and public television.

The three of them almost hit the ceiling when I hopped over the sectional and landed in their midst.

'Gathering research for a current events project, are we?' I said.

'We saw you!' Trent screamed after taking his hands away from his face. 'On the TV! It's on every station.'

'You're still busted,' I yelled back at him.

Brian, my eldest son, was so into his MLB game on his computer in his room, he didn't hear me enter. The ninja holds nothing on the father scorned. I flicked off the tower of his Dell as Barry Bonds was in mid-grand-slam swing.

'Hey!' he said angrily as he looked up. 'Dad? Dad!' he said.

'Brian?' I said back. 'Brian!'

'I was . . . uh,' he tried.

'About to throw yourself on the mercy of the court?' I said.

'Sorry, Dad. I'll start my chores,' Brian said, '*forth-with.*'

I almost knocked down Mary Catherine when I stepped back into the hall.

'Mr Bennett. Mike, I mean. I'm so sorry,' she said frantically. 'I was trying to get them into bed when Bridget needed my help. She told me . . .'

'Let me guess,' I said. 'She had an arts-and-crafts project due for school.'

'How'd you know?'

'Okay, I forgot to tell you,' I said. 'Bridget is clinically addicted to arts and crafts. We've been trying to wean her off glue, sparkles, and beads for years now, but nothing seems to work. If you let her, she will destroy the earth in her unquenchable desire to make key chains and ankle bracelets and wall hangings. I've gone to work with sparkles on my face and clothes from her confounded glitter paint so many times, the guys in my squad thought I was in a glam band. She knows you're new, so she took advantage. Arts and crafts are *severely* restricted to weekends.'

'I didn't know,' Mary Catherine said sadly. 'I should have done a better job.'

'Good God,' I said. 'You're still alive and still here? You should try out for the Navy SEALs.'

Chapter Forty-Seven

After I relieved Mary Catherine of command and ordered her upstairs to bed, I found a priest in my kitchen.

The squat white-haired man in black was holding a steaming iron ready as my seven-year-old Bridget put the finishing touches on a pink-and-white plastic-bead pony that covered the entire top of our kitchen island.

'Well, if it isn't *Father Shame-less*. I mean, *Seamus*,' I said.

Nope, it wasn't Halloween. My grandfather Seamus was *a priest*. After Seamus's wife died, he decided to sell the Hell's Kitchen gin mill he'd owned for thirty years and become a man of the cloth. Lucky for him, vocations to the priesthood were at an all-time low, so he was accepted. 'Gone straight from hell to heaven,' as he liked to say.

He now lived in the Holy Name rectory around the block, and if he wasn't attending to parish business

– which he was very good at – he was sticking his nose into mine. Because Seamus wasn't content to merely spoil my children. If he wasn't actually devilishly encouraging mischief, priest or not, he felt he was slacking off.

Even Bridget's freckles seemed to drain of their color when she saw me standing there.

'*Goodnightdadgoingtobediloveyou,*' she somehow managed to get out before sliding off the stool she was kneeling on and disappearing. Fiona, holding Socky under her arms, shot out from the other side of the island and managed to exit a step behind her twin.

'Having a senior moment, Monsignor? Forget how to read a clock? Or did you forget it's a school night?'

'Did you not take a look at this fine steed here?' Seamus said, passing the iron back and forth over the plastic to melt the collection of beads together. It was nearly the size of a real horse. Too bad there wasn't a barn in the apartment to keep it in.

'That girl is pure artist,' Seamus said. 'And like they say, it takes more than books to inspire creativity.'

'Thanks for that little nugget of wisdom there, Seamus, but if these kids don't get their sleep and stick to their schedules, we're all doomed.'

Seamus unplugged the iron, propped it loudly up on the butcher block, and squinted at me. 'If that's the case, why bring someone new into the house now?' he said. 'That Mary Catherine tells me she's from Tipperary. There's a queer breed come from Tipperary. All the wind off the North Atlantic isn't good for the mind. If you ask me, I don't like the looks of her or the situation. Young, single woman in a house with a married man.'

That was it. I snapped. I snatched up the plastic pony. Seamus ducked as I Frisbeed it across the kitchen and knocked the chore chart off the fridge.

'Where do you want me to file your concern, Gramps?' I yelled. 'To my wife on her deathbed, or maybe to the thirty-three celebrities in St Paddy's with guns to their heads?'

Seamus came around the kitchen island and put his hand on my shoulder.

'I just thought I was the one who was going to help you,' he said in one of the most tired voices I had ever heard him use.

I understood now. Why he was being such a pain in the butt about Mary Catherine. He thought he was being replaced, pushed out of our family picture.

'Seamus,' I said, 'if I had a staff of twenty, I would still need your help. You know that. There'll always be a place for you here. I need you to help us by helping Mary Catherine. You think you could do that?'

Seamus's mouth pursed as he thought about it.

'I'll try,' he said with a melodramatic, agonized exhalation.

I stepped across the kitchen and picked up the chore chart. When I lifted the plastic pony, I noticed that it was missing its tail.

'Plug that iron back in, Seamus, would you?' I said, bringing it quickly back over to the kitchen island. 'If we don't get this thing fixed, Bridget will kill both of us.'

Chapter Forty-Eight

When I arrived back at the bedlam scene in front of St Patrick's, I saw that two FBI Hostage Rescue Team trailers had been parked next to the NYPD one. With all the mobile command buses, the staging area was starting to look like a huge tailgating party.

A party in the parking lot of hell, maybe.

I checked in with my boss, Commander Will Matthews, and then with the other negotiators. Still no word had come back from the gunmen inside. Nothing new from Jack.

So I poured myself what could have been my twentieth cup of coffee that day and sat.

I hated this part, the waiting, the feeling of powerlessness. It was one of the reasons why I'd transferred out of the Hostage Negotiation Team. In Homicide, there was never a second when there weren't a hundred things you could do, never a lack of angles to work a case, always countless outlets to pour your persistence and neuroses into.

I sat up suddenly in my swivel chair. There actually was one thing I could do to get me away from the oppressive face of the clock, and it could possibly help us.

I found Commander Will Matthews sitting in the rear of the bus with a glass of fizzing water in one hand. 'Hey, boss,' I said. 'Remember what I said about Caroline Hopkins? My hunch about her so-called accident? L'Arène, that restaurant where it happened, is three blocks away. I was thinking of swinging by to talk to the kitchen staff.'

Will Matthews rubbed his eyes and nodded. 'Okay,' he said. 'Take twenty minutes to see what you can dig up if it makes you happy. Then get your butt back here.'

I patted my pocket. 'I have my cell. And a backup.'

The recent tragedy there, and the siege up the street, must have spoiled the appetites of New York's rich and famous because L'Arène looked empty when I jogged in off Madison Avenue. The marble stairs I climbed in the vestibule were draped with a red, white and blue carpet that seemed more French than American. On either side of the stairs, sumptuous pyramids of lemons and apples sat on top of antique champagne boxes.

Maybe on some other night, the elegance of the

setting might not have been so off-putting. And if I hadn't been grinding so hard in the last few hours, the arrogance that seemed to pulse from the tall, tuxedoed maître d' posted beyond the inner door wouldn't have filled me with such anger.

The dark, curly-haired Frenchman looked like he'd just eaten a bad snail when he spotted me in front of his dictionary-size reservation book.

'The kitchen is *closed*,' he spat, and returned to writing notes in his book.

I closed the tome for him and put my badge on top of it. I savored the shock on his face.

'No,' I said. 'Actually it's not.'

When I told him I was there to investigate the First Lady's accident, the maître d' instantly handed me a business card.

'Gilbert, DeWitt and Raby represent us in all legal matters. You will refer your inquiries to them.'

'Wow, that's really helpful,' I said as I immediately dealt the card back past the sharp tip of the maître d's long nose.

'But I'm not from the insurance company, I'm from the Homicide squad. Now I can either talk to you and your kitchen staff here, informally, or call my boss and we can go the formal route.

'If we go by the book, everyone will have to be

brought down to the station house, and of course, you'll make sure each and every staff member has all his proper immigration papers available for identification purposes. You know, now that I think about it, there was a request from the Justice Department to play a part in this case. You know, the FBI, the IRS? You do have L'Arène's tax receipts from the last five years? And, it goes without saying, your own personal ones?'

The maître d's expression underwent an almost instantaneous transformation. It was amazing how warm a smile he'd been able to hide behind his Gallic scowl.

'I am Henri,' he said with a bow. 'Pray, tell me. How can I assist you, Detective?'

Chapter Forty-Nine

After I told him I needed to interview the kitchen staff, *mon ami* Henri promptly led me through a set of swinging Tiffany blue doors and translated my questions for the chef.

The chef looked like Henri's shorter and pudgier older brother. He seemed affronted by the questions. He'd personally fixed the First Lady's meal, and there was no way, he said angrily, that he had put any peanuts in her foie gras.

The only explanation he could fathom was that a foolish prep cook had spilled peanut oil on the dish during the controlled chaos of a busy night, but even that seemed patently absurd to him. The chef then said something in heated French before sweeping a couple of pots off the stainless-steel counter and storming off. I caught the word *American*, and thought I heard the word *Snickers*.

'What was that last part?' I said to Henri.

Henri blushed.

'The master chef suggested perhaps that the First Lady snacked on a . . . candy bar before her meal arrived.'

So much for repairing French and American relations tonight, I thought.

'Has there been any turnover in the staff since the night she was here?' I said.

Henri tapped a long finger against his bloodless lips.

'Yes,' the maître d' said. 'Now that I think of it. One of the prep cooks, Pablo, I believe was his name, stopped showing up for work a day or so after the terrible accident.'

'Any last name on Pablo? An address? Off his employment application perhaps?'

Henri squinted as a pained, sorrowful, almost penitent expression crossed his features.

'It was like you were saying before about *formal* and *informal*. Pablo was more of an informal hire. We have no application per se,' he said. 'His leaving was not even a real concern. Our turnover rate for prep staff, like in most restaurants, is quite high.'

'I'll bet,' I said.

'Wait,' Henri said. 'I believe he left some things in his locker. Would you like to come down and take a look?'

I did, and downstairs in Pablo's old locker I discovered two items.

A pair of dirty sneakers and a crumpled Metro North Hudson line train schedule.

The case of the dirty sneakers, I thought. Encyclopedia Brown would have been impressed.

Yet another dead end, or so it seemed at that moment anyway.

I stuffed the kitchen helper's things into an empty Duane Reade bag I found under the locker. Maybe we could ID Pablo from prints. If he wasn't already back in Central America.

It was a pretty sad lead, I realized, but better a sad one than none at all.

'Do you have a clue?' Henri asked excitedly, and I lifted the bag of 'evidence.'

I slammed the locker with a resounding bang.

'Very rarely, Hank,' I said.

Chapter Fifty

In her dream, Laura Winston, the *Vogue* magazine-dubbed 'Fashion Queen of the *New Millennium*,' was out on the lake at Ralph Lauren's estate in northern Westchester. She was lying alone in a canoe dressed in a sheet of white muslin, and she was floating beneath a sky of bright, endless blue. The boat skimmed along the shore beneath the boughs of a stand of cherry blossom trees, and a blizzard of falling white petals, fine as angel eyelids, softly landed on her face, her throat, her breasts. When she tried to sit up in the canoe, she realized that the muslin was wrapped tightly around her arms. She was dead and in her funeral boat, she realized – and she began to scream.

Laura Winston woke with a start and banged her head hard on the wooden arm of the church pew she'd propped it against.

There was a heavy *clop-clop* of booted feet, and two ski-masked men with bandoliers of grenades strapped across the front of their brown robes passed slowly up the center aisle of the chapel.

What an idiot, she thought. Right now, if she had wisely begged *off* the funeral, she'd be thirty thousand feet above the South Caribbean in a Gulf Four, banking toward her twenty-one-million-dollar French Renaissance palace in St Bart's to put the finishing touches to her New Year's Eve celebration. Giorgio, Donatella, Ralph, and Miuccia had already RSVP'd.

Instead, she had ignored that little voice, her prudent inner survivor that had piped up just the night before: *Hel-lo! High-profile NYC event, neon bull's-eye terrorist target. Stay away!*

And then, of course, there was that other little secret voice that was just starting to warm up its dry, agonizing pipes.

She was out of her pills.

The OxyContin had originally been prescribed for a lower-back tennis injury. A month later, after learning that her doctor was more than willing to keep prescribing, she was taking them with her multivitamins. The ultimate energy boost, the ultimate stress eraser.

Laura didn't want to admit it, but for about the last hour or so, she'd been jonesing. It had happened once before on a shoot that had gone a day over in Morocco.

The withdrawal had started out like a tiny itch in her blood. Soon the itch got much worse, and she had started throwing up. After dry heaving for an hour or so, she couldn't stop shaking. After ten hours, she would have gladly pulled out her own hair to make it stop. She'd managed to survive that episode with half a bottle of Valium mercifully given to her by the photographer.

But now, *here,* she had nothing.

Maybe some of the others had something, she thought quickly. These Hollywood types were known for their Dr Feelgood prescriptions. She could politely inquire, couldn't she? They were all in the same boat. Share and share alike.

No! she thought, shuddering. Her 'Itness' was all she had. To lose it was simply unacceptable. No one could know about her 'hillbilly heroin' addiction. She had to think. Think!

Bottom line. What did the hijackers want? Either money or some political aim, she reasoned. Either way, her being alive was important to them, wasn't it?

What if she staged some kind of illness. A heart attack? No, all they'd have to do was take her pulse to see that she was faking. What other kinds of medical emergencies did people suddenly suffer from? Diabetic fits, panic attacks?

That was it! A panic attack! Wouldn't have to fake too hard there, either. She was already sweating; her heartbeat was elevated.

Withdrawal hidden in a panic attack. A brilliant plan that would salvage her potentially billion-dollar reputation. Worst case, she'd be separated from the rest of the celebs to vomit in peace.

Laura Winston relaxed her resistance against her shaking, and *went with it*.

Chapter Fifty-One

Eugena Humphrey was so deeply zoned into her soothing Pranayama yoga breathing that at first she didn't even notice when Laura Winston stood up. Eugena's breath escaped from the high part of her lungs in a definitively non-Tantric gush when the elegant fashion guru suddenly started moaning like a rabid squirrel.

A second ago, the fashion diva had been sleeping blissfully. Now, with her pasty face and her exquisitely colored hair in a rat's nest, she looked like she might have been sleepwalking. Except that her eyes were open.

'Sit down, Laura,' Eugena said. 'You saw what happened to Mercedes. These men aren't playin'.'

Eugena tugged the hem of the fashionista's butter-soft black suede Chanel skirt.

'Get your hands OFF ME!' Laura Winston screamed.

Hysterical, Eugena thought. She had to calm the woman down before she got herself killed.

'Laura, what's wrong?' Eugena said as calmly as she could. 'Just talk to me. It's okay. I can help you.'

'I can't TAKE IT!' Laura yelled, jogging out into the aisle. 'HELP ME, PLEASE! Pleeeeeaaaaase! SOMEBODY!'

The short, stocky lead hijacker appeared by the rail as Laura dropped, wailing, to her knees.

'We can't have her bugging out like this,' he called to Little John across the chapel. 'Take care of her.'

The extra-large hijacker stepped over and lifted Laura up from the marble floor by her lapels.

'Ma'am? You'll have to get back in your seat,' he said.

'PLEASE HELP ME!' she yelled after a loud, rattling sob. 'You can help me, can't you, please? I can't breathe. My chest. I need air. So hot in here. I need to go to a hospital.'

'To Bellevue maybe,' the big hijacker said with a chuckle. 'Ma'am, you're hysterical. The only way I know how to deal with hysterical people is to slap them. You don't want to get slapped, do you?'

The hijacker grabbed the middle-aged woman by her wrist when she tried to bolt past him. He turned her bony arm around behind her, then took her by the back of her haute couture top and led her out beyond the rail.

'If that's the way you want to play it,' Little John said, shaking his head.

Next to an enormous statue of Jesus in Mary's lap, he opened up a confessional door and pushed the now screaming Laura Winston inside. When she tried to rush out, he put a combat boot to her chest, sent her flying, and slammed the door shut.

'Jeez,' Little John said, shaking his head at the other hostages. 'Some people, huh?'

Chapter Fifty-Two

Seconds later, as Little John strutted down the center aisle like a conquering hero, comedian John Rooney lost it. Being forced to idly watch the gunman abuse Laura Winston had set some deep chord within Rooney humming. He forgot about his safety, about the resistance plan, about the police outside. He just sprang up from his seat and jumped the hijacker.

Little John stumbled and dropped when Rooney slammed into the back of his knees. Rooney then managed to wrap an arm around the hijacker's neck and squeeze with every ounce of his pent-up fear and rage.

Rooney was still on top of Little John when the other gunmen started kicking him. Steel-toed boots struck his shoulder, his neck, his forehead. Instead of letting go, he closed his eyes and concentrated on one thing: *the pressure of his arm on the hijacker's windpipe.*

The kicking stopped suddenly. Then Rooney heard

a metallic snapping and felt something cold and hard press against his temple.

He opened one of his eyes and saw Jack, the lead hijacker, smiling at him from the opposite end of an M16.

'I'm only going to ask you once,' Jack said. 'Let him go.'

'Shoot me!' Rooney found himself saying. Adrenaline burned like acid in his blood. 'I'm not going to sit and watch you animals beat up on old people and women!'

Jack squinted at him between the holes in his mask. Finally, he slowly lowered the M16.

'Okay, Mr Rooney,' the hijacker said. 'Point taken. I'll take measures to tone down the aggressive crowd control. Now, if you would please release my colleague. If he dies, I'm afraid it'll start quite a bad precedent.'

Rooney released the big man and stood up, breathing loudly. His cheek was bleeding from where a bootlace had scratched it, and his right arm felt like it had been in an industrial accident, but his blood sang. *He'd actually done something about this outrage.*

Jack checked Little John in the chest with the rifle when he leapt up like a Doberman off the floor. 'Go get something to eat and some rest,' he told him.

'Mr Rooney, please retake your seat. I'd like to address everyone.'

Rooney sat as Jack went to the podium and cleared his throat. Then the hijacker smiled, and with his suddenly cheerful demeanor, he could have been an airline spokesman updating terminal passengers about a delay.

'Hi, everybody,' he said. 'We've started the negotiation process, and it seems to be working quite smoothly. If things continue to go this well, there's a shot of getting you back home to your families by Christmas morning.'

There was no applause, but Rooney definitely thought he detected a collective sigh.

'Now, unfortunately, the bad news,' Jack went on. 'If things deteriorate, we'll more likely than not be forced to kill a number of you.'

A low moan rose from the back of the chapel.

'Since we are here in a house of worship,' Jack continued, 'I'd advise any of you who have religious aspirations to get your prayers in now.'

Linda London, the reality TV socialite, doubled over and began sobbing.

'People,' Jack chided amiably. 'People, please. You act like we're going to torture you. You have my word. All executions will consist of a quick, humane shot to the back of the head.'

Jack stepped back down from the pulpit and stopped beside where Rooney sat.

'Oh, and one more thing,' he said, stabbing Rooney in the throat with a stun gun. Rooney's eyes shut of their own accord as every muscle in his body clenched at once. But instead of black, all he saw was sizzling television fuzz. A dry heave of a scream was lost in his throat as he bounced numbly off the floor and rolled under the seat.

'We're not your lifestyle coaches or your Pilates instructors, and this isn't Letterman's greenroom.' Rooney heard Jack through his semiconsciousness. He even came up with one coherent idea when he managed to gather the scraps of his pain-ravaged thoughts: *I should have let him shoot me.*

'I thought you had to have some brains to be successful in this country,' Jack complained. 'Which part of "step out of line and we'll kill you" are you morons not getting?'

Chapter Fifty-Three

It was ten to seven in the morning when eleven-year-old Brian Bennett tapped on his sister's door.

'Julia?' he whispered. 'You up?'

Julia came out, combing her wet hair. Already showered, Brian thought with disappointment. He'd wanted to be the first one up, the leader of the family. He was the oldest boy, after all. When had Julia the Great woken up? Six?

'I was just about to get you,' Julia said. 'Dad still sleeping?'

'Like a dead . . . I mean, like a rock,' Brian said quickly. 'Who knows when he came in last night. You want me to start getting the cereal out and you wake the monsters?'

'Okay, but if you're finished before I get the girls up, go in and get Trent and Eddie and Ricky,' Julia said. 'It's going to take me a while to get the girls dressed right and do their hair.'

'Okay,' Brian said. He began to turn in the dim hall, but then stopped.

'Hey, Julia,' he said.

'What?'

'I feel bad about when Dad came in last night and busted us. I really think this will make it up to him. Great idea to get up early and get everyone ready.'

'Why thanks, Bri,' Julia said. 'That's really nice of you to say.'

Man! Brian thought, wincing. She was right. What the hell was he doing being all fuzzy and nice to his sister?

'Last one to get their team ready is a retarded loser,' Brian called over his shoulder as he left.

He threw open the door to the boys' room after he had quickly set the kitchen table. He was shaking Ricky's foot at the bottom bunk when Trent swung out from the top and hung upside down like a bat.

'Did he come? Did he come?' Trent asked urgently.

'Did *who* come?' Brian said, flipping his five-year-old brother out of his bed and onto his bare feet.

'SANTA!' Trent screamed.

'Shhhh!' Brian said. 'No.'

'What?' Trent said sadly. 'Santa didn't come? Why not? Are you lying, Bri? I know I was a little naughty, but I was nice, too.'

'It's not Christmas yet, you little maniac,' Brian said, heading toward the closet. 'Wake up, Ricky, and go brush your teeth. Brush and flush. Now.'

Brian smiled when he opened the bedroom door five minutes later. The girls were just coming out of their room. He'd thought Ms Perfect in Every Way Julia would have the little ladies doing calisthenics or something by this time. *But no. Snag. It was a tie.*

Brian laughed when he flicked on the kitchen light. Even though it was corny, he had to admit, seeing everyone with their costumes on was also hilarious.

It was dress rehearsal today at Holy Name for the Christmas pageant, and everyone had a part to play. Chrissy, Shawna, Bridget, and Fiona were garland-haloed angels. Trent and Eddie were shepherds. Ricky had scored the part of Joseph and was sporting a totally fake and funny black beard. Even Jane and Julia, who were in the choir, were wearing long silver robes. Of course he himself had the coolest, most uncorny costume, being one of the three wise men.

'Look at them,' Brian said, standing at the head of the table next to Julia. 'They're almost, like, cute or something.'

Julia took a camera out of her robe and snapped a picture of the little Bennetts. What was up with girls?

Brian thought. How did they always know the right things to do?

Julia showed Brian the screen on her camera.

'Do you think Mom will like that one?' she said.

'Maybe,' Brian said. 'How the heck should I know?'

Chapter Fifty-Four

When the muted *clunks* and giggles and bangs and cries of my family getting ready woke me that morning, I sensed the absence on my wife's side of the bed and was grateful. The workday-morning deal between Maeve and me was that she would get them dressed and I would take them to school. To let me sleep in while she did the much heavier work of getting our double-digit familia together was the type of kindness by omission only people who are long married can understand.

I tossed around and was reaching for the warmth of her body pillow when I felt the cold, stiff sheets beside me, and I remembered.

As I lay there, taking my first morning sip of personal horror, a chilling question occurred to me.

I swung my bare feet onto the cold hardwood and grabbed my tattered and holey robe off the bedpost.

If Maeve wasn't getting the kids ready, who was?

It's hard to describe how I felt when I stepped into

the kitchen and saw my children fully dressed for their Christmas pageant. I was convinced I was dreaming, or maybe even dead, seeing the kids transformed around our breakfast table into some surreal Renaissance painting of a heavenly multitude. Then Trent knocked his SpongeBob cereal bowl off the table – and everyone turned around.

'*DAD!*' they said at once.

How could they have gotten themselves ready? I thought. What a bad father I was. I hadn't even remembered about the play. I didn't know why I started crying when I stooped to pick up Froot Loops off the linoleum. Then I did know.

The kids being able to take care of themselves felt like Maeve had done her job. Like she had tied up all the loose ends and was now ready to go.

I wiped my tears on the sleeve of my robe as Chrissy hugged me hard and gave me a butterfly kiss by fluttering her eyelashes on my neck.

A deep breath helped me pull myself together. If Maeve saw me cry in front of them, she'd kick my ass.

And so I felt a joyful smile invade my face when I looked at them again. My kids really were angels. They were completely unreal. I nodded at Julia and Brian. Had anyone, let alone a couple of kids, risen to a horrible occasion with such selflessness? I gritted my teeth to kill another wave of sorrow; then I cleared my throat.

'I know it's not Sunday,' I yelled with enthusiasm, 'but who needs a Sunday breakfast as much as me?'

The cries of 'We do' and 'Me' rang off the walls as I slapped two cast-iron frying pans up on the stove.

Seamus arrived in the kitchen as I was dispensing my bacon, egg, potato, and green onion hash to my guys.

'Ock. Faith and begorra,' he said, glaring wide-eyed at the costumed kids. 'Halloween already?'

'NO!' the kids cried, giggling at their grandfather.

Mary Catherine came in a minute later, a quizzical look on her face. I handed her a plate.

'I warned you we were nuts,' I said, smiling.

For a few glorious seconds I just stood at the stove, staring out at my family, listening to them eat and laugh. My bliss lasted until I spotted my cell phone and keys on the counter next to the coffee machine.

Damn world, I thought. I wished it would just lay off already.

I thought of the hostages and how the clock was ticking against them. It was the hostage-takers themselves that finally got me to uproot myself and head for the shower. I smiled bitterly as I felt the heavy, black resentment in me shift away from myself and toward them like the cannon of a tank. Jack was the one responsible for taking me away from my loved ones, I realized.

You don't know who you're messing with, buddy, I mentally e-mailed him. *You might think you do. But you have no idea.*

Chapter Fifty-Five

The Bennetts stopped some NYC traffic again when we did our morning dash for the front doors of Holy Name half an hour later. A brunette model crawling out of a taxi in a sequined black dress, no doubt worn the night before, stopped at the curb, put her hand to her décolletage, and actually said, *'Ohhhh!'* at the cuteness of my family pageant. Even a passing metrosexual in a *GQ* camel-hair overcoat couldn't help gaping open-mouthed at my crew as he exchanged his iPod earpiece for his ringing cell.

And far better than both of those reactions was the one I got from none other than Sister Sheilah.

'God bless you, Mr Bennett,' she called with a smile, *an actual smile,* as she unhooked the door.

I was feeling pretty warm despite the cold when I got back into my van. I decided to sit for a minute. I lifted the *Times* I'd picked up from my doorstep to look at it for the first time.

The spark of holiday joy fizzled instantly in my chest

when I looked at a picture of myself under the FIRST LADY CAROLINE HOPKINS'S FUNERAL HIJACKED headline. 'We Don't Know Anything' was the cheerful caption under my picture. I looked at the byline of the hatchet job.

Cathy Calvin.

Who else?

I shook my head, and felt my stomach filling with acid. She'd hamstrung me but good. Even the picture was bad. There was a pensive, searching expression to my face that could easily be misinterpreted as utter confusion. They must have snapped it when I was looking for the cathedral caretaker.

Thanks for my fifteen minutes of fame, Calvin, I thought. You really shouldn't have. I couldn't wait to see Commander Will Matthews. It was going to be such fun receiving the commendation for the top-notch PR job I had done with the *Times*.

And on that note – this case just kept getting better and better, didn't it? – I violently hurled the paper over the seat and downshifted into drive.

Boy, oh, boy, was I glad to be in the white-hot center of this mess.

Chapter Fifty-Six

It was precisely eight twenty-nine when the Neat Man placed his coffee on the frosted ledge of the pay phone kiosk on the corner of 51st and Madison.

Though he'd gotten the cup from one of those Porta-Potty-like corner carts, he was heartened by its blistering temperature as he took a scalding sip.

Between the ash-colored buildings down 51st, the gray morning sky looked like a giant shard of dirty glass. The dull light did very little to illuminate the dark arched windows of St Pat's, kitty-corner across the barricaded street.

The Neat Man smiled for a moment, savoring the misery, the too hot, too horrible coffee, the biting cold on his face, the ear-drilling clatter of the police generators. As if on cue, a bum stirred from a rag-and-bag pile beneath a sidewalk shed halfway down the block and yawned before loudly air-blowing his nose, one nostril at a time, into the gutter.

Ah! Morning, New York-style, the Neat Man thought as he picked up the pay phone.

Learning all this raw, in-your-face grittiness was going to be a jolt, he thought. But maybe if he reached way down deep into his soon-to-be seven-figure bank account, he might have a shot of finding a way.

'What's up?' a voice said.

'Same old, same old, Jack, my man,' the Neat Man said cheerily. 'You see the new trailer out front? Hostage Rescue is in the house.'

'That's what I'm talking about,' Jack said, pumped. 'Everyone's sticking right to the script.'

'How are the guests? Everyone have a pleasant night?'

'The rich really aren't like you and me,' Jack said. 'They're a trillion times softer. The truth, a kindergarten class would be more trouble.'

'Didn't I tell you?' the Neat Man said.

'That you did,' Jack said. 'That you did. Keep your eyes open out there. Stick to the plan.'

The line went dead. The Neat Man hung up the phone and smiled as a couple of uniformed cops walked by. Despair, gray as the dawn, was in their bag-eyed faces.

When he closed his own eyes a vision of *a huge, sun-washed bathroom appeared before him, acres of gleaming marble, steam rising off a bubbling jacuzzi, a blinding white pyramid of meticulously folded towels beneath a window filled with a blue-green sea.*

He lifted his lava-temperature coffee again as he turned toward the church. There were pigeons in the nickeled light, fluttering about the sharp spires. His stomach churned as he remembered the pigeons his father used to fly off the roof of their Brooklyn tenement.

If he never laid eyes on another flying rat, the Neat Man thought, or his low-class excuse for a father for that matter, he would die a very happy man.

The Neat Man blinked away his rare lapse into memory and moved the coffee cup up and down and side to side over the church like a priest conferring a benediction.

'For the gifts which I am about to receive,' the Neat Man said, 'may the Lord make me truly thankful.'

Chapter Fifty-Seven

Funnyman John Rooney didn't know what time it was when he decided to stop trying to fake sleep, but by the wan light glowing behind the stained glass above, he guessed it was somewhere near nine.

With the thin pews proving almost impossible to get comfortable in, the hijackers had allowed them to take the seat and kneeler cushions and sleep on the floor in front of the chapel's altar. The cushions were small, though, and the body-heat-sucking marble floor made a city sidewalk seem like a Tempur-Pedic mattress in comparison.

May I have a side of exhaustion with my terror, please? Rooney thought, rubbing his fists into his eyes as he sat up against the altar rail. *Yeah, supersize it. Thanks, abduction-dudes.*

At the back of the chapel, three masked hijackers sat in folding chairs, drinking coffee from paper cups. He couldn't see Little John or the lead gunman, Jack, anywhere. With the masks and robes, it was hard to tell how many hijackers there actually were. Eight, a dozen. Maybe more. They seemed to work in shifts, everything very organized.

Rooney watched with rising anger as one of them leaned to his side and lit a cigarette off a votive candle.

A hand fell on his shoulder as Charlie Conlan sat up next to him.

'Mornin', kid,' Conlan said quietly without looking at him. 'That was brave of you to fight back like that last night.'

'You mean stupid,' Rooney said, fingering the scab on his face.

'No,' Conlan said. 'Ballsy. Thing now is to do it again, only at the right time.'

'You still want to fight them?' Rooney said.

Conlan nodded calmly, and Rooney did a double-take at the star's patented steely-eyed squint. In real life Charlie Conlan seemed to be an even bigger badass than the rock-and-roller persona that had made him famous around the world.

'Yo,' whispered a voice behind them. *Source* magazine-dubbed 'Bubblegum Ho' Mercedes Freer, who'd been released from the confessional the night before, sat up from where she'd been sleeping.

'You bad boys gonna try something?' she said.

Rooney debated letting her in on it, then finally nodded. 'Just being prepared.'

'Amen to that shit,' the singer said. 'Check it. One of those g's is into me. He was talking to me through the confessional door last night. Skinny one with the shotgun, sitting in the middle up there. Yo, we could use that. I could play like I want to do him or something.'

Just then, Little John arrived from the back of the chapel with a cooler and a cardboard tray of coffees.

'Rise and shine, campers,' he yelled as he came up the aisle. 'Asses in the seats. It's chow time.'

A sudden sustained booming sound started from Reverend Solstice three rows behind Rooney. At first he thought the black minister was having a heart attack. But the sound turned into a note and soared, and Rooney realized that the man was singing.

'Ahhhhhhhhhhmayzing grace, how sweeeeet the sound.'

Reverend Sparks, sitting next to Solstice, started singing a kind of backup.

Rooney rolled his eyes. How absurd was this?

But after a while, even he could see that the impassioned voices of the two men seemed to infuse a soothing warmth into the cold church. Other people began to join in, and when Rooney saw Little John shake his head in disapproval, he began singing along too.

It got even more shocking when Mercedes Freer stood afterward and started singing 'Silent Night.' Rooney's mouth gaped at the pure classical beauty in the girl's voice. The foul-mouthed tart could have been a soloist in an opera.

'Sleep in heavenly pe-eace,' she sang. 'Slee-eep in heavenly—'

The explosive, crisp *snap* of a gunshot replaced Mercedes's last note. There was a rumbling as everyone turned back in the pews toward the larger church – where the shot had come from.

The chilling reverberation of the shot pressed some reset button in the core of Rooney's mind. He felt his resolve go out like a hard-blown candle.

God help us, he thought, feeling for the first time the true weight of that three-word plea.

The killing has started.

Chapter Fifty-Eight

What the hell is this? How could it have happened? With his back flat against one of the cathedral's sequoia-thick marble columns, Jack gripped his nine millimeter and listened closely.

He'd been walking the perimeter when a figure in black had bolted out from the gift shop entrance. Thinking that the FBI's Hostage Rescue Team had somehow breached the church's interior, he'd drawn his pistol and fired.

They'd gotten in somehow, Jack thought. There had to be some angle he and the Neat Man had missed. He waited for the sound of a boot falling against marble. On whispered orders. He scanned himself for the red dot of a laser sight, which would mean, essentially, that he was dead.

'What happened?' Little John said, arriving down the center aisle with two men at a run. A grenade was in one hand, his own nine millimeter in the other.

'Man in black just popped out of the gift shop.

I don't think it was Will Smith. Think I hit him, though.'

'Feds?' Little John whispered, glancing up at the stained-glass windows. 'How?'

'I don't know,' Jack said, peeking around the column. 'There's a body down by the baptismal font. I'll take that one. You guys check the gift shop. Shoot first.'

The men split up and rushed toward the front of the church. Jack swung his body out into the aisle, pistol trained on the figure on the marble floor. It didn't move.

He tapped the warm barrel of his gun hard against his forehead when he saw who it was he'd shot. *What have I done?*

Jack looked down at an elderly priest. Candlelight flickered in the dark pool of blood beneath his head. *Shit.*

Little John almost ran into him.

'No one in the gift shop,' he said. He looked down at the slain cleric and his still, saucer-sized eyes.

'Holy shit!' he said.

Jack crouched down on his heels next to the body and stared at the priest's dead face. 'Look what you made me do,' he said angrily.

Little John holstered his gun.

'What are we going to do now?' he asked.

At least the boys had his back, Jack thought, looking down at the innocent he'd just murdered. He had told them that killing might be a possibility, and still they'd all agreed.

At least he'd have company in hell.

'We use it,' he said. 'Didn't want to do this the hard way – but it's looking like we don't have a choice anymore.'

'Use it?' Little John said, looking down at the dead priest. 'How?'

'Grab the good father's arms and legs,' Jack said. 'I'm tired of all this waiting anyway. Time to speed up the clock with a little pressure. It's hardball time.'

Chapter Fifty-Nine

It was just past nine when I arrived at the POLICE DO NOT CROSS barricade of the command center. Before I was tempted to construe that message as a standing order for me to return home to my family, I cut the Chevy's engine and opened the door.

I shook my head at the ongoing life-and-death siege as I threaded my way through the growing media encampment, then was waved through each of the three checkpoints.

Reflected in the graphlike black glass of the modern office building neighboring to the north, the spire of the cathedral looked like a stock that had spiked and was now plummeting. A couple of reporters were doing stand-ups for feeds into their stations. When there was news, the print reporters typed into their laptops, the TV folks did stand-ups, and the radio people filed – very loudly – over their phones.

I had just turned away from the media folks and their bullshit when I caught the movement of the cathedral doors across Fifth. *The doors were opening again!*

At first it seemed as if the figure that flew from the arched shadow was another person who had been released. When I noted how fast the black-suited man was moving, my pulse quickened. I thought maybe somebody was escaping.

Then I saw the body go facedown on the stone stairs without any attempt at breaking its fall, and I knew something was very wrong.

I didn't allow myself to think too much as I skimmed the bumper of the dump-truck barricade and crossed the avenue at a run.

It was only as I was coming up the cathedral steps and kneeling beside the fallen figure that it occurred to me, coldly, that I wasn't wearing my Kevlar vest.

The fallen body had plowed through a section of the street shrine that had been left for Caroline Hopkins the day before. The upended votive candles now looked more like tossed beer bottles than solemn offerings. A bouquet of wilted roses lay just beyond the downed man's outstretched hand, as if he'd dropped it in his fall.

I couldn't get a pulse out of him. A needle of ice spiked my heart when I turned the body over to perform CPR.

My eyes went from the priest's white collar to the hole in his temple to his open, lifeless eyes.

I closed my own eyes and covered my face with one hand for a second. Then I turned and glared at the already closed bronze doors.

They'd murdered a priest!

ESU lieutenant Reno was at my side. 'Mother of God,' he said quietly, his stone face faltering. 'Now they're murderers.'

'Let's get him out of here, Steve,' I said.

Reno got the man's legs, and I got his arms. The priest's hands were soft and small, like a child's. He hardly weighed anything. His scapula, hanging down from his lolling head, scraped the asphalt as we ran with the corpse to the police lines.

'How come all this job is anymore is pulling out bodies, Mike?' Reno said sadly as we rushed past the barricade.

Chapter Sixty

I heard a phone ring from the open front door of the command bus as I laid the murdered priest down on an EMS stretcher. I didn't need caller ID to figure out who it was. Instead of sprinting to grab the phone, though, I let it ring on as I carefully closed the priest's eyelids with my thumb.

'Bennett!' I heard Commander Will Matthews bellow.

I zombie-stumbled past him without acknowledgment and made my way farther into the bus. For the first time, I didn't have any butterflies as I accepted the phone, any latent fear that I would somehow screw something up. Quite the opposite.

I was dying to talk to the son of a bitch.

FBI negotiator Martelli must have sensed my fury. He grabbed my wrist.

'Mike, you need to relax,' he said. 'No matter what happened, stay calm. Unemotional. You go ballistic, we lose the rapport you've established. Thirty-two people are still in jeopardy.'

Unemotional! I thought. The worst part about it was that Martelli was absolutely right. My job was to be Mister Super Calm. It was like getting your nose broken and having to apologize for getting blood on your sucker-punching attacker's fist. I was really starting to hate my current role.

I nodded to the com sergeant at the desk.

'Bennett,' I said.

'Mike,' Jack said merrily in my ear. 'There you are. Listen, before you guys get all upset, I can explain. Father Stowaway must have been hitting the house wine pretty hard yesterday morning because we told everybody to leave. He jumped out at the wrong time and tried to run for it. With that black suit of his, we thought he was one of you SWAT guys trying to crash the party.'

'So you're saying what? It was just an accident? Not really your fault?' I said, my grip threatening to pulverize the plastic cell phone.

'Exactly,' Jack said. 'One of those wrong place–wrong time deals, Mike. Not that there's any real big loss, if you think about it. Fudgepacker takes a dirt nap. Way I see it, there's a lot of altar boys out there who'll be sleeping a little easier tonight.'

That was it, I thought. Role or not, I was done listening to this monster.

'You son of a bitch,' I said. 'You absolute piece of shit. You killed a priest.'

'Do my ears deceive me?' Jack yelled happily. 'Or did I actually just hear a little real emotion. I was starting to think I was speaking with a voice-mail computer there, Mikey. All that psychotherapy, all that calming negotiating strategy crap you've been spouting almost made me want to eat my gun. *Finally! Let's put it all out on the table, laddie.* We want the money and to get away, and you guys want to blow our heads off with high-powered rifles at your earliest convenience.'

Jack laughed easily.

'We're not friends. If there ever were enemies on this earth, they're me and you. And you're right, Mike. We're sons of bitches. In fact, we're the evilest sons of bitches you ever had the misfortune to cross paths with. If we're willing to kill a priest over nothing, how much more willing do you think I am to bodybag one of these worthless celebrities over seven figures? *Either kill us, or get us our money.* Just stop wasting my time!'

'You sure you don't want to choose that other option?' I said suddenly.

'What option is that, Mikey?'

'Eating your gun,' I said.

'Fat chance,' Jack said with a laugh. 'I'm not that hungry. But you keep messing around with me, you better watch out. Before this thing is over, I might just decide to feed it to you.'

Chapter Sixty-One

A connection-cutting dial tone howled in my ear – just as Mike Nardy, the cathedral's care-taker, entered the trailer.

'I'm afraid I have a confession to make,' he blurted, looking out over the assembly of cops and agents. 'There *is* another way into the cathedral.'

The FBI HRT commander, Oakley, stepped forward to handle this himself.

'Tell us about it, Mr Nardy,' he said.

The old man was seated in a swivel chair and handed a coffee.

'The reason I didn't say anything before was, well, it's kind of a secret. Kind of embarrassing for the Church, too. The only reason I'm even here is that Father Miller, the priest who was just shot, was a friend of mine, and well, I have your word that it won't get out? The passageway?'

'Of course,' Oakley said immediately. 'Where's the way in, Mr Nardy?'

'From the Rockefeller Center concourse,' the care-taker said. 'There's a passage that cuts under Fifth into a, um, bomb shelter. Back in the sixties, Cardinal Spellman, God rest his soul, got quite, I guess the word is *paranoid*, after the Bay of Pigs incident. He was convinced New York was going to get nuked. So he allocated some funds for an undisclosed construction project.

'A bomb shelter was built off the archbishops' crypt. With the Rockefellers' permission, an alternate escape passage was dug to the lower concourse of Rockefeller Center, where they now have shops and such. I've never been through the passage; no one has since they built it.'

'Why didn't you tell us this before?' I butted in angrily. 'You knew we were looking for a way to get in, Nardy.'

'I thought things could be resolved peacefully,' the caretaker said quietly. 'Now I know otherwise. Poor Father Miller. He was a good soul.'

One thing I loved was when citizens decided to manipulate the police for their own political reasons. I was about to tear into the old man for obstructing justice when Oakley cut me off with a shake of his head.

'Do you think you could show us the way in, Mr Nardy?' Oakley said calmly.

'Absolutely,' the caretaker said.

Oakley called into his radio and ordered half of his commando team to the command center.

Finally, some action, I thought. Finally a break for the good guys.

I was sick of talking, too. Just like Jack.

'Going somewhere?' Oakley said, eyeing me with surprise.

'With you,' I said with a tight smile. 'You never know when you might need to negotiate.'

Chapter Sixty-Two

A fter twenty minutes of weapon loading and intense strategy briefing, I joined a dozen joint task force FBI and NYPD commandos. We followed the caretaker, Nardy, into 630 Fifth Avenue.

I was all but swimming under a borrowed night-goggle headset, heavy vest, and tactical shotgun. Only the occasional creak of a combat boot could be heard as we moved quickly through the red marble chamber of the Art Deco lobby and down the stairs.

Commander Will Matthews had cleared the concourse below at the beginning of the siege, and it was a little creepy as we trooped through the silent, deserted mall-like corridor. There were Christmas decorations and lights blinking through the plate glass of upscale clothing stores, toy shops, and a food court, but the aisles and the tables were empty.

It reminded me of an old horror movie my son Brian had made me watch with him the Halloween before about people running away from zombies in a mall. I quickly dispelled the déjà vu when I remembered the title.

Dawn of the Dead.

Nardy stopped at an unmarked steel door beside a Dean & DeLuca gourmet food store. He removed a prodigious ring of keys from the pocket of his rumpled slacks. His lips moved as he sorted through them, in prayer or counting, I wasn't able to tell. He finally selected a large, strange-looking key from his ring and handed it to Oakley.

'That's it,' he said, crossing himself. 'God bless you.'

'Okay, everyone,' Oakley whispered. 'Radios off and my team in front. Make sure the suppressors are screwed down tight. Have your night goggles ready for going in lights-out. Single file, space yourselves out. Listen for my signal.' He turned to me. 'Mike, last chance to go back.'

'I'm all in,' I said.

Chapter Sixty-Three

There were metal flicks of weapon safeties being released and then a slightly louder one as Oakley turned the lock.

The door made a loud creaking groan as it swung in. We stared over the barrels of our weapons into an unlit concrete-lined corridor.

'Mom always said if I played my cards right I'd make it to Fifth Avenue,' Oakley whispered as he flipped down his night goggles and stepped into darkness behind his MP5.

When I turned down my goggles, the lightless tunnel went to an eerie lime green. Twenty feet in, we had to duck under a thick bank of rusting iron cable ducts. Another thirty feet after that, we passed along a teakettle-hot steam pipe that was as big as the side of a gasoline truck.

The grade of the tunnel took a sharp pitch downward, and we arrived at a long set of spiraling iron stairs also heading down.

'I always wondered what they spent the second collection on,' Oakley said as he descended. 'Anybody who spots a dude with horns and a pitchfork has standing orders to squeeze until he hears a click.'

At the bottom of the two-story staircase was a riveted metal door with what looked like a steering wheel in its exact center. If I didn't know better, I would have said we had somehow arrived at the engine room of a ship.

The door moved inward as if it were on oiled hinges when Oakley put his hand to it. Suddenly, we were in a small, odd concrete room. It was a church, with painful-looking concrete pews and a cement altar. The only thing not made of concrete was the crucifix fashioned of a dull gray metal that might have been lead. To the right of the crucifix was an iron ladder heading up into a kind of chimney in the ceiling.

Oakley motioned for silence as we moved toward the ladder.

The vertical passage was about two stories high, like some strange silo built underground. I don't know if they trained in ladder racing at the FBI, but if there was an Olympic event, the Hostage Rescue guys would have gotten the gold.

From the bottom of the ladder, I could make out

another steering wheel opener at the roof of the chimney above the commandos' heads.

Then I saw it spin with a screech.

A few seconds later, I couldn't see anything because a circle of light burned down from above, and I was blinded – blind and then deaf as the world around me shattered with the crackle of gunfire.

Jack was onto us.

Chapter Sixty-Four

I reared back from the chimney. I tore off my night-vision goggles. Bullets pocked holes in the concrete floor as gunfire rained down into the cramped slot.

It was a miracle I wasn't hit as I pulled the jumping, falling, and sliding members of the retreating tactical team away from the kill-zone base of the ladder.

The blue-white flashes from the continuing gunfire pulsed like strobe lights as team members performed CPR on their fallen brothers.

I heard Oakley swearing and counting heads as I flicked my MP5 to auto and jogged back to the chimney.

Then I shoved the machine gun up into the hole beside the ladder, one-handed, and pulled the trigger. The MP5 jumped like a jackhammer in my hand until I heard a click. I didn't know if I'd hit anything, but it seemed to momentarily stop the attack.

A second later, there was a loud, whistling clang, and a smoking canister landed at the base of the ladder. Then another. I pulled my Windbreaker up around my face as acrid smoke burned my eyes and lungs.

'Tear gas!' I shouted. 'Fall back!'

I almost tripped on a fallen cop behind me. 'Hit,' he said in a whisper. I lifted him up into a fireman's carry and headed back for the door we'd come in through. I banged one of my shins on a stair of the spiral staircase and felt blood seep down into my boot.

I nearly brained myself, and the cop I was carrying, when I ran into one of the iron ducts near the tunnel entrance.

It was surreal back out in the corridor of the mall. Under the blinking red and green holiday lights and sappy Christmas Muzak, the blood and filth on our guys looked like makeup.

I laid the man I had carried out on the polished marble floor of the concourse. Then I gasped as I stared into his lifeless blue eyes. He was a burly, black-haired NYPD ESU cop, no more than twenty-five.

Now he was dead, gone while I'd tried to carry him to safety.

Oakley was putting a helmet over the face of a fallen FBI commando to my left.

What had happened? Two good men, good cops. Down.

I looked around, stunned. There was an advertisement for a clothing store through the plate glass above the cop's corpse. Some laughing teenage blonde in a Santa hat and red catsuit sandwiched between a couple of shirtless male models on the hood of a vintage car.

That absurd tableau, coupled with my shock, snapped something inside of me. A rattling burglar alarm went off as I shattered the store window into a million pieces with the butt of my MP5.

I slid down the wall into the puddle of green broken-glass diamonds. I bit my lip as I looked back at the black hellhole we'd just climbed out of.

God help us, I thought. And then – *How do they know so much about St Patrick's? How do they know so much about us?*

Chapter Sixty-Five

The Neat Man folded his cell phone closed as an ambulance hopped the curb of 630 Fifth right in front of him. He had to take a step back and actually prop his back against the cold, filthy side of the crisis trailer in order to let out the female EMT from the front cab. He did a double-take and then walked away with his head down.

If it isn't I-need-a-hug Yolanda, he thought, stealing another glance at the side of the Hispanic paramedic's face.

He shook his head, remembering her from outside the hospital where Caroline Hopkins had breathed her last.

Of all the sieges in all the cathedrals in all the world, she had to drive her meat wagon into mine.

The Neat Man smiled as he tilted his coffee at her.

Here's looking at you, bitch. Six degrees of separation and all that crapola.

He watched her rush across the plaza, pushing a

wheeled stretcher. The tactical team emerged from the revolving door just as she got to the entrance.

The Neat Man counted heads quickly. Thirteen had gone down. Now there were nine standing. His boys inside had taken care of business! Against Hostage Rescue, too! And Hostage Rescue was supposed to be the best of the best.

Thank God he'd been able to tip Jack off.

He winced a little when he saw asshole hotshot detective Mike Bennett was still among the living. Yolanda was pulling up his pant leg and wiping at a cut on his shin.

What happened, Mikey? Got a boo-boo?

He watched as Bennett shrugged her off and hobbled, shell-shocked, toward the trailer. Cops and FBI agents patted him on the shoulder as he passed.

'Not your fault,' the Neat Man called from the crowd at Bennett's back as he passed. 'It's those bastards inside. This is all on them.'

Chapter Sixty-Six

This was a tragedy. The first one for the good guys, thought Jack as he looked down on a fallen pal.

The bleeding hijacker rested his head against the false stone casket and moaned as Jack violently slammed shut the concrete lid to the bomb shelter.

Learning of the existence of the secret escape tunnel from the cathedral's crypt was one of the major factors that had swayed him and the Neat Man to finally go through with the hijacking. It was how most of them had snuck in, and the way they were thinking of getting out.

Jack rubbed at the bridge of his nose and closed his eyes as panic began to bulge in his chest.

Had to calm down. He wasn't allowed to panic. He'd allowed for this, remember? Practically expected it. It would still work out.

He took a breath, and let it out.

Thank God he had come up with a plan B.

He opened his eyes as his dying comrade moaned again.

Fontaine, he thought. *You unlucky son of a bitch.*

'Calm down now,' Jack said as he unseamed the man's brown robe with a Ka-Bar knife, then freed the Velcro straps of his bulletproof vest with a loud rip.

'You're going to make it,' he lied without hesitation or request.

One of the return-fire rounds shot up from the bomb shelter had ricocheted off the lead-lined lid of the hatch. Fontaine had caught the bullet in the back just above the collar of his Kevlar vest, to the left of his spine. That wasn't even his worst problem, Jack thought. Because either he'd just spilled a couple of gallons of Benjamin Moore high-gloss red over the front of his pants, or he was rapidly bleeding to death from where the round had left his body.

When Jack peeled the heavy vest off Fontaine's chest, he spotted the blood-gushing exit wound above his friend's right nipple. Jack looked at the dying man with a wondrous respect. The fact that Fontaine was still breathing seemed to defy logic.

'Don't lie to me,' Fontaine said. 'I'm all sliced to shit inside. I can feel it. I can feel the blood.'

'We'll put you outside,' Jack offered. 'You'll be caught, but at least you'll be breathing.'

'Yeah, right,' Fontaine said. 'They'll patch me up so I can be good and healthy when they put the needle in me. Besides, they ID me, we're all screwed. Just do me a favor, will you, when you get out?'

'Anything,' Jack said.

'Give my share to my girl, Emily. Hell, not even a full share. Just something.'

The hijacker sobbed suddenly.

'It ain't the dying that hurts so much as the dying for nothing.'

Jack sat in the man's blood as he got behind him, cradling him.

'You have my word, dog,' Jack said in his ear. 'She gets a full share. She'll go to college, Fontaine. Just like you always wanted. Ivy, right?'

'For sure,' Fontaine said with a soft nod. 'She got fifteen hundred on her boards. I ever tell you that?'

'Only about a thousand times,' Jack said, chuckling into his buddy's ear.

'Knocking up her worthless mother was the only thing I ever did right,' Fontaine said, smiling. He seemed peaceful now, as if he were drifting off to sleep after a hard day's work. Jack saw a final tension jolt through the dying man, followed by a palpable slackening. Fontaine was gone. They had lost a good man.

Jack was dry-eyed as he stood and handed his Ka-Bar to one of the hijackers who had watched it all.

'Cut his hands and his head, and bag 'em,' he said. 'We take them with us. We can't take the chance they'll identify him.'

Chapter Sixty-Seven

'**B**ut *I* want to be the car. I *have* to be the car!' five-year-old Trent Bennett whined across the Monopoly board. Nine-year-old Ricky, sensing trouble, immediately snatched the piece off the GO square and clutched it to his chest. Trent started to cry.

Brian Bennett rolled his eyes. Here he was, doing his job, keeping the squirts busy. He'd busted out an actual board game, and would they cooperate? No way, Jose.

Mary Catherine, their new nanny or whoever the heck she was, had told him she needed to run out and get something from the store. Grandfather was at church. So that left Brian pretty much in charge.

He got up from the dining-room table when he heard the front door open. He could see a massive Christmas tree being pushed in through the door when he stepped into the hall. Mary Catherine took off her hat and wiped her hand across her red, sweating, though kind of pretty, face.

Brian gaped at her. She'd gone out and gotten them a tree for Christmas.

That was, like, *nice*.

'Brian, there you are,' she said in her funny Irish accent. 'Do you know where your mom and dad keep the decorations? We've got work to do.'

Twenty minutes later, all of the kids were in the living room, assembly-lining ornaments up to Mary Catherine on the shaky painting ladder. It wasn't the same as their mom, Brian thought. Mom did a tree nicer than the ones in the window at Macy's. But he had to admit, Mary Catherine's was a lot better than nothing at all.

Chrissy, still dressed as an angel, passed by in the kitchen doorway, struggling to hold up a sloshing Brita water pitcher.

'What are you *doing*?' Brian asked.

'Hel-lo, *my job*,' she said matter-of-factly. 'Socky needs his water.'

Brian laughed. With the influence of her sisters, sometimes Chrissy acted more like she was thirteen instead of three. He watched the littlest angel come back into the living room and turn on the TV.

'Ahhhh! Look! *Look!*'

'What is it?' Brian said, rushing over to his sister.

On the screen, their father stepped onto an outdoor

podium between a cluster of microphones. Just like Derek Jeter after a baseball game, Brian thought excitedly.

Concern replaced his pride when Brian looked closer. His father was smiling, but it was his bad smile. The one he made when he was pretending not to be sad or angry.

His dad looked like Jeter all right, Brian thought.

After a big loss.

Chapter Sixty-Eight

It wasn't just the biting cold of the day that made me feel numb as I stopped before the checkpoint media podium. Usually, making a routine statement before the local news outlets filled me with butterflies. But when Will Matthews said that the commissioner had ordered an immediate press conference, I actually volunteered.

I knew those murdering bastards inside were watching – and I wanted them to see me, to hear what I had to say.

I looked out over the avenue-filling clutter of national network and worldwide press cameras and gazed dead ahead into the black lens of the camera in front of me.

'Within the past hour,' I said, 'a rescue attempt was made to free the hostages. Gunfire was exchanged, and two men, an FBI agent and an NYPD ESU officer, were slain. Two other officers were wounded. Names will not be released until the families are notified.'

A concentrated wave of motion and sound swept through the newsies, starving wolves just tossed prime rib.

'Why was such a rash move authorized?' a male network reporter with chief-executive hair called out from the front ranks.

'The decisions of the on-scene command cannot be commented on in light of the ongoing situation,' I told him.

'In what part of the cathedral did the rescue attempt take place?' asked a pretty middle-aged female reporter behind him. She had a microphone in one hand and an open cell phone in the other.

'Again, tactics can't be divulged at this juncture,' I said. It was scary, even to me, how calm I sounded. A few minutes before, I was in a firefight. Now I was as collected as Colin Powell doing a troop assessment. Whatever the reason, I was proud of myself. To let the scum inside see that they had gotten to us in the slightest degree would have been an insult to the fallen men.

'This is a difficult situation, ladies and gentlemen,' I continued. 'I know everyone wants to know what's going on, but now's not the time for full disclosure. It runs contrary to our purpose. We want to extract the thirty-two hostages safely.'

'And the hostage-takers as well?' someone called from the back. 'What about them?'

I looked steadily into the camera again. I could almost feel my eyes making contact with Jack's inside.

'Of course,' I said. 'Of course we do. We want this to be resolved peacefully.'

I ignored the barrage of shouted questions as I stepped down from behind the wheeled podium. I almost knocked down a tall brunette reporter as I tripped over a taped-down media cable alongside the curb.

'C'mon, Mike,' Cathy Calvin said. 'Who are these guys? You have to tell us what they want. What's their angle?'

'Why are you asking me?' I said, putting an almost cross-eyed, confused look on my face. 'Don't you read your own paper, Ms Calvin? I don't know nuttin', remember?'

Chapter Sixty-Nine

I had already arrived back in the command center bus and was sitting calmly with the phone in my hand when it rang, and I almost dropped the damn thing. I was still boiling, but I knew how useless that emotion was now. Anger felt good, but it wasn't working. What I had to do now, I knew, was to repair things, salvage the bloody mess somehow.

And most of all, I had to keep Jack talking instead of shooting.

'Mike here,' I said.

'YOU LYING SON OF A BITCH!' Jack screamed.

'Now, now, Jack,' I said. 'There was a mix-up. A communication flub. I wasn't told about the raid until after it happened.'

I wanted to be as honest as possible in order to reach some middle ground, but under the circumstances, it was impossible. Truth was, I'd just tried to kill Jack and his accomplices and was pissed that we'd failed.

But I had to distance myself from all that. Act like I was just a cog in a large wheel that I couldn't control.

'And please, Jack,' I said. 'You were the one who was asking for straight talk a little while ago. What did you expect? Blowing away a priest, tossing him out on the steps like a Hefty garbage sack, wasn't going to have any consequences?'

'That was an accident! I told you!' Jack said. 'One of you pricks killed my friend. He died in my arms.'

'And one of you guys killed two cops,' I said. 'This is a dead-end game we're playing, Jack. I thought you wanted money. Killing people isn't going to get it for you. It's only going to get my trigger-happy, now completely pissed-off fellow cops to come in there shooting. I mean, let's face facts. If you force us to raid the church, in the end, you're not going to make it. You made a mistake with the priest. I can see that now. And we made a mistake too. Let's put what's happened behind us and get this thing back on track.'

I waited. Though I'd made it up on the spot, it was a decent argument. Anyway, we needed more time to regroup, think up a new strategy. The secret tunnel had seemed like our one good shot, but maybe there was another way. What we needed now was for the clock to kick back into slow.

'Only part of the track I'm putting this on from here

is the third rail, you lying sack of shit,' Jack just about spat in my ear. 'You screwed up, Mike, and now I'm going to punish you for it. Come to the front door and pick up the trash.'

Chapter Seventy

I had cleared the entrance of the bus and was running flat out across the street when the immense cathedral door began inching open again. I knew another victim was about to be ejected from the cathedral. Part of me wanted to believe I could save a life if I acted fast enough, but I knew better.

I was crossing the wide sidewalk when a human form suddenly flew out the black space of the open door. I couldn't tell whether it was a man or a woman.

The body skidded across the flagstone paving and landed facedown on top of a wilted flower arrangement. Male, I registered. Dark suit. Which hostage had been killed?

Breath scorching in my chest, I fell to my knees in front of the victim. I didn't even bother looking for a pulse when I saw the torso. The lower back had been ripped apart and was horribly torn and bloody.

I was too late.

The victim was a middle-aged man. His shirt had been removed, and dozens of large, ragged stab wounds covered his back. What looked like cigarette burns went up and down his forearms. I'd seen my share of bodies, and I recognized that someone with a sharp knife, maybe even a box cutter, had taken out a lot of anger on this one.

The first thing I saw when ESU lieutenant Steve Reno helped me flip the victim was that the poor man's throat had been slit.

My heart seized hard in my chest as I looked at the victim's beaten and bloody face.

I turned to Reno beside me. 'This is so wrong,' the big man said, staring at the corpse. Reno's voice was small and wounded, as if he was speaking to himself. 'As wrong as it gets.'

I nodded my head as I continued to stare down, unable to take my eyes away.

Andrew Thurman, the mayor of New York City, peered up lifelessly into the leaden sky. A pulse of cold shuddered through me as I glanced up into the dark, towering arches where he seemed to be looking for some answer as to why this could have happened.

Steve Reno pulled off his Windbreaker and wrapped it around Mayor Thurman like a blanket. He crossed himself silently before he closed the mayor's eyes with his thumbs.

'Grab his legs, Mike,' Reno said. 'Let's get him out of here. Don't let the press get any shots.'

Chapter Seventy-One

The noon Angelus bells started tolling from the cathedral as we carried the mayor of New York down the front steps. Everything that had happened up until now paled in comparison to this brutal, horrifying, and unnecessary murder.

There was an instant hush in the crowd of law enforcement. The bell continued its ominous pealing as the police and emergency personnel we passed in the cordoned-off street either gaped, goggle-eyed, or stiffened in ramrod postures of respect.

Cold kneaded my stomach violently as I remembered how police and firemen stopped and stood in the same reverential way in the WTC rubble whenever a service member was brought out of the pile. I looked up at Rock Center's glorious seventy-foot Christmas tree right after we laid the slain mayor on an EMS stretcher.

The hits just kept on coming, didn't they?

Enough, I thought. What the hijackers had done

was precedent-setting in the savage department, but I had to get myself beyond shock. It was time to put up the wall and focus. Get out ahead of this thing. Figure Jack out somehow.

Why the mayor? I thought, staring again at his badly tortured body.

Was Jack so overwrought by the death of one of his fellow hijackers that he'd chosen the mayor as the one victim who would make us the angriest? Or was the whole thing another ploy to push our buttons, to get us to react in a certain way? Was this murder actually a clue for us? Our first? Why did they pick Andrew Thurman as the one to die?

As I was trying to figure it out, a captain from Midtown North came down between the white wicker angels and rows of poinsettias and grabbed me. Borough Commander Will Matthews had moved the command center to an office in 630 Fifth, the Rockefeller Center building to the west, directly across from the cathedral. He wanted me to report there immediately.

I ran all the way, and I don't know what I expected when I stepped into the boardroom of the second-floor office – but it wasn't that Commander Will Matthews would be the lowest-ranking cop in the room.

Normally, I would have been a little rattled to receive NYPD Police Commissioner Daly's curt nod of hello a second before Bill Gant's, the special agent in charge of the FBI's New York office. But my shock reserve was bone dry that afternoon. I just nodded back at both of them.

'Afternoon, Detective,' the commissioner said.

He was tall, aristocratically handsome, and seemed more like a banker than a cop in his broad pinstripe navy suit. Some said, with his tailored clothes and his Columbia MBA, he was just another glory hound, far removed from the rank and file. This was the first time I'd gotten close enough to make any kind of judgment.

'We just heard about the . . . my God, I can't believe I'm saying this . . . Andy's . . . I mean, the mayor's murder,' Daly stammered. He seemed genuinely upset, and that touched me. 'You've been speaking to the individuals responsible. What do you think this is all about?'

'Frankly, sir,' I said, 'I can't get a bead on them. It looked like a straight-up money deal, at first. A group of professional criminals trying to pull off an audacious mass kidnapping.

'But then, for some unknown reason, they shot a priest. I guess you could chalk up shooting the tactical team officers to defense, but what they did to the mayor shows a great degree of rage. Maybe at first it was for money, but now, since they see how surrounded they are, they're losing it.'

'Do you think all or a part of this might have had something to do with a personal grudge against the mayor?' Gant asked. With his basset-hound eye bags, the short FBI chief looked like the antonym of Daly. Pudgy and pale in a dark Sears single-breasted suit, Gant could have been a bartender at a funeral.

'I don't know,' I said. 'It's possible.'

'You don't know too much, do you?' Gant came right back at me.

'You think I volunteered for this detail?' I said, unclipping the crisis phone off my belt and sliding it across the boardroom table at him. 'Be my guest, pal. Step right up. You guys sure showed 'em how it was done down in Waco.'

And minutes before, I'd thought I was in a place beyond anger. I guess not.

'I'm sorry,' Gant said, backing away from the crisis phone as if it might bite him. 'That was a cheap shot.'

'Yes, it was,' the commissioner said, eyeing the FBI leader like he was looking for a soft place to hit him with a billy club. 'Detective Bennett is going above and beyond in this case, and he's staying on it. Is that clear?'

Screw what *they* said about the commissioner putting on airs, I thought, hiding a smile. *They* were wrong.

Gant looked taken aback, but he nodded agreement. A second later, Gant's phone rang. He shot out of his chair and into the hall after he looked at the caller ID.

He came back a moment later with an even paler look on his face. 'That was the director. He just got off the horn with the president. Military intervention has been authorized. Delta Force has been mobilized and is en route.'

Chapter Seventy-Two

I was still trying to come to terms with what I'd just heard as I staggered out of the boardroom inside Rockefeller Center. I'd been on some big cases before, but this was the first time I'd heard war declared.

Just when I thought things couldn't escalate any further, I saw that the whole of the command center operation had been moved into the hallway for more space. I spotted my fellow NYPD negotiator, Ned Mason, placing a sheet of computer paper up on a corkboard filled with them. The FBI negotiator, Paul Martelli, was on the phone at a desk beside him.

'So it's true? Thurman is *dead*?' Mason asked. I'd noticed that he always needed to know what was going on, to be in the loop.

I nodded solemnly. 'He was dead when they threw him out on the street.'

Mason looked like a brick had just hit him in the face as he nodded back.

'How could this be happening here?' Martelli said.

He looked shocked too. 'Russia. Baghdad, maybe. But Midtown Manhattan? Jesus. Hasn't this city been through enough?'

'Apparently not,' I said. 'How's the money-gathering going?'

'We're getting there,' Mason said, gesturing toward the papers on the board. Each one indicated an individual hostage, their representative, and the amount of the ransom.

'I just got off the horn with Eugena Humphrey's people in LA,' he said. 'In addition to Eugena's ransom, they're going to put up the money for the two reverends inside as well.'

'That's generous,' I said.

'If only the rest of them could be that cooperative,' Mason continued. 'Rooney's business manager refuses to release any money until he *personally* speaks with one of the hostage-takers. When I told him that was impossible, he hung up and is now refusing to take my calls. Can you believe it? It's like he thinks he's negotiating a contract instead of taking his client's life out of danger. Oh, and one of Charlie Conlan's kids has started legal action to block the transfer of any funds. The asshole's argument is that maybe his father is already dead, and he's refusing to put his inheritance in jeopardy.'

'Family values at work,' I said.

'You said it,' Martelli agreed.

'How much do we have collected so far?' I asked.

'Sixty-six million in escrow,' Mason said, after punching buttons on a desk calculator. 'Another ten makes seventy-six, and we'll be ready to wire it.'

'Did you subtract the mayor's ransom?' I said.

Mason's eyes widened as he looked up at me. 'You're right. Okay. Take away his three million, the total goes from seventy-six to seventy-three. Only seven million dollars to go.'

'Only,' I said. 'You know you've been hanging out with the rich and famous too long when you use the word *only* before the words *seven million dollars*.'

'It's like the man said,' Martelli added, putting the phone in the crook of his neck. 'A million here, a million there. Pretty soon you're talking *real* money.'

Chapter Seventy-Three

J ack sat on the steps of the high altar with his cell
phone antenna clenched between his teeth. He'd
quit smoking eight years before, but he was seriously
considering starting up again. He'd known the operation would be stressful. He'd even predicted the
attempted breach.

But that was on paper. Actually dealing with it in
real life, he thought, the blood pounding in his head
as he scanned the surrounding jewel-colored windows
for snipers, was a-whole-nother ball of wax.

Maybe I pushed it too far, he thought, gazing at the
flag-covered casket of the First Lady in front of him.
Maybe they'd storm the place now, celebrities or not.
He'd wanted to make a statement with the mayor, but
he wondered if he hadn't gone a little over the top on
that one, too.

The pathetic whimper Andrew Thurman had made
when Jack slid the Ka-Bar into his back still echoed
in his ears. The saints on the holy windows seemed

to stare down at him sternly, their strange dead eyes brimming with a malevolent disapproval.

No, no, no, Jack thought with a violent sneer. No way could he even think about going soft now. He knew what he had to do, and he was doing it. Killing the mayor had been nothing. Part of a formula that would end with his getting very rich. *Besides, the prick deserved it,* he reminded himself.

There was a time when Jack had badly needed the mayor's help and had been left twisting in the wind. *Hizzoner had it coming,* Jack thought with a nod.

And there would be more killing before this was over. No doubt about that.

'Jack? Come in,' came a voice from his radio.

'What now?' he answered.

'Come back to the chapel right now!' the radio said. 'One of the fish has fallen and claims he can't get up.'

Jack shook his head with a snort of disgust. His guys were great come ball-crushing time. They had guts and were loyal and obedient to a fault. But have them make a decision on their own about the tiniest shit, you were asking for a confirmed miracle.

He keyed the Motorola.

'On my way,' he said, getting to his feet.

Not again, Jack thought when he arrived at the rear chapel rail.

Another big shot was slabbed out on the marble floor.

Chapter Seventy-Four

Real-estate tycoon Xavier Brown's eyes were rolled way back in his head, his open silk shirt showing an expanse of snow-blind white belly. The talk show woman, Eugena, was sitting almost on top of him, compressing his chest with the heels of her hands, saying, 'Hold on, hold on, Xavier.'

'What the hell did you do to him?' Jack said to Little John.

'Nothing,' Little John answered defensively. 'That's just it. Fatty got up, complained his arm was hurting him, and then boom, down he goes. Beached whale.'

Jack knelt next to the talk show lady. He had to admit, even given how much he despised these worthless, privileged wimps, it was a little weird. He was starting to *respect* some of them – like Eugena.

'How's he looking?' he asked her.

'Very bad,' Eugena said, continuing CPR. 'His pulse is very weak. If he doesn't get to a hospital, he'll die. *No.* I don't know that for certain, but it's what I think.'

'Damn,' Jack said, standing directly over Brown. Another snag. Potentially a very costly one. What to do to protect his investment?

Jack snatched up his phone and hit redial.

'Mike here,' came the detective's voice. Jack had to admit the cop was good. They just sent out the mayor carved up like a Halloween pumpkin, and the cop sounded like a concierge at a four-star hotel. *You know it, pal. The hijacker is always right.*

'You got a problem,' Jack said. 'Hot-shit honcho Xavier Brown's stock has just taken a sudden nose-dive. I think his ticker's having trouble keeping up with all the fun and excitement. Tell you what, Mike, I'll let him out of here before his aorta explodes, but you have to pay his ransom first.'

'We don't have it all together yet, Jack,' the detective said. 'You have to give us more time.'

More time, is it? Jack thought. Wonder why. To figure out another way in and take us out, perhaps? These dolts couldn't help sticking to the dusty playbook, could they? No wonder he was going to get away with this.

'Go ahead and send his money first then,' Jack said. 'Or then again, don't. But tell his people they better decide quick. X. Brown is looking like the next time he makes it into the *Wall Street Journal*, it's going to be on the Obit page. I'll be watching the account. I see my money, I open the front door.'

'I'll let them know,' the negotiator said.

'You do that,' Jack said.

It took five of his men to drag the heavy financier up the aisle toward the main entrance of the cathedral. His guys looked like a radical tree-hugging order of monks trying to save a manatee. Eugena Humphrey tagged along the whole way, even dropping down to give the tycoon CPR in the vestibule. She was turning out to be a pretty good chick.

He turned when one of his men called to him from one of the little security rooms off the main altar. A laptop sat on a beat-up desk before the man.

'They did it!' the gunman said with excitement. 'They moved it already. The money is there.'

Jack smiled as he came over and looked at the screen. A three followed by six zeros was in the column next to their Costa Rican bank account number. By way of a half dozen Cayman Island, Isle of Man, and Swiss banks; untwisting the pretzel of dummy accounts and wire transfers would be impossible.

Three million. He was a millionaire.

Before he was forty, too.

He was almost giddy when he lifted his radio.

'Release the Fat Man,' he said.

Chapter Seventy-Five

Jack was so juiced by the progress, he helped pass out lunch to the hostages himself. Actually, he took great pleasure in providing a cold Mickey D's-only menu for the fussy celebrity gourmands. 'Dah, dah, dot, dah, dah – I'm lovin' it.'

He paused at the front of the chapel, staring out at his favorite captives. Funny, they didn't look like they were ready for the red carpet anymore. Had to be a real bitch and a half, trying to face the day without their maids and personal trainers and lifestyle coaches. Pale and crumpled and baggy-eyed, munching on their fast food, they reminded him of something.

Oh yeah, he remembered.

Human beings.

He took the microphone off its stand.

'Hey, everybody,' he said. 'Finally things are starting to break our way. Ransoms have begun rolling in. Won't be long now. Hope all your stockings are hung over the chimney with care.'

Jack paused. His amplified sigh was almost wistful.

'Got to hand it to you as a whole, guys,' he said. 'I really thought a bunch of soft celebrities like yourselves would freak out under the circumstances. But for the most part, you've proved me wrong. You held up better than expected, and for that you should be proud. And I really do hope the authorities continue cooperating. You can take this experience with you and get on with your lives. And even if a couple more of you have to be eliminated, you can go down realizing how lucky you are to die in your prime. It'll be James Dean, Marilyn Monroe, and you. You might have made yourselves stars, but think about it. A couple in the back of the head on the steps of St Paddy's? It'll turn you into legends.'

As Jack stepped down from the pulpit, Eugena Humphrey stood.

'Sir,' she called out bravely, 'may I communicate with you about something? Can we talk?'

Jack reached into his robe for his Taser, then stopped himself. There was a mesmerizing sincerity in the talk show host's face that even he couldn't deny was compelling.

'Make it snappy,' Jack finally said.

'Thank you,' Eugena said. She cleared her throat and looked directly into Jack's eyes.

No wonder this lady was so successful, Jack thought, feeling the weight of her confidence and intensity. It was as if the two of them were together in a small, cozy room – instead of yelling at each other over guns and hostages.

'What I want to say is this,' Eugena said. 'We're all truly sorry if who we are and what our lifestyles are all about have hurt you in some way. I'll be the first to admit that I am sometimes consumed with things instead of other people's feelings. But, honestly, after this ordeal, I do feel different. I'm going to enjoy the simple things in life again. I've learned from this experience, as I'm sure all of us have, and in some strange way, I'd actually like to thank you. But please, don't kill anybody else. Because deep down, you're right. We're *not* special. We're just people. Like you.'

Jack stood there, just staring at the woman. He would have thought it was impossible, but he almost felt guilty for a second. This stupid broad's somewhat eloquent plea had almost unnerved him. He didn't even watch her stupid show.

Jack was about to announce that whatever happened, she herself would be spared, when Little John, standing beside Eugena, drew his nine millimeter. He pressed the steel barrel to the talk show host's cheek.

'That was really emotional,' Little John said, cocking the hammer with his thumb. 'I'm crying so hard, I wet my panties. But you must have missed the e-mail about nobody giving a crap. Now, you either put a sock in it, or I'll put a bullet in it. This isn't your talk show, lady. This is *our* show.'

Jack called out to his compatriot, 'Little John, I couldn't have said it any better myself.'

Chapter Seventy-Six

How could it be Christmas Eve? I thought.

I stood on the corner of 50th Street and watched as snow began to fall, but not the soft, feathery flake variety. I flipped up my collar at the gritty bits of frozen rain that scoured at my face like sand tossed in a wind tunnel.

Over at the command center, I'd heard about a new problem for us to contend with. Along the lines of barricades, tourist crowds had gathered and were resisting being dispersed. Having been denied a peek at the Rock Center tree, which had been cordoned off, they were content to stand around and gape at the unfolding spectacle.

I watched a group of teenage girls, cheerleaders from Wichita, Kansas, arrive at the northwest corner of 51st, laughing as they pumped handwritten FREE MERCEDES signs into the air. A few had SIEGE OF ST PAT'S T-shirts over their sweaters.

I shook my head. You knew you were in trouble

when somebody was selling T-shirts. I could see every member of my Manhattan North Homicide squad sporting them when I returned to the squad room. *If I returned*, that was.

I wandered over toward Lieutenant Reno and HRT chief Oakley, who were commiserating in front of the black FBI tactical bus. Oakley had a folded blueprint in his hand.

'Mike,' Oakley said, 'we're going over that first idea you had about the north spire again. Figuring out some way to get into the cathedral up there.'

I looked at the commando chief. His face was drawn and weary, but even in the cold murk there was no mistaking the determination in his eyes. Oakley had lost one of his men, and it didn't look like he would be slowing down until something was done about it.

'It's probably the next best tactical option,' I said. 'But after what happened in the concourse, I'm worried about getting ambushed again. And it might be a lot harder to fall back from three hundred feet in the air.'

'We've spoken to Will Matthews and the FBI special agent in charge,' Reno said. 'The next decision to go tactical will be a full-force breach from every side. Next time they send us in, we won't stop until every hijacker is taken out, Mike.'

I was standing there, trying to shrug off the implications of what Reno had just said, when I heard the squall of feedback coming from the north. I rubbed my eyes, trying to register what I was seeing. Here we go again.

Beyond the barricades and news trucks, a group of young black men was standing on top of a yellow school bus. A short boy tapped at the microphone stand in front of him.

'One, two,' came his amplified voice. Then there was a pause, and he started singing.

The song was 'I Believe I Can Fly.' It was like a punch in the chest when the choir joined the soloist.

I could read the banner on the side of the bus. BOYS CHOIR OF HARLEM. Most of them were probably from one of the kidnapped reverends' congregations.

All we needed was a Ferris wheel and cotton candy, and we could start charging admission to this freak show on Fifth Avenue.

Though I had to admit, the boys' soaring voices brightened the gloom somehow.

Reno must have thought so too, because he grinned as he shook his head.

'Only in New York,' he said.

Chapter Seventy-Seven

A makeshift mess hall for the army of law enforcement had been set up right in the main lobby of Saks Fifth Avenue.

I went in through the revolving doors under the neon snowflakes to grab a quick bite to eat. The Four Seasons restaurant's recent offer of hostage meals had been rejected by Jack, so they had given the food to us instead. Christmas Muzak blared down from garlanded ceiling speakers as I spooned duck prosciutto and turkey hash onto my daisy plate. It wasn't the continuing surrealism of the siege situation that was alarming so much as the fact that I was starting to get used to it.

I could hear that the Boys Choir still believed they could fly as I came back out onto the street. I brought my food past the animatronic Santa in Saks's plate-glass window and back to the trailer. I was on my second bite of tuna tartare when the crisis cell rang on my belt.

What now? I thought. *What's your pleasure, Jack? At your service, of course.*

'Mike here,' I said.

'How's it hanging, Mickey?' Jack said. 'Cold enough for you? Kind of toasty in here.'

For a moment, I thought of the various strategies I could use. I could go passive or aggressive. Ask some questions to feel out his present mood. I was tired of strategies, though. Jack was the one toying with us, and I was sick of pretending it was the other way around. At this point, I was sick of talking to Jack, period. And it didn't matter *what* I said, did it?

'Killing the mayor was a mistake,' I said, lowering my plastic fork. 'You wanted us to believe you're a psychopath not to be trifled with? Well, you did a good job. Only that just makes storming in there more of a foregone conclusion. Which, according to you, blows up the cathedral. Which will kill you. Which makes spending all that money kind of hard. So, you really are crazy? Help me out here. I'm having trouble keeping up.'

'So glum, Mick,' Jack said. 'It's like you're giving up, and it's only the third quarter. Check it out. You've finally started paying. That was good. Real good. Now, all you have to do is come through with the rest of the dough-re-mi. Then it will get real interesting, I promise. How do the bad guys get away with it? So, stick with me here. Reach way down deep. Oh, and by the way, before I forget. There'll be another celebrity body at midnight.'

'Jack, listen. Don't do it,' I said. 'We can work something—'

'*Shut up!*' Jack yelled.

I immediately stopped talking.

'I'm tired of your bull, my friend,' Jack said. 'The delays. The stalling. You guys took your best shot and missed, and now it's time for you to pay for messing with us. Piss me off a little more, and instead of one dead celeb, I'll make things so bad, Prada will be coming out with a body bag this season.

'You receiving my transmission loud and clear, Mike? I repeat, there will be another famous body at midnight. No more easy ones like the worthless mayor either. I've already made my selection. You'll like this one. Oh, and stop that singing right now, or *I believe I will kill all the female hostages.*'

Chapter Seventy-Eight

With another block of excruciating downtime in front of us, I grabbed the opportunity to hand over the crisis phone to Ned Mason. Then I headed uptown to see Maeve.

I noticed a change when I came into her room. The sheets were different, flannel, new, and crisp. There was a vase full of fresh flowers, and she was wearing a new bathrobe. They were nice additions, so why did they creep me out?

Maeve was awake, watching CNN, which now had ongoing coverage of the siege. What ever happened to the Yule log? I found the remote and clicked off the set before I took her hand.

'Hey, you,' I said.

'I saw you on the tube,' Maeve said, smiling. 'You always look so handsome in that suit. Whose christening did you wear it to? Shawna's?'

'Chrissy's,' I said.

'Chrissy,' my wife said with a sigh. 'How is my little Peep?'

'She came into the nest the other night,' I said. 'I forgot to tell you. I forgot to tell you a lot of things, Maeve. I . . .'

My wife raised her hand and put her finger to my lips.

'I know,' she said.

'I shouldn't have been so concerned with my stupid job. I wish . . .'

She stopped me with a hurt look.

'Please don't wish,' she said quietly. 'It hurts more than cancer. I knew full well how dedicated you were to your job when we first met. It was one of the reasons I married you. I was so proud, seeing you speak to the press. My God. You were inspiring.'

'Who do you think inspires me?' I said, tearing up.

'No, not on these nice new sheets. Wait. I have your present.'

We always exchanged gifts on Christmas Eve, usually around 3:00 a.m., after putting together a bike or train set or some other God-awful toy.

'Me first,' I said, taking a wrapped box out of the bag I had stashed in the trunk of my car. 'Allow me.'

I tore off the paper and showed Maeve the portable

DVD player and the stack of DVDs I'd gotten her. The movies were old black-and-white noirs, Maeve's favorites.

'So you don't have to constantly watch the idiot box,' I said. 'Look, *Double Indemnity*. I'll sneak us up some Atomic Wings. It'll be just like old times.'

'How awesomely devilish of you,' Maeve said. 'Now mine.'

She produced a black velvet jewelry box from under her pillow and handed it to me. I opened the box. It was an earring. A single gold hoop. I used to wear one back in the late 'Guns N' Roses' eighties when we first met.

I started to laugh. Then both of us were laughing hard, and it was wonderful.

'Put it in. Put it in,' Maeve cried through her laughing fit.

I maneuvered the earring into the latent hole of my left ear. Miraculously, after nearly two decades, it slipped right in.

'How do I look? Totally tubular?'

'Like a well-dressed pirate,' my wife said, wiping a rare happy tear from her eye.

'Arrrrrrr, matey,' I said, burying my face in her neck.

I backed away when I felt her stiffen. Then I shuddered at the distant look in her eyes. Her breathing became irregular, as if she was hyperventilating without any hesitation. I blasted the nurse's button half a dozen times.

'I've spilled the water from the spring, Mother,' I heard my wife say in the Irish accent she'd fought so hard to erase. 'The lambs are all in the ditch, every last one.'

What was happening? Oh God no, Maeve! Not today, not now – not ever!

Sally Hitchens, the head of the Nursing Department, came rushing in. She shined a light into Maeve's eye and reached under her robe for her pain pack.

'Doctor upped her meds this morning,' Sally said. Maeve closed her eyes when the nurse put her hand on her forehead. 'We have to watch her closely until she adjusts. Can I speak to you a second, Mike?'

Chapter Seventy-Nine

I kissed the top of my wife's head and followed Sally out into the hall. The nurse looked directly into my eyes. Bad sign. I quickly thought of the unsettling difference in Maeve's room. The nice new sheets. The fresh flowers. Some kind of preparations were being made.

No. Not acceptable.

'We're getting very close to the end now, Mike,' she said. 'I'm sorry. I'm so sorry.'

'How long?' I said, looking at the hall carpet first, then back up at Sally.

'A week,' the nurse said gently. 'Probably less.'

'A week?' I said. Even I knew I sounded like a spoiled child. It wasn't the nurse's fault. The lady was an angel of mercy.

'Impossible as it is, you have to prepare yourself,' Sally said. 'Didn't you read the book I gave you?'

She'd given me Elisabeth Kübler-Ross's famous book *On Death and Dying.* It described the stages in the death process: denial, anger, bargaining, depression, acceptance.

'I guess I'm stuck in the anger part,' I said.

'You're going to have to unstick yourself, Mike,' the nurse said, annoyed. 'Let me tell you something. I've seen some cases in this place that, I'm ashamed to say, haven't affected me all that much. Your wife is not one of those cases. Maeve needs you to be strong now. It's time to deal. Oh, and Mike, love your earring.'

I closed my eyes and felt my face flush red with anger and embarrassment as I heard the nurse walk off. There was something unending about the pain I felt pass through me then. It seemed incredibly powerful, as if it would burst out of my chest like a bomb blast, stop the world, stop all life everywhere.

It passed after a moment when I heard someone in one of the other rooms click on a TV.

Apparently not, I thought as I opened my burning eyes and headed for the elevators.

Chapter Eighty

I called home on my cell phone as I left the hospital and hurried toward my car. Julia picked up.

'How's Mom?' she said.

In homicide interrogations, sometimes it takes lying very convincingly in order to extract a confession. At that moment, I was glad I'd had some practice.

'She looks great, Julia,' I said. 'She sends her love. To you, especially. She's so proud of the way you've been taking care of your sisters. So am I, by the way.'

'How are you, Dad?' Julia said. Was that static or extremely mature concern in my baby's voice? I remembered that she'd be heading to high school next year. How the heck had my little girl grown up without me noticing?

'You know me, Julia,' I said into my cell. 'If I'm not actually freaking out, I guess I'm doing pretty good.'

Julia laughed. She'd been front row center for my classic comedy, *Dad Meltdowns*.

'Remember that time when everyone was fighting

on the way to the Poconos, and you told me to close my eyes and look out the window?' Julia said.

'I wish I could forget it,' I said with a laugh. 'How are things in the barracks?'

'There's quite a line behind me, waiting to tell you,' she said.

As I drove through the cold city streets, I spoke briefly to each of my kids, telling them how much their mother and I loved them. I apologized for not being there for their pageant or Christmas Eve. I'd missed holidays working cases before, but there was never a time when neither Maeve nor I had been there. As usual, the kids were taking things in stride. Chrissy was sniffling when she got on the line.

Uh-oh. What now? I thought.

'What is it, honey cub?' I said.

'Daddy,' Chrissy said, sobbing, 'Hillary Martin said Santa can't come to our apartment because we don't have a fireplace. I want Santa to come.'

I smiled with relief. Maeve and I fortunately had heard this lament at least twice before and had devised a solution.

'Oh, Chrissy,' I said into the phone with mock panic. 'Thank you so much for reminding me. When Santa comes to New York City, because people in a lot of apartments don't have fireplaces, he lands his sleigh on the roof of the building and comes down the fire escape. Now, Chrissy, do me a real big favor, okay? Tell Mary Catherine to make sure the window in the kitchen is unlocked. Can you remember that?'

'I'll tell her,' Chrissy said breathlessly.

'Wait a second. Wait, Chrissy,' I said, turning up the police radio under my dash. 'Oh, wow! I just got an official report from our police helicopter. Santa's approaching New York City right now. Quick! Get to bed, because you know what happens if Santa shows up and children are awake, right?'

'He keeps going,' Chrissy said. 'Bye, Daddy.'

'Mr Bennett?' came Mary Catherine's voice from the receiver a few seconds later.

'Hi, Mary,' I said. 'Where's Seamus? He should have relieved you by now.'

'He did. He's holding court in the living room with "'Twas the Night Before Christmas."'

Reading that story had always been my job, but I felt more gratitude than sadness. Despite the negatives, my grandfather Seamus was a wonderful storyteller and wouldn't hesitate to do anything to make sure the kids were getting the best Christmas they could under the awful circumstances. At least my kids were safe, I thought. They were surrounded by angels and saints. I wished the same could be said for me, but the job I'd chosen often involved the sinners. *The very worst of them.*

'Please, Mary. Feel free to get out of there,' I said. 'And thank you so much for picking up all the slack. When this craziness at the cathedral is over, we'll sit down and figure out a sane schedule.'

'I'm glad I could help. You have a wonderful family,' Mary Catherine said. 'Merry Christmas, Mike.'

I was speeding south past the wreath-and-holly-decked Plaza Hotel when she said it, and for a second, I wanted to believe that it could be. Then in the distance down Fifth, I spotted the harsh glow of the siege tinting the black sky.

'Talk to you later,' I said, and snapped my phone shut.

Chapter Eighty-One

In the dark confessional, Laura Winston lay curled on the cramped floor, sweating and shivering. *The most fashionable woman on the planet,* she thought, *is in desperate need of a makeover.*

In the twenty hours she'd been confined, she'd drifted in and out of consciousness. But ever since the dim light had retreated from the stained-glass skylight above her, six or seven hours ago, she'd been completely and atrociously awake with the fever and pain of withdrawal.

It was around noon when she had noticed her reflection in the polished brass kick plate of the door. Makeup eroded by tears and sweat, honey-blond razor cut flecked with vomit. At first Laura thought she was staring at some kind of religious carving, the image of a deranged, skeletal demon triumphantly slain by an angel. She recalled the last lines of Sylvia Plath's poem 'Mirror' as she lay there, unable to look away from the terrible image. *In me she has drowned a young girl, and in me an old woman/Rises toward her day after day, like a terrible fish.*

It had taken a kidnapping, a violent ordeal of historic proportions to do it, but now, finally, she realized the truth.

She was *old*.

And she'd actually hurt people, hadn't she? Laura thought. Women especially. Month after month after month in her magazine she'd perpetuated the hurtful myth of eternal chicness and supposedly attainable beauty. Draped impossibly expensive clothes on fourteen-year-old genetic freaks and called it normal, then implied to her readers that if they didn't look like them, they were worthless, or at least not living up to their potential.

When she got out of this, *if she did*, she was going to change, she decided. Pack it in. Go to a good rehab facility. Downsize. Instead of building an empire, she was going to establish a charitable foundation. Insane as it was, this awful experience had fundamentally changed her for the better.

Give me one last chance, Lord. The fashionista prayed for the first time since she was a little girl. *At least give me the chance to change.*

It felt like something tore inside her ear when the gun went off just outside the confessional door.

When the ringing subsided, she could hear people screaming. The sulfurous stench of cordite wafted under the door and mixed with the sour smell of her vomit.

Her breath jammed in her throat as she heard a muffled curse and a body being dragged past her door.

God have mercy. They'd shot somebody else!

Laura felt her heart wallop against her chest.

Who could it have been? Who? Why? She hoped it wasn't Eugena, who had been so kind to her.

The hijacking wasn't really about money, was it? Laura concluded with numb horror. One by one, they'd be taken off to slaughter. Made to pay for their stupid, decadent sins.

She was running out of time. *I'm next,* Laura thought with a dry heave.

Chapter Eighty-Two

Eugena Humphrey, unfortunately, had seen dead bodies before.

Her grandmother's was the first, and she remembered how angry the withered, sadly questioning change in the face of her beloved Gram had made her. More recently, with her philanthropy work, she'd been shown pictures of atrocities throughout the world that needed somebody's attention, and she had tried her best to help.

But even the garish images of the hacked-up villagers in equatorial Africa couldn't prepare her for what she had just witnessed with her own eyes.

Just shot him, Eugena thought. *Stepped up to the pew and just shot him through the head.*

Why? How could one human being do that to another?

Now she watched the gunmen drag the body along the marble. What a horrible sound it made, like blood being squeegeed off glass. A hijacker at each side pulled at the body's rag-doll arms as though it were some nonsensical schoolyard game.

A shiny black loafer came off one foot. Terrible detail. The open eyes of the lolling head seemed to make contact with Eugena as the corpse was pulled into the shadowed gallery beside the altar.

Why me? the lifeless eyes seemed to accuse her as he was pulled out of sight. *Why me and not you?*

They just killed my dear friend, Eugena thought, and then she began to sob uncontrollably, and she knew she would be changed forever by this.

Chapter Eighty-Three

As I came through the checkpoint, I felt a hard punch right to my heart. I could see Oakley and a couple more ESU cops running like madmen across Fifth toward the cathedral steps. That could only mean one thing, I thought, angrily racing ahead to catch up.

I checked my watch. What the hell? Jack had said midnight. *It was only ten thirty.*

I was already at the ambulances in Rock Center when Oakley and the other cops arrived with a suit-clad body. I couldn't see the face as the medics scrambled desperately over the victim on the stretcher. Who the hell was it? Who had they killed now? Why do it before the deadline?

After a moment, the paramedics stopped. One of them turned away with tears in her eyes. The oxygen mask she was holding fell from her fingers unheeded. She sat down in the gutter, and the flashes from news photographers outside the cordon and in the windows of buildings overlooking the cathedral rudely invaded her grief.

I felt my heart flash-freeze when I finally saw who it was – the latest murder victim. I remembered other times I'd experienced this same awful shock . . . with Belushi, Lennon, River Phoenix.

John Rooney, the movie-star comic, lay sprawled on the stretcher, eyes and mouth wide open.

What felt like a slow electric current crept along my spine.

Another person slaughtered for no good reason, just for show.

I glanced back at the crowds and press straining to see past the barricades. I almost sat down next to the grieving paramedic at the curb.

How the hell were we expected to go on with this?

I remembered how my kids had worshipped Rooney. Maybe they were watching the live-action DVD he'd been in only last Christmas – *Rudolph* – right now.

Who would be next? I thought. Eugena? Charlie Conlan? Todd Snow?

Rooney had millions of fans, many of them children. Being such a star, he'd become part of the country and the world's consciousness, and those bastards had just erased him and all the warm feelings he'd miraculously been able to generate.

I glanced back again at the cathedral, the crowd stretching beyond it, the microwave towers of the news vans.

For the first time, I wanted to pack it in. I ached to just take the phone off my belt and walk away. Find a subway. Go lie in my wife's room, holding her hand. Maeve could always soothe me somehow.

'My God!' Oakley cried in outrage. 'How the hell are we going to deliver this bombshell? First we drop the ball with the mayor. Now we let poor John Rooney get killed.'

Then it dawned on me.

There it was.

That was the whole point.

I suddenly understood why the hijackers were wiping out celebrities, one grueling murder at a time.

They wanted things to go slow, methodically slow. That way, the crowds would gather. That way, the media, along with the rest of the world watching at home, would come together to put the pressure on so that this thing would be resolved. But the pressure wasn't on them, I realized.

It was on us.

Someone had finally done it. Someone had devised law enforcement's worst nightmare. As time went by and the bodies piled up, we looked worse and worse.

It made any decision to breach the cathedral in a rescue attempt almost impossible. If we screwed up, and *boom,* the place went up, people wouldn't blame the hijackers, they'd blame us.

I let the crisis phone ring four times before I answered it.

'Hi. It's Jack,' he said, and actually sounded gleeful. 'Hi-Jack. Get it? Sure, it's not as funny as Rooney, but I'm thinking his stand-up days are over. Time's up, Mike. No more excuses. No more delays. If all the money isn't in my account by nine o'clock tomorrow morning, there'll be so many dead rich and famous people under the ol' tree this Christmas, Santa'll have to leave all the presents in the fireplace.'

Chapter Eighty-Four

It was coming on two in the morning when I slowly, painfully lifted my head off the laptop keyboard I'd been using for a pillow. I was aware of the earring Maeve had given me. Also, that for the first time in hours, the activity in the makeshift Rockefeller command center had died down to a murmur.

Our work was almost done here. It had taken every ounce of finagling and begging and negotiating, but we'd somehow gotten all but four of the seventy-three million dollars together.

Delta Force had arrived around midnight and was working with the FBI and NYPD tactical people, trying to find some weakness, some helpful detail that had been overlooked. I'd heard that a mock-up of the cathedral was being built at an army base in Westchester to assist the commandos to plan for a breach.

As a kid, the thought of ever seeing soldiers patrolling the streets of New York was ridiculous, a scene from a B science-fiction movie. Seeing the soldiers on the perimeter of Ground Zero and watching the F-14s buzzing the Midtown skyscrapers as they flew air cover after 9/11 still didn't seem real to me, *but it was.*

I sat up as an army general came past my desk. Seeing combat boots on NYC ground twice in one lifetime, I thought as I watched the officer and his entourage enter the command boardroom, seemed unfair.

'Why don't you take a breather, Mike?' Paul Martelli told me with a yawn. He'd just come back from catching some sleep. 'Nothing going on here for a little while.'

'We're coming down to the end of this thing,' I said. 'I don't want to be missing if I'm needed.'

Martelli patted me on the shoulder.

'Listen, Mike,' he said, 'we all know about your wife, your family situation. I can't even imagine the stress you're under. We'll call you the second something develops. Now get out of here. Go be with your family. Mason and I have you covered.'

Martelli didn't have to tell me twice. Anyway, I felt the negotiations were over – *they'd won.* We still had to negotiate the hostages' release and whatever kind of transportation the hijackers thought they would need to get them to safety. But all that could wait.

Maeve was sleeping when I came in. I wasn't about to wake her from such a peaceful state. On her bedside table, Jimmy Stewart was reluctantly receiving a cigar from Potter on the screen of the portable DVD player. I shut it off.

I stood there staring at my dear, sweet wife, the treasure of my life.

I smiled as I remembered our first date. I had just taken my finger off the bell to her apartment when she threw open the door and kissed me. There was a flash of her honey-brown eyes, the spiced sweetness of her perfume, and without preamble, soft lips hit me and my heart smacked against the back of my chest like a handball.

'Thought I'd save us a little awkwardness later,' she'd said, her smile beaming as I stammered a bit, reeling against her threshold.

'Sweet Maeve,' I whispered now from the foot of her bed. 'There'll never be a man as lucky as me. I love you so much, my queen.' I touched a finger to my lips, then to hers.

Minutes later, I swung crosstown again. There wasn't a soul on the windswept streets. Even the homeless had gone home for Christmas, I guessed.

I went into the kids' rooms and checked on them. There were probably visions of PlayStation and XBox dancing in their heads instead of sugarplums, but at least they were snug in their beds as required. Seamus was snoring to beat the band on top of the chaise in my bedroom, cookie crumbs on his cheeks. My eleventh kid. I tossed a throw on him and turned out the light.

My biggest shock came when I stepped into the living room. Not only was there a grand tree, but it had been decorated to the nines. The kids' gifts had been pulled from the back of my closet, expertly wrapped, and stacked in ten piles under it.

There was a note on the DVD remote sitting on the sectional. HIT PLAY, it said. MERRY CHRISTMAS! MARY CATHERINE.

I did as instructed. A video shot of Chrissy, dressed as an angel and proceeding up the aisle in Holy Name's gym, filled the screen.

I teared up, but not angrily this time. What an awesome job Mary Catherine and my grandfather had done. What could be more beautiful than this?

Duh, how about Maeve there, healthy, beside you? a voice inside me said.

I didn't have the strength to listen to voices right now. It would all be over soon. I wiped my eyes to watch as my boys, now shepherds, came wandering from afar toward the stage. *God save the Bennetts.*

Chapter Eighty-Five

I don't know what I appreciated more when I woke up early on Christmas morning. The unmatchably wonderful smell of coffee and bacon wafting through my open door or the barely stifled giggling coming from the other side of my bed.

'Oh no,' I said, sitting up after a particularly loud titter. 'All my children are sound asleep . . . and there's Irish ghosts in my room!'

There was an explosion of laughter as Shawna, Chrissy, and Trent tackled me back onto my pillow.

'It's not ghosts,' Trent said, kangaroo-bouncing up and down beside my head. 'It's Christmas!'

Tugging one hand apiece, Chrissy and Shawna got me to my feet and pulled me out into the sweetly pine-scented living room.

I got my Christmas present right there and then when I looked down at my two little ones. Norman Rockwell couldn't have painted it any better. Christmas-tree lights softly illuminating the breathless, saucer-eyed wonder of two little girls on this special day of days.

'You were right, Daddy!' Chrissy said, letting me go as she clapped her hands over her head. 'I left the kitchen window open, and Santa made it!'

I saw Trent shaking a box.

'How about you little guys wake up the big ones first,' I said. 'Then we'll open presents together, okay?'

Three little comets rocketed out of the room simultaneously. I headed for the kitchen, following that wonderful smell. Mary Catherine smiled at me as she poured pancake batter into a skillet.

'Merry Christmas, Mike,' she said. 'Do you like your fried egg on top of the pancake or on the side?'

'Whatever's easiest,' I said, stunned to learn that having both pancakes and eggs at once was within the realm of the possible. 'I don't know how I'm ever going to thank you for all you've done for my family. The tree, taping the pageant, wrapping the gifts. Heck, I'm starting to think maybe Santa is real. You sure you're not from Tipperary by way of the North Pole?'

'Please,' Mary said with a wink. 'Father Seamus did most of it. Wait, I hear the children. Take that tray out. I poured the hot chocolate, and your coffee is there on the island.'

I did as I was told and headed back to the living

room. I thought everyone would be tearing into the gifts like wolves on a heifer by this point, but they were just standing there. What was up?

'You didn't have to wait for me, guys,' I said. 'Merry Christmas. Let the wrapping paper fly!'

'Well, Dad,' Brian started. 'We had a kids' meeting and . . .'

'What Brian is trying to say,' Julia said, 'is that we decided that we don't want to open our gifts until we see Mom. We know you have to go back to work, but we're willing to wait until you get home so we can all go over and see Mom together.'

I stepped over and wrapped as many of my kids into my arms as I could.

'Game over,' I said, closing my eyes tight in the center of the scrum. 'You guys are the best kids who ever lived.'

After I ate my egg pancakes, I reluctantly hopped in the shower and got changed. The last thing I saw after I hugged my way to the front door of my apartment was Mary Catherine charging the video camera battery. How I was ever going to repay this girl, I couldn't begin to fathom.

I almost knocked down Seamus, who'd gone home early to shower and change, as he stepped out of the elevator. He was dressed all in black, with his Roman collar tight at the neck. Damn if he didn't look holy and pious and very nice.

'Merry Christmas,' he said. 'Off to work, are we? That's a fine, fine job you have for yourself there. Real conducive to family life, it is.'

'Oh, 'tis, 'tis,' I said in my grandfather's brogue.

Right. As if I wanted to go to work. I almost laughed after I took a breath. It wouldn't have been a holiday without my grandfather busting my chops about something.

'Hey, thanks for what you did for the kids, you nasty old bat,' I said with a smile. I stopped the door as it started to slide closed. 'Oh, and bah humbug to you too.'

Chapter Eighty-Six

Inside the semi-darkened cathedral, Eugena Humphrey woke on a hard wooden pew. She sat up, rubbing the cold out of her arms. She widened her eyes reluctantly and let out a breath of disappointment as she eyed the cathedral's all-too-familiar stark stone. Finally, she turned her head toward the votive candles that had given her a sense of peace and hope over the last forty-eight hours.

The rows of golden light were gone, she saw immediately. Every flame completely snuffed out.

She'd had some pretty bad Christmases before, she thought, closing her eyes again. But this was worse than getting regifted.

Though she knew it would be painful, she couldn't help thinking about what she would have been doing back home at this very moment.

She could almost see her husband, Mitchell, coming into the bedroom of her cozy penthouse apartment above Wilshire Avenue with a heaping breakfast tray just for the two of them. Because of the occasion, the chef and nutritionist would have the day off, and Mitch's diet be damned. Blueberry pancakes, apple-smoked sausage, pecan bacon, oversized mugs of Kona coffee. After they ate heartily, they'd do their *exchange*. Because they had unlimited resources, it had come to pass over the years that even very expensive gifts, such as diamonds and new cars, had become – impossible to believe as it was – well, boring. She and Mitchell had come up with a new strategy that had proved to be joyful and meaningful for them both. They were each allowed to spend up to one hundred dollars, and the idea was to purchase the most beautiful or meaningful objects they could find.

It stressed simplicity. Got them back down to the basics. Plus, it was just fun.

One year, he had bought her a dozen perfect red roses. The effect was to make her really look at the flowers. Actually see their elegance and richness and fleeting beauty in a way that she hadn't since she had received her first bouquet.

This year, she'd gotten him a twenty-one-dollar watch she'd found at a pharmacy she'd done some stealth shopping in. It was a retro design. Quite simple. A circular white face with regular black numerals. She thought that it was simple in an eternal way, though.

The kind of watch God might wear if he needed to, and it seemed to her, at least in a profoundly understated way, to represent the preciousness of time, of life, of love with someone like Mitchell.

Eugena opened her eyes as something hard speared into the back of her neck.

'Hey, lucky you, Eugena. Santa got you a cheeseburger this year,' Little John said as he dropped a greasy paper-wrapped bundle in her lap.

Maybe the other hijackers were doing this for money, but that son of a bitch, Eugena thought, glaring at the back of the gunman's hood, got off on inflicting pain. He was the one who had walked up and killed John Rooney in cold blood.

An overwhelming sense of despair threatened to overtake her.

Who was she kidding? How in the name of God could she take another hour of this? Another minute?

She moved her 'Christmas breakfast' to the bench beside her and tried to start up her yoga again to calm herself down, lift her spirits. A growl came out of her with the first exhale.

No! she thought, searching around hatefully for the gunman. Enough damn tolerance. It was time to get pissed off.

But didn't other people feel this way all the time?

came an errant thought. Cold, angry, depressed, dirty, in need of just about everything. So many around the world suffered so much harder on a day-to-day basis. Who was she to complain?

Even if she was a celebrity, she was a goddamn person too! And one who wasn't going to take it anymore.

There's no use talking to these evil bastards, Eugena could see now. No way to resolve this thing peacefully. She sat up, clenching and unclenching her fists. She finally decided that if she got the opportunity, she was going to fight for her life.

Chapter Eighty-Seven

A cross the aisle from Eugena, Charlie Conlan checked his watch, then checked it again. He looked up as the skinny hijacker who liked Mercedes Freer came strolling past, doing his rounds.

Conlan turned and saw a lone hijacker sitting on the rear rail. He watched as the punk put his shotgun in his lap and took something out of the pocket of his robe. It was a jeweled cell phone he'd grabbed from one of the celebrities. Was he making a call? Who would he be calling now?

No, Conlan realized as the hijacker stared at the screen and started pressing buttons with his thumbs. He was playing a video game.

Conlan coughed twice. His signal. Todd Snow in the front pew sat up and shot him a look. Conlan nodded as Mercedes, sitting at the end of one of the middle pews, tugged the passing hijacker's robe.

Let's roll.

When the hijacker turned, Snow bolted over the front pew, hopped silently over the rail, and disappeared under the skirt of the altar.

Conlan swiveled his head to see if the hijacker at the rear had noticed. Nope, still into his game.

Conlan could hear Mercedes chatting up the other punk.

'I'm going a little crazy,' Mercedes hissed. 'C'mon, you and me. I'm serious. Give me a kiss at least.'

The hijacker's Adam's apple bulged. He glanced back at his partner, then leaned down and started tongue-kissing the pop singer through his mask. His hands were all over her chest.

'Not here in front of everybody. Behind the altar,' Mercedes whispered breathlessly.

The hijacker squinted back at his partner.

'What? I'm not worth it?' Mercedes said. She walked her fingers down the gunman's robe. Stopped right above his crotch. 'Believe me, I'm *worth* it.'

'Behind the altar?' he said. 'You're even dirtier than your videos. All right, let's go.'

Conlan exhaled as Mercedes rose in her pew. This was it.

Two things would happen now. Snow would stomp the hijacker behind the altar, and Conlan would rush the gunman at the back rail. Then they would have

JAMES PATTERSON & MICHAEL LEDWIDGE

two guns, and maybe they'd have a chance to get out of this alive.

Charlie Conlan wiped the sweat from his palms. He knew how risky this was. But it was either fight or wait to be shot like Rooney.

He glanced up at the altar again. Mercedes and the hijacker were glued together as they hurried up the steps.

Now.

Conlan stood in his pew. Suddenly there was an unexpected explosion. What felt like a steel fist slammed into the small of his back.

There was another explosion, and an iron blow caught him in the chin. Without knowing how it had happened, he was down on his back, numb and bleeding, struggling to stay conscious.

He heard Todd Snow yell out. Snow had been rushing toward the gangly hijacker when three others suddenly appeared. They fired on him – rubber bullets!

Conlan watched, horrified, as the quarterback dropped. Then Little John walked out from the larger church. He stepped up to Snow.

'You thought you could take us? *You? That old man?'* Little John said as he put his boot on Snow's chest.

Slowly, almost ceremoniously, he took a rubber bullet gun from one of his colleagues. He placed its bore between the athlete's eyes. Then he seemed to reconsider. Instead, he placed the muzzle on the star's right hand, his throwing hand. He stepped on the wrist to hold it still.

'Interference,' Little John yelled in a canned ref's voice. 'Ten yards. First down. And I'm placing you on the permanent Disabled List.'

The pop of the gun firing was swallowed by Snow's scream.

Conlan looked on as Mercedes Freer walked up to Little John. What the hell was she doing now?

He watched as she was handed a cell phone. Then a cigarette. He realized what had happened as Little John chivalrously lit it for her.

'You sold us out,' Conlan croaked. 'You insane little bitch.'

Mercedes rolled her eyes at Conlan.

'Merry Christmas, Momma,' Conlan heard her say into the cell phone as the numbness in his face started to warm. 'Stop cryin',' he heard her say. 'It's okay. These boys aren't so bad. They'll let me go, don't you worry about it. One thing you taught Mercedes is how to take care of herself.'

Chapter Eighty-Eight

With the absence of traffic on Christmas morning, I got back to St Patrick's in near record time. Even the pedestrian and media crowd had thinned out considerably, but I had a feeling that after they finished opening their presents, they'd be back for their fill of blood sport.

As I was coming across the plaza of 630 Fifth, a red-suited Santa walked past with a tray of coffee and a submachine gun strapped across his back. It was Steve Reno.

'Where you delivering presents, Santa? Fallujah?' I said.

'Trying to keep up morale, Mike,' Reno said through his cotton-ball beard.

'You have a harder job than me,' I said.

Paul Martelli almost tackled me as I got off the elevator at the command center.

'We did it, Mike,' he said. 'Five minutes ago, we got the last of it. All the money. It's ready to go.'

'Any chance we'll be able to trace it?' I asked.

Martelli shrugged his shoulders. 'We know it's set to go to an account in the Caymans. They will wire it somewhere else immediately, then somewhere else. Eventually, we could probably put enough political pressure on the bank down there to tell us where it was sent, but by then it will probably have been shot to another numbered account in Switzerland or who the hell knows where. The white-collar crime guys are working on it. If we are able to trace it, it's going to take some time.'

Well, at least we had gotten the money together, I thought. That was something.

I turned as Commander Will Matthews came out of the boardroom. I winced at his stubbled cheeks, the red-rimmed eyes. All he'd gotten this Christmas was an ulcer.

'We ready to go?' Will Matthews said to Ned Mason.

Mason stood up, cupping a phone receiver, and said, 'Bank's just waiting on you to give the final word.' He looked eager to get this over with, too. He hadn't been much help, but at least he had stayed around to observe.

Will Matthews took off his five-point cap and clawed a hand through his flattop before he took the receiver.

'This is Borough Commander Will Matthews,' he said. 'I hate like hell to say this. *Wire the money.*'

I followed my boss back into the boardroom and stood with him as he silently gazed at the cathedral.

Finally he turned to me.

'You get those bastards on the phone one more time, Mike. Tell them they got their blood money. Now let these poor people go.'

'How do you think they're going to try to get away, Commander?' I finally said.

'Let's just see, Bennett,' Will Matthews said, gazing malevolently across Fifth Avenue. 'The suspense is killing me.'

Chapter Eighty-Nine

I went back out to the communications desk in the outer office. The sergeant who had been the lead tech guy since this thing began nodded at me with anticipation. 'What's up, Mike? What now?'

'Can you ring me into the cathedral?' I said.

The sergeant blinked repeatedly, then nodded. He stood immediately, swept the paper off his desk, and flipped open a laptop.

'Give me a minute,' he said, which was about all it took.

'Yello,' Jack said as the sergeant handed me a phone.

'It's Mike,' I said. 'The money's been wired.'

'All of it?' Jack said.

'All of it. You got what you wanted.'

'Let me see about that,' Jack said skeptically.

I could hear some key clicks in the background. They were checking up on the account from inside the cathedral. Wasn't the Internet just the best?

'Mikey, me boyo. What a wonderful gift,' Jack finally

said after a minute. 'I'm about to explode with Christmas joy.'

'We fulfilled our part of the bargain,' I said, ignoring yet another of his wiseass comments. 'We've done exactly what you wanted. Now you have to do your part. It's time to let the hostages go.'

'All in due time, Mike,' Jack said calmly. 'All in due time. The hostages will be released all right, but on our terms. What would be the point of getting shot like dogs after all this good work? You know what I'm saying? Here's what we're going to need. You got a pen?'

'Tell me,' I said.

'Okay. Here goes. In twenty minutes, I want eleven identical black sedans with dark tinted windows, gassed and ready, parked out front at the Fifth Avenue entrance. The doors will be left *open*, and the engines left *running*. Fifth Avenue will be cleared all the way to One-thirty-eighth, and Fifty-seventh will be cleared river to river. It goes without saying that any effort to stop and detain us will result in a vast amount of death. If all our demands are met, the remaining hostages will be released unharmed.'

'Anything else?' I said.

'Nope, that's it,' Jack said. '*Arrivederci*, Mikey. It's been a real hoot.'

I almost couldn't believe it when I heard a dial tone in my ear. That was it?

All they wanted was eleven cars? Where did they think they were going to drive? Mexico?

Behind me I heard the borough commander speaking into his radio, telling the task force cops to clear Fifth and 57th and to block the side streets off. He got on another radio and told all the rooftop snipers to get ready.

'When they come out, we'll take them down,' he said. 'Anyone who has a clear line of sight has a green light.'

'Roger that,' came back one of the Delta Force guys.

'Oh, and I want GPS on those sedans,' Will Matthews told one of his captains.

'Bennett,' Will Matthews told me, 'get up on the roof and into a helicopter, in case we have to pursue.'

Not exactly overjoyed about heights, I can't say I was extremely psyched about that task, but I nodded okay.

As I stepped into the elevator headed to the roof, I couldn't imagine how the hijackers were planning on getting five steps out of the cathedral without getting massacred. I hit the button for the top floor.

Guess we'll find out soon enough.

Chapter Ninety

I don't know how gung ho I would have to have been to climb into a helicopter that was *on the ground*, never mind fifty-one stories up. If I wasn't so pressed for time, I would have crawled to the open doors to avoid the low, heavy chop of rotors.

The pilot must have noticed the green tinge of my face, or had a healthy sadistic streak. The second I was strapped in, the aircraft dropped off the side of the building, express elevator down, leaving my stomach back on the fifty-first floor.

After we slowed and stopped to hover four hundred feet over the intersection of 50th and Fifth, and I was done congratulating myself on not throwing up, I took in the whole of the cathedral for the first time.

It really was a beautiful structure, its spires and ornamentation as delicate and intricate as a wedding cake's, which was mind-boggling, considering the whole thing was made out of stone. Instead of being dwarfed by the Midtown glass office monoliths it was surrounded by, it seemed to shame them and somehow make it seem like the skyscrapers were out of place.

As I looked down, eleven black Chevy sedans rolled slowly in from the north. They stopped in front of the cathedral, and the uniformed cops driving them jumped out, leaving the doors open.

Squad cars were parked at every intersection to the southern horizon up Fifth, their cherry tops flashing as they blocked the streets on both sides.

What a scene.

'Doors!' someone called over the police-band crackle.

Down below, the tall front doors of the church began slowly opening.

A figure in a head-to-toe brown hooded robe and ski mask stepped out and stopped beside the stair railing.

I stared at the lone figure, waiting for just about anything to happen next.

Despite the fact that I was one of an army of cops, I was strangely anxious. One thing these sick puppies had taught us was that they were capable of anything, at any time.

There was a frenzied spattering of police radio chatter from my headset as another subject, dressed in the same brown robe and ski mask, stepped out a moment later. Was it the hijackers? What the hell was going on?

I twisted toward a flash of movement by the church doors.

A second later, my jaw dropped harder than the helicopter had off the roof.

Spilling out of the cathedral, walking in two straight lines down toward the waiting sedans, was a group of twenty-odd people.

All dressed in brown robes.

All wearing ski masks.

There was no way to tell the hostages from the bad guys.

Chapter Ninety-One

'**D**oes anybody have a shot?' Will Matthews cried out over the radio.

There were maybe thirty figures in brown robes out in front of the bronze doors of the cathedral now. They were moving slowly down the steps toward the waiting sedans.

'*Hold!*' called a voice. 'We're scanning with radar for concealed weapons.'

On the roof of Saks, a sniper set down his rifle and raised what looked like an extra-long pair of binoculars. He lowered the binoculars finally and called into his sleeve.

'Stand down,' he said. 'We have no shot. Heat signatures indicate that *they all seem to have weapons on them.* We have no safe shot. We can't tell who is who.'

My earphones almost fell off as I shook my head. Jack and his hijackers had done it again. They'd anticipated how dangerous it was for them to get from the church to the cars. They'd anticipated our next move and somehow disguised everyone. Our snipers didn't have a shot.

Down below, the brown-robed mass of people was climbing into the cars, three and four per vehicle. After a moment, the tinted-windowed doors started to close one by one. That was that. Another golden opportunity lost, or taken away from us. The bad guys could be the drivers in each car – or they could be in the backseat, holding a gun on a hostage in the driver's seat. There was no way to know.

I noticed for the first time that from the windows of the buildings on both sides of Fifth, citizens and media people were watching, transfixed. From where I was, it almost looked like a ticker-tape parade, only with celebrity hostages instead of sports or war heroes.

I stared at the idling cars. The big question remained: How did the hijackers think they were getting off the island of Manhattan? With the strange way that things were winding down, I was beginning to believe that nothing short of a bloodbath would resolve this.

It wasn't just airsickness that made my stomach roll a few seconds later.

'Goddamnit to hell!' I heard Will Matthews cry over the radio. 'Bennett, don't lose them!'

When I glanced at the pilot beside me, I noticed

that it was a woman beneath the aviator sunglasses and helmet. I knew I was in for it the second I saw her cocky smirk.

'What are you waiting for?' I said, and we fell.

Chapter Ninety-Two

W̲e stayed at a low hover over the convoy of black sedans. The whirling edges of the rotor couldn't have been more than twenty feet from the smooth glass and ornate stone building façades on either side of the avenue. I swallowed hard. Driving a car in this city was nerve-racking enough for me.

The hard, constant vibration of the helicopter made the cars below appear to tremble through the windshield when they finally pulled away from the cathedral. Now where the hell were they going?

The seat harness bit hard into my chest as we tilted forward and began to pursue.

We inched along in the air behind the convoy as it passed classy Fifth Avenue shops – Cartier, Gucci, Trump Tower. What, were they getting in a little last-minute window shopping?

An even stranger thing happened when the cars arrived at Tiffany's on the corner of 57th Street.

They stopped!

Were they going somewhere for breakfast? Maybe Jack planned to rob the famous jewelry store as a parting gesture. Anything was possible at this point. The helicopter's rotors thumped in time with my pulse as I waited and watched.

After a pause of a full minute, the lead car finally inched out from the curb and made a left – heading west on 57th Street. As the next four cars began to follow, I thought maybe the whole strange procession was going to take a slow rolling tour of the West Side. But the sixth car surprised me by turning east on 57th. The remaining cars behind it followed east as well.

I reported the bizarre new twist over the radio.

East Side, West Side, all around the town, I thought, watching the black sedans split away from one another.

Was one group the celebrities and the other the hijackers? There was no way to know from up here.

'Is there any way for you to distinguish who's who?' Will Matthews asked in an anguished voice.

I stared at the two lines of cars, struggling to figure it out. The combination of diesel fuel, vertigo, and the constant pounding of the helicopter wasn't exactly helping things in the focusing department. I gave up for the moment.

If there was any clue at all, I couldn't see it right now.

'There's no difference I can make out,' I finally called into the radio.

'Which way?' the pilot asked, annoyed, as we just sat there over the intersection at 57th.

'West,' I decided. 'Hang a left.'

At least if I was wrong, and I got fired, I thought as Bergdorf's swung under my right shoulder, it would be a shorter subway ride back to my apartment.

Chapter Ninety-Three

Straightening the wheel of the lead sedan heading east on 57th Street, Eugena Humphrey sucked in a deep breath. The heat of the cramped car was making her sweat, and the gamy stench of the ski mask the hijackers had made her wear was another distraction. Just what she didn't need right now.

She glanced at two uniformed cops, just standing there on the sidewalk, gaping at the passing sedans from in front of an art gallery on the north side of the street.

Nobody was doing anything! How could they?

Frightened as she was, sick and tired, she knew she couldn't break down now. She couldn't crack. And she wouldn't.

When was the last time she'd actually driven herself around? she thought. Ten years ago? She remembered a red Mustang she'd bought herself after her transfer out of the Wheeling, West Virginia, affiliate to LA. What a wild ride she'd been on since then.

And this was how it would end? Unwashed on Christmas Day at the mercy of some degenerate criminals. After all she'd done. All the hard work and astute decisions, pulling herself up out of nothing. She not only had risen above what the world tried to enforce as the limits of her race and class, but had tapped into the higher limits of human potential. Become a force for good in the world, a strong force.

But at least she'd lived a full life, hadn't she? Done just about everything there was to do.

Eugena gasped as the gunman in the front seat jabbed her violently with the pipe of a sawn-off shotgun.

'Speed it up,' he yelled at her.

At that moment, Eugena felt her despair pop and her adrenaline surge.

Speed it up? No problemo. I can certainly do that.

She hit the gas, and the V-8 engine seemed to cry as buildings and windows began to blur past. The sedan briefly left asphalt as it hit the hump of Park Avenue.

'That's it, momma. Punch it!' the hijacker howled as they landed, showering sparks.

As they hurtled toward Lexington, Eugena's eye caught the gleam of one of those steel telephone company nitrogen tanks on the corner. She fantasized about hitting it head-on.

Outside the windshield, it was as if New York City – the world itself – was coming at her now at warp speed. An unstoppable force at an immovable object.

Chapter Ninety-Four

The lineup of sedans was still doing a slow crawl west on 57th Street. Through the gap of sky up and down Seventh Avenue, I spotted at least half a dozen news helicopters shadowing us. There hadn't been this much attention on slow-moving vehicles since OJ's white Bronco.

I watched with more intensity as the convoy of cars seemed to slow by the subway entrance on Sixth Avenue. All we would need was for them to bail out into the labyrinth that is the New York City subway system.

But then the cars passed through the intersection, returning to parade speed.

Why wouldn't they do something, make their move?

It was as if the hijacker convoy was reading my mind as it came parallel with the Hard Rock Cafe a minute later.

There was a scream of engines and a bark of

spinning tire rubber, and the five cars suddenly peeled out.

The cops blocking the intersection at Broadway looked like stunned NASCAR spectators as the vehicles rocketed past them.

The sedans seemed to be drag-racing as they shot across Eighth. By the time they hit Ninth Avenue, they looked like they were taking a shot at the land speed record. The turbine of our chopper had to kick it up several notches just to stay on them.

I thought this sudden need to be somewhere in a hurry a tad peculiar, since they were speeding toward a dead end. There were maybe two blocks of Manhattan left.

Then what?

I could feel the blood leave my face as I watched the sedans scream down the final slope of street heading directly toward the Hudson River.

Would they try to ram one of the barricades? I didn't know, but I was certain of one thing: A deadly crash was coming in seconds. And there was nothing I could do except watch from a front-row balcony seat.

Chapter Ninety-Five

Hog-tied in the front passenger seat of the lead car heading west, rocker Charlie Conlan felt the cut on his chin reopen as the speeding vehicle bounded off a world-class pothole.

Conlan knew that the car was going way too fast. This was it, he thought. How it would happen. The End of a Legend.

As the sedan's engine roared, Conlan was struck with anger at the animal sitting beside him. Then at himself. He was still breathing, which meant he could still fight, still resist. But his arms and legs were taped together. So what could he do?

He glanced at the hijacker behind the wheel to his left. His mask was still on, but the hood was down.

Conlan nodded to himself as he figured it out. *Maybe I'll die, but it won't be on my knees to these bastards.*

The car had just lifted off from a steep crest along Tenth Avenue when Conlan leaned over and bit down into the driver's ear. The horrified scream the hijacker made almost drowned out the engine.

What this worthless vermin had put them through, Conlan thought, tasting blood. He'd killed his friend Rooney, then dragged him outside like a bag of garbage. Conlan wished he could inflict a world of pain on his sorry ass. But then the front tires shredded as the car touched down off-kilter, turned sideways – and began to flip.

Seconds later, the plate-glass window of the BMW showroom on the northeast corner of Eleventh seemed to evaporate as the sedan's spinning ton of steel crashed through it.

A horrible crunching sound blasted out Conlan's eardrums, and the world went *black.*

Then gray.

Then fluorescent white.

Conlan came out of the fog of shock and found himself blinking up into a bright ice-cube-tray light fixture. He was in an operating room, right? Or maybe he was having an acid flashback. The pile of glass in his lap made a tinkling sound as he turned around to see what was up.

Damn, he was inside a car showroom. They had somehow landed right-side up. He gaped at the twisted metal inches away from his throat. The sedan was now *a convertible*, since the roof had been ripped away.

When he looked out the hole in the shattered windshield, his first thought was that the hijacker driver, who was hunched over one of the showroom motorcycles, was trying to escape.

Then he noticed that one of the handlebars was sticking out the middle of the hijacker's back. 'One down,' said Charlie Conlan. 'That's for John Rooney.'

He turned toward the backseat next. The rest of the passengers looked to be all right. Todd Snow undid his seat belt, crawled across broken glass, and ripped at the tape on Conlan's wrists. They stared as the third passenger in the backseat took off a ski mask.

'Great job, fellas,' Mercedes Freer said with a big, bleached-out smile. 'You saved us!' She grinned – just before Todd Snow punched out the two-faced diva's front teeth.

Chapter Ninety-Six

Blinking Christmas lights strung on the fire escape of a brownstone tenement streaked past the copter's window as we hurtled toward the car dealership that the lead sedan had just plowed into.

I gawked from above at shattered glass and ripped metal, spinning police lights, running cops.

Another day, I thought, struggling to absorb the insanity I'd just witnessed, *another war zone.*

I turned to my left, away from the milling chaos at the dealership, just as the four remaining cars hit the emptied intersection of the West Side Highway near the Hudson.

They hadn't slowed!

I thought that they were going to try to turn at the last second and smash their way through the road-block. The cops manning the barricade must have thought the same thing because three or four of them dove out of the way.

But we were all wrong.

The world seemed to gray out as I watched help-lessly. The adrenaline and sleep deprivation, the caffeine overdose and stress, finally took their toll. I thought I was hallucinating.

The black sedans didn't swerve left or right. It was like they were on rails as they rocketed dead straight for the fence bordering the Hudson River.

Even from inside the chopper, I heard the front tires of the cars explode like pipe bombs as they struck the high concrete curb before the fence. The sedans seemed to crouch down and coil; then they bounced high and hit the fence.

Chain links parted like wet tissue paper, and suddenly the cars were in the air above the icy river. It sounded like sheet metal landing on concrete when they hit the water simultaneously, *upside down.*

I don't know what I had been expecting before that.

But it wasn't mass suicide.

'They're in the water!' I heard on the radio then. 'All six cars are in the East River! It's totally insane. This can't be happening. But it just did!'

I thought the report was from a cop watching on the ground beneath me – until I realized they were talking about the other cars. The ones that had headed east.

The hijackers had crashed *all* the remaining cars into two rivers!

The helicopter was already swinging down toward the water as I pointed. We got there just in time to see brake lights disappear under the surface.

'As low as you can go,' I yelled to the pilot as I popped my harness and the latch of the helicopter door. Frigid wind howled into the cabin as I leaned out above choppy gray water.

'And radio the Harbor Unit,' I said.

Then I was free-falling.

Chapter Ninety-Seven

The water wasn't so bad.

If you were one of those Coney Island polar bear people, maybe.

The temperature, or lack thereof, went through me all at once like an electric shock. Then I bobbed in the ice water. But my feet finally found something like a bumper, and I turned myself down into the all but lightless polluted water, reaching forward with my hands.

I don't know how I found the door handle in the opaque water, but I did. I pulled hard, and the door swung open and a form brushed by me, then another.

I was out of breath, and *heat*, by the time a third and fourth shadow bobbed past me toward the surface, so I kicked up off the sunken car's roof.

My clothes felt like they were made of lead, *frozen* lead, as I dog-paddled. I counted twelve people floating in the water. They'd taken their masks off, and I recognized most of them as the VIP hostages. How many had gotten into each car? Were they all safe now?

'Is there anybody else stuck in the cars?' I yelled to Kenneth Rubenstein, who was flailing in the water beside me.

He stared at me as if I were speaking Chinese. He was in shock. I decided I could do no more, except try to get everyone on the surface out of the water.

That's where the helicopter pilot came in. She was amazing, the best. Using the skid like a gaff, she managed to lift our gasping, hypothermic butts out of the drink and pop us on a nearby dock.

An army of burly sanitation workers had arrived from their truck depot beside the river, and they dragged us inside a thankfully warm building. A blanket was thrown over my back. A hulking sanitation worker gave mouth-to-mouth to a pale middle-aged woman for a moment before she stiff-armed him in his hairy chest.

I realized it was the fashion magazine editor, Laura Winston. A young woman beside her started vomiting all over herself. The reality TV wild child, Linda London.

It was maybe half an hour later when I received a call from Commander Will Matthews. All the remaining celebrities who'd gone into the East River had been plucked out of the water and were accounted for. The VIPs were bruised and wet and still in shock, but it seemed as if everyone would survive.

The hijackers, though, were glaringly unaccounted for at both crash sites. Whether they were drowned in the cars or still back at the cathedral had yet to be determined. Before I hung up, Will Matthews ordered me to go to the crash site at the car dealership up the block to see what the hell was going on.

Why not? I thought, my wet hand shaking as I gave a task force sergeant his cell phone back. I needed a little excitement this morning.

At least everyone had made it, I thought, heading back outside to the edge of the dock. Except for the people who'd been murdered at the church, of course.

I tried to let that small victory calm me, but it was a stretch.

Jack's promise from the beginning of the ordeal galled the hell out of me as I gazed out at the helicopters searching the fuzzy gray surface of the frigid water.

He said he'd get away with this, and he had.

Chapter Ninety-Eight

A t an abandoned dock just north of the new Hell's Kitchen Sports Pier, twenty blocks south of where half of the cars had driven into the water, a black shape bobbed up from among the rotting piles.

With his eyes just above the surface of the water, Jack carefully scanned the choppy gray Hudson behind him for the NYPD Harbor Unit, but there was nothing. And just as important, no one along the shoreline beside the sports complex.

From inside his lightweight Scubapro wetsuit, he took out a Ziploc bag. He removed the cell phone inside it and hit redial as he took out his air tank mouthpiece.

'Where?' he said.

'They're still concentrating on the crash sites, still looking to save hostages,' the Neat Man said. 'They haven't started looking for you yet. Window's open, m'boy, but closing. Move now!'

Jack didn't have to be told twice. He slipped the

cell phone back into its bag and himself back under the briny water and tugged on the tow rope.

Five minutes later, Jack and the other four hijackers with him were up on a concrete ledge beneath a walkway on the south side of the sports complex, peeling off the wetsuits they'd worn under their brown robes, dumping the air tanks they'd hidden under the water at the crash site. The tanks were small, only thirty cubic feet of air, but enough for the ten to fifteen minutes they had to be under water.

The most hazardous part, he thought, had been the actual crash itself into the river. But the rest – their extraction from the cars and finding the tanks – had gone off like clockwork. Not only was it probably the greatest hijacking of all time, now they were about to pull off the greatest escape!

And not just him, he thought.

His sweet knuckleheads had managed not to screw it all up, and he was proud of them. But this was no time to celebrate. They had to go to Queens to pick up the rest of the gang, who'd dumped into the East River. Hopefully they had fared as well.

Jack glanced up at the busy West Side Highway. He smiled as he noticed his pulse racing. He'd seen his share of action, but none of it compared with the razor's-edge euphoria he was feeling now. Nothing even came close. If they hadn't lost Fontaine and Jose, this job would have been perfect.

He turned and looked back as the last member of his crew shed his wetsuit, revealing a track outfit beneath. *Just do it,' right?* Now they looked just like everybody else coming off of the sports pier. Yuppie office mates who'd decided to spend Christmas playing and partying instead of with their corny-ass families.

'Okay, ladies,' Jack said to his men with a wink. 'Let's move 'em out. We're almost home. We won the Super Bowl.'

They had to keep themselves from sprinting as they climbed the short fence and came out alongside the main building, waiting at a light to cross.

Jack swallowed hard, his blood going as cold as the water they'd just climbed out of, as a police car, its siren screaming, approached from the south. He started breathing again when it blew right past them, speeding uptown. No doubt heading back to 57th, where they'd started their little *Dukes of Hazzard* stunt.

It was thirty-five minutes later when they were in a van picking up the rest of the hijackers by the dock of an abandoned bottling plant in Long Island City. Little John grinned triumphantly as he and the other five men threw themselves in through the sliding door to back slaps and high fives.

'What the hell took you so long?' the big man said, accepting an ice-cold Heineken that Jack handed him from a cooler. 'Where's Jose?'

'He lost it as we were coming across Eleventh Avenue,' Jack said, punching a hand into his fist. 'Jose's gone.'

Little John looked down at the van floor, ruminating. 'What about his prints?' he said after a moment.

Jack smiled.

'Remember we told him about the need to not leave any evidence?' he said. 'Well, the crazy mother said he wasn't taking any chances. So he spent the last month and a half burning off his fingertips with a Zippo.'

'*To Jose!*' Little John said, lifting his beer bottle, happy again. 'That *gato* had some balls.'

'And Fontaine,' Jack said, remembering his friend who'd been downed in the firefight in the crypt. He glanced at the man's hands in the Ziploc, sitting on ice beside the beers. Kind of looked like chicken wings.

'What do we do now?' Little John said.

'I don't know about you, but after three days wearing the same drawers and that little dip in one of the most polluted rivers on Earth,' Jack said, 'I could go for a hot shower.'

'And some hot you-know-what too,' one of his compadres called to howls as the van slipped onto the Brooklyn–Queens Expressway.

'I meant after that,' Little John said.

'We stick with the plan. Two, three months of waiting to make things look good, and then it's a one-way first-class trip to Costa Rica.'

So they'd really done it, Jack thought, grinning at the sound of the *Arriba! Arriba! Ándale!* calls in the van. It was hard to believe. They'd held the world off. The next part was a joke. Incredibly easy. They just had to sit back and wait, and not spend their millions.

Chapter Ninety-Nine

I had to borrow some clothes, so I was decked out in a spiffy green sanitation worker's uniform when I arrived back at the car dealership on Eleventh.

It looked as if two medical examiners in white Tyvek suits were playing a game of tug-of-war as they attempted to remove a brown-robed hijacker from the handlebars of a motorcycle. Only after an ESU cop arrived with some bolt cutters did they finally manage to pull the motorcycle out of the dead man's chest.

Over by a pulverized soda machine, one of my favorite rock singers of all time, Charlie Conlan, and Giants quarterback Todd Snow were being interviewed by detectives from the Major Crimes Unit. They didn't look like they were much in the mood for autographs. From the look of the shredded car, I was surprised the only injury I saw was a black eye and fat lip on the pissed-off-looking pop star, Mercedes, who stormed by with an EMS medic, and not a word of thanks to anybody.

I knelt beside what was left of the hijacker as the assistant MEs laid him on the showroom carpet. I borrowed a pair of rubber gloves and slowly pulled off his mask. The back of my fist flew against my forehead when I uncovered a second black rubber mask beneath it.

A skin-diving mask.

That's how they did it! How they had gotten away. They'd used scuba-diving equipment to escape under the water.

I borrowed a phone and told Will Matthews about my discovery. After some choice expletives, he called in more harbor units from Jersey and the Coast Guard.

After I hung up, I pulled off the hijacker's rubber mask. The deceased was a Hispanic man in his late thirties, early forties. Nothing in his pockets. A nine-millimeter Beretta pistol in an underarm holster, but the serial number had been filed away. I groaned when I looked at his hands and saw his fingerprints were gone, too. I'd seen similar prints on the hands of crack-heads, ridges melted down to a nub from holding too many hot pipes.

No! I thought, these bastards weren't going to disappear without leaving me at least one lead. I found Lonnie Jacob, a crime scene investigator I'd worked with several times. I showed him the jacker's hands.

'Think you can get anything?' I said.

'Maybe a partial,' Lonnie said skeptically. 'I'll have to work on him back at the morgue. I really doubt we'll get anything, though. This dude *did not* want to be identified.'

'What's up, Mike?' Commander Will Matthews said moments later as he came across the broken glass toward me. 'You transferring to Sanitation on me?'

'Thought I'd put out some feelers after this home run,' I said.

'We did all we could, Mike,' Will Matthews said, staring at the carnage all around us. 'That's the truth, and it's the story I'm sticking to. I advise you to repeat after me during the impending shit storm.'

'Will do,' I said. '*We did all we could.* Happens to be the truth.'

'Now get out of here and see your family. My driver's outside waiting for you,' Will Matthews said. 'That's an order.'

A cold wind was whipping down 57th when I stepped outside. I had hardly noticed it before, but this Christmas had turned out to be one of those stainless-steel-colored December days when you have the feeling winter will never end. As I got into the back of the cruiser and my thoughts shifted toward my wife, I decided I didn't want it to.

If Maeve wasn't going to see another spring, why the hell should anybody else?

Chapter One Hundred

Some say nothing compares to Christmas in New York, but I'd never seen the city look grimmer. After I got home and changed, I drove my brood to the hospital. I couldn't see the wreaths and lights anymore, only the endless gray corridors of blank windows, the grimy concrete, the steam rising from the broken streets. Some Irish writer once referred to Manhattan as a 'cathedral,' but as I stopped our van in front of the hospital, it looked more like a sad construction site to me, cluttered and cold and pitiless.

I had to hold myself up against the van's door frame in order not to fall over from exhaustion as Mary Catherine fed my kids out in their good clothes, clutching their brightly wrapped presents.

Even the stern nurses, stuck there on Christmas, seemed teary-eyed as our cosmically sad procession passed through the lobby to good ol' Five.

'Wait a second,' I said, patting my pockets as we

approached Maeve's corridor. *'The pageant tape.* I forgot to . . .'

'It's right here, Mike,' Mary Catherine said, handing me the small plastic case.

I was about to thank her yet again for being such a lifesaver. Au pair, I thought. Was that Gaelic for fairy godmother? She would have had a cheerier Christmas in Afghanistan than here with my crew, but she'd jumped right in up to her neck.

'Give my love to Maeve,' the amazing young woman said quietly. 'I'll be in the lounge if you need me. Go.'

I could see Seamus kneeling beside Maeve in her wheelchair when we turned into her corridor.

A lump formed in my throat when I saw the open Bible in his hand. I stopped when I watched him make the sign of the cross on her forehead. *Last rites?* I thought.

How was I going to get through this? Today of all days?

Somehow Maeve was smiling when I knocked on the door frame. She was all dressed up as usual, this time a red Santa hat replacing her Yankees one.

Seamus closed his Bible and hugged me hard. 'God give you the strength, Michael,' he said in my ear. 'Your girl is a saint. You are too.' Seamus paused. 'I'll be back. I need to get some air.'

I guess my heart wasn't already broken, because I felt something snap like a guitar string in my chest when Maeve scooped Chrissy and Shawna into her withered lap.

I glanced up at the ceiling. My family's story could become a new holiday classic, couldn't it? I thought ruefully. *Christmas in the Terminal Ward.*

It wasn't fair. Maeve had always exercised regularly, ate right, didn't smoke. I bit my lip as a searing pressure built in my chest. I wanted to, needed to, scream my guts out.

But something strange happened when my son Brian helped her back onto her bed and put the pageant on the TV. Maeve started laughing. Not polite little giggles either, but gasping-for-breath belly laughs. I moved next to her, and her hand found mine behind the wall of our kids.

For the next ten minutes, the hospital room disappeared, and we could have been on our beat-up couch at home, watching the Yanks or one of our favorite old movies.

My useless anger exploded into guffaws as Shepherd Eddie tripped over his staff halfway up to the gym's stage.

'What a great job you did!' Maeve said, throwing high fives all around after the tape had ended.

'Bennetts bringing the house down. I'm so proud of all you guys.'

'Would you listen to the shameful amount of ruckus coming from this room?' Seamus said to giggles as he came back.

Maeve beamed as he gently took her hand and kissed it. 'Merry Christmas,' he said, smuggling a gold box of Godiva chocolates behind her back with a wink.

It looked like someone had rolled a hospital bed into a Hallmark store after the handmade gifts and Christmas cards were handed out. Julia and Brian stepped forward with a black velvet box. Maeve's smile, when she opened it, seemed powerful enough to banish the illness from her body forever. It was a thin gold necklace. The attached pendant said #1 MOM.

'We all chipped in,' Brian said. 'All of us, even the little ones.'

She kissed him on the cheek as he did the necklace's clasp for her.

'I want you to keep on chipping in, guys,' Maeve said, leaning back, struggling to keep her eyes open. 'Many hands lighten the load, and if it's one thing we have a lot of, it's hands. Little hands and big hearts. You couldn't have made me prouder. Dad will show you what I got for you later, kids. Merry Christmas. Never forget, I love you all.'

Chapter One Hundred and One

I stayed behind after Seamus took the kids back home. For some reason, I felt strong all of a sudden, calm, completely alert, not even tired. I closed the door to the room and sat behind Maeve in the cold bed, hugging her. After a while, I held her hand, staring at where our wedding rings touched.

When I closed my eyes, I pictured Maeve from my first days of courting her in the hospital emergency room. She had always been holding someone's hand then, too, I remembered. Black, white, yellow, brown, young, old, mad, maimed, broken, bloody. I thought about all the human hearts she'd lifted in her life. Mine most of all. And our ten children.

As I stood up to stretch around midnight, Maeve opened her eyes wide and crushed my hand in hers.

'I love you, Mike,' she said urgently.

Oh God! I thought. *Not now. Please, not now!*

My hand went for the nurse's button, but Maeve batted it away. A tear rolled down her taut face as she shook her head.

Then she smiled.

Stop!

She looked into my eyes. It was as if she could see some distant place within them. Some new land she was about to travel to.

'Be happy,' she said.

Then she let go of my hand.

As her fingertips left the surface of my palm, I felt as though somewhere deep inside me something shattered and a hole opened.

I caught Maeve as she tipped back. She was so light. Her chest was already still. My hand lowered the back of her head toward the pillow as gently as it did on our honeymoon night.

This is it, I kept thinking. *This is really it.*

The room spun as I stood there gasping. It felt as if the wind had been knocked out of me, all of my air, my spirit gone.

Everything I had ever felt happy about, every laugh, every sunset, every hope, every good thing there was or ever would be shook loose and tottered and plummeted out of my heart.

I looked up suddenly when I heard the singing.

The pageant tape had come on again somehow, and on the TV screen above, Chrissy was making her way across the Holy Name gym stage in her silver angel costume as the whole school sang 'Silent Night.'

I shut it off, along with the light, and lay down beside my wife. Snow was falling lightly in the dark outside the window.

How can I still be alive? I thought, feeling my heart beat on and on selfishly in my chest.

When I found Maeve's hand, I felt the cold of her wedding ring. I remembered the happy tears in her eyes, in the small church we were married in, as I slid it on her finger. The rice that mixed with spits of snow as we came hand in hand outside and down the old wooden steps.

As I closed my eyes, I could no longer hear anything. The sounds of the hospital faded in the dark, and so did the sounds of the world outside. All that was left in the universe was my wife's cold hand in mine and a nothingness that hummed through me like high voltage.

Chapter One Hundred and Two

The head nurse, Sally Hitchens, came in at 4:30 a.m. She smiled as she helped me to stand up. She'd take care of my Maeve now, she promised as I stood disoriented and crazy-eyed over my wife. She'd protect her and keep her for as long as it took.

I *walked* the thirty blocks home from the hospital, the cold burning my skin in the predawn dark. A bartender, slamming closed the steel shutters of a bar on Amsterdam Avenue, crossed himself as I passed.

All the kids were up in the living room as I stumbled in.

I was instantly surrounded by them as I sat down. I thought I had purged away some of the pain from hours before, but I was deluding myself. My heart got heavier and heavier as my eyes slowly passed over each of my kids' faces. My sorrow was as dense as a black hole as I looked upon the tears in my little Chrissy's eyes.

Death notices are perhaps the hardest of realities for homicide detectives. Now, here I was having to deliver one in my own living room, to my own kids.

'Mom's gone to heaven,' I finally said, gathering them in my arms. 'Mom's in heaven now, guys. Say a prayer.'

After rising from their sobbing ranks, I stumbled into the kitchen and broke the news to Seamus and Mary Catherine.

Then I went into my room, quietly closed the door, and sat on the edge of my bed.

When Seamus came in, maybe ten hours later, I was still sitting there in the same clothes and hadn't slept.

That's when he sat down next to me.

'When I lost your grandmother,' he spoke very quietly, 'I was ready to murder. The doctors who'd told me she was gone. All the people who came to her wake. Even the priest at her funeral made me unbelievably angry. Because of how lucky they were. They didn't have to go home to an empty apartment. They didn't have to listen to the roar of silence as they took down her abandoned things. I even seriously thought about picking up the bottle Eileen had pulled me out of. But I didn't. Do you know why?'

I shook my head. I had no idea.

'Because of how insulting it would have been. Not to Eileen's memory, I realized, but to Eileen herself. That's when I realized she hadn't really left for good. She'd just gone on ahead a little.

'One thing Eileen had taught me by her example was that you get up and put your clothes on and do what you can do until the day you don't get up. I guess what I'm trying to say is that Maeve isn't really gone. She's just ahead, waiting for you, Mike. That's why you can't shut down. We Irish don't always succeed, but we're pretty decent at grinding it out.'

'Grind it out until you're dead,' I said blankly after a moment. 'Gentle words of inspiration from Seamus Bennett. You're the new Deepak Chopra.'

'Ah, sweet, undiluted sarcasm,' Seamus said, punching my knee softly as he rose. 'That's the lad. Maeve'd be proud of ya. Music to her Irish ears.'

So after I took a shower, we made arrangements. Or, I should say, Seamus and Mary Catherine did. They called the church and then the funeral home, and I just nodded or shook my drooping head. *Grind it out until you're dead.*

Chapter One Hundred and Three

It was stone wall to stone wall with friends and relatives inside Holy Name Church two days later for Maeve's funeral. At the wake the night before, and now here at the church, my wife had managed to draw a crowd that rivaled the one at St Patrick's for the First Lady, despite the fact that there wasn't a news van or celebrity in sight.

In the sea of sad faces, I made out her former coworkers, past patients, even most of our snooty neighbors. Not only did my Homicide squad show, but most of the NYPD, it seemed, was there, giving their support for a brother in blue.

At the wake, so many people had shared touching vignettes I'd never heard before about Maeve. Story after story about how she had comforted their kid or wife or parent as they were wheeled into surgery or giving birth or dying. The compassion she showed at the hardest of moments. The strength she'd provided when people were most alone.

There are times when New York can be the loneliest place on earth, but as I watched Seamus in his robes come down from the altar and encircle Maeve's casket with incense and heard the sincere weeping of the people behind me, I could feel a sense of community that I would put up against the smallest of small towns.

After the Gospel, Seamus did the eulogy.

'One of my favorite memories of Maeve comes from, of all places, Ground Zero,' he said from the pulpit.

'We were both volunteering on the *Spirit of New York,* moored off Battery Park City, helping to give out hot meals to the rescue people. It was during the fourth game of the 2001 World Series, and I was on the open top deck of the boat, comforting a distraught battalion chief who had lost one of his men, when we heard this earsplitting howl from below deck. We thought someone had been shot or fallen overboard, but when we arrived below in the dining room, all we could see was Maeve, wearing headphones, jumping up and down so hard she was nearly rocking the boat.

'"Tino Martinez tied it up," she was screaming. "He tied it up!"'

'Someone got a TV and set it up on the buffet table. Now, I've listened to people say that they've never heard Yankee Stadium louder than when Derek Jeter hit that walk-off home run in the tenth to win it, but they weren't any louder than the group of us crowded around that beat-up set. When I think of Maeve, I will always see her in the middle of those tired men with her fist pumped in the air. Her energy and hope and life transforming that black place and time into something unique, something I think on the verge of holy.'

Seamus's cheeks clenched then. He, along with the rest of the church, was losing it.

'I won't lie to you. I can't say why God would take her now. But if the fact that she was sent here among us doesn't point toward a loving God, then I can't help you. If we bring away anything from today, it should be the lesson that Maeve herself showed with every full, spent day of her life. Hold back nothing. Leave nothing in the tank.'

All through the church everyone, including myself, was crying shamelessly. Chrissy, beside me, brushed my overcoat out of the way and wiped her tears on my knee.

The sun came out for the burial at Gates of Heaven Cemetery up in Westchester. The kids filed past Maeve's casket with roses. I almost lost it again behind my sunglasses when Shawna kissed her flower before she put it down with the rest. And again when the high, bittersweet skirls of an NYPD piper's 'Danny Boy' blew off the headstones and frozen ground.

But I didn't.

I asked myself what Maeve would do, and I swallowed my tears and hugged my kids and promised myself and my wife that I would somehow get us through.

Chapter One Hundred and Four

I'd offered to stay home from work with the kids, who were off on Christmas break, but Seamus and Mary Catherine wouldn't hear of it.

'Sorry, fella,' Seamus told me. 'These kids need to be spoiled like no one has ever been spoiled before, and with the mood you're in, you're going to have to leave that job to me and Mary C. Besides, you need to get outside of yourself there, Mick. Throw yourself into something positive. Stop sitting around and go and collar those pathetic mopes who jacked the cathedral.'

'Collar the mopes?' I said with a faint grin. 'Jacked?'

'So I watch *NYPD Blue* now and then,' Seamus said with a fantastic roll of his eyes. 'Is it a sin?'

So the Monday morning after the funeral, I arrived back at my desk inside Manhattan North Homicide in East Harlem. Harry Grissom, my boss, and the rest of my squaddies were irritatingly supportive and polite. Who would have ever thought that you'd miss being the butt of practical jokes? Soon enough, I thought, knocking the dust off my mouse.

I put in calls to Paul Martelli and Ned Mason. And I learned that nothing really new or promising had been discovered. Every square inch of the church's granite, marble, and stained glass had been searched and dusted for latent prints, but there had been nothing. These criminals had been extremely tidy.

There had been some excitement when a hijacker's body was found in the archbishops' crypt under the altar, Martelli told me, but it ended when it was discovered that the man's hands and head, along with any chance at identifying him, had been removed by his cold-blooded partners.

No traces of explosives had been discovered in the church either, so it seemed that Jack's threat about blowing everyone to smithereens had been just a bluff. Another hand he had won.

I found a Post-it on my computer to call Lonnie Jacob, the NYPD CSU investigator working the car dealership where the sedan had crashed. Around noon, I lifted the phone and dialed the fingerprint lab at One Police Plaza.

'Mike,' Lonnie said after he answered. 'I was just about to call you. I just did it.'

'Did what?' I said.

'It wasn't easy, but by sodium hydroxiding our John Doe's hands, I was able to dry them out and peel off the top layer of his charred skin. The second dermal layer is harder to ID because there's this kind of doubling of the ridges, but at least we have something. I already spoke to my contact down in Latent Prints at the FBI. Should I fire it down to DC to cross-reference?'

I told him yes, and he told me he'd call me back with the results. These criminals had gone nutso about covering their tracks – which could only mean they were definitely trying to hide something.

Chapter One Hundred and Five

The following day word got back to us that when the police commissioner heard the meager results of our investigation at St Patrick's he had a simple response: *Do it again. Do it better.*

First, the Emergency Service Unit guys returned to the cathedral and repeated exactly what they had done to stabilize the crime scene. They even checked for booby traps and hazmats again.

NYPD detectives, along with the Crime Scene Unit – *CSU, not CSI* – did another thorough search for evidence like latent prints and fibers. Everything was swabbed down a second time for DNA. A check was made to see if any religious relics had been defiled – anything that might provide a psychological or behavioral clue.

Everything that could be checked was examined a second time.

Bloodstains.

Hair, fibers, and threads.

Loose glass – from windows, bottles, eyeglasses.

Firearms.

Tool marks, evidence of flammable liquids.

Controlled substances found anywhere, but especially in the archbishops' crypt, where the hijackers hid out before the attack.

Two patrolmen were stationed at St Patrick's solely to act as messengers to get possible evidence to the labs as quickly as possible.

And after three more exhausting days, the end result – not a clue about Jack and his team.

Chapter One Hundred and Six

I felt too cooped up sitting in the squad room, so I decided to go for a ride one morning. I smiled, looking out at the chaotic hustle and bustle of loud vehicles and even louder pedestrians surging around St Patrick's when I pulled up on Fifth Avenue in front of it. Our city had survived riots, blackouts, 9/11, Mayor Dinkins, and now this, I thought as I headed up the cathedral steps.

The church was closed to the public for repairs. The uniformed Midtown North cops stationed at the door stepped aside when I showed them my tin.

I walked up the center aisle and genuflected before sitting in the front pew.

I sat looking out on the solemn, austere, empty church. You'd think I'd be sick of churches by this point, but for some reason, I felt comforted just being there in the candle-scented darkness. I felt oddly consoled.

My high school graduation from Regis had taken place here. I smirked, remembering how wretched at Greek and Latin I'd been. One thing, though, perhaps the only thing I'd picked up from the Jesuit priests who taught us, was their stress on the importance of *reason*. Time and again, they preached the necessity of using our God-given rationality in order to cut through to the essence of things. I guess it was the reason I chose philosophy as my major when I went on to Manhattan College, a small, very fine school in the Bronx. And the ultimate reason I had become a detective. *The need to get at the truth.*

I stared up at the main altar, thinking about the case.

We knew the *when, where, what, why,* and *how.* The only thing left was the *who.*

Who would have done it? Who was capable of the brilliance, and the brutality? Men with a lot of will, for one thing, I decided; and men not afraid to use extreme violence as a means to a selfish end.

They had killed five people during the siege. An ESU officer and FBI agent had been shot in the tunnel firefight. A priest had been shot in the side of the head, by accident, according to Jack. John Rooney had been executed at point-blank range. Interviews with the hostages who had witnessed it confirmed that.

Finally I thought about the mayor. *Why had they stabbed Andrew Thurman to death?* The cigarette burns over his arms meant that he'd also been tortured. These men were nothing if not efficient. Why change their killing method for the mayor? It would seem that shooting a man, however unpalatable, was better than stabbing him, right? Why get personal with the mayor?

I laid my hands against the polished wood in front of me as I squeezed the rail hard.

There was a reason. I just didn't know what it was. Yet.

I stopped by the row of votive candles at the Lady Chapel before I left. I lit one for each of the souls that had perished here, and an extra one for my wife. The dollar bills made a shuffling sound in the silence as they dropped into the offering box. *Angel wings,* I thought, stifling a tear. I hunched onto the velvet kneeler, closed my eyes against my clenched fists.

Dear Maeve, I prayed. *I love you. I miss you terribly.*

I was still waiting to hear from Lonnie about the prints, and when I returned to my desk he still hadn't called. I poured myself a coffee and stared out my window at East Harlem as I waited.

In an empty lot right across from the precinct, kids had set some already discarded Christmas trees on fire, their charred trunks like a pile of black bones.

There was still a lot of investigating left to do. We knew the makes of the guns left behind by the kidnappers, and maybe that would turn into something. We'd found shells and spent cartridges. And half a dozen guns that shot rubber bullets. That was an interesting twist for me. They'd thought to bring crowd-control weapons. We still needed to figure out exactly how they had stored oxygen tanks in the river. Not that it really mattered.

I was hip-deep in hostage interview reports when the phone on my desk rang two hours later.

'Sorry, Mike,' Lonnie told me with disappointment. 'Nothing doing. No hits on the prints. The dead guy doesn't have a criminal record.'

As I laid the phone back into its cradle, looking at the tiny black holes in the earpiece, I thought I caught Jack's cocky laugh.

Chapter One Hundred and Seven

The phone was ringing on my desk when I came in the next morning.

I heard a familiar voice when I picked up, and certainly not one I was expecting.

'This is Cathy Calvin from the *Times*. May I speak to Detective Bennett?'

I debated between telling the hatchet-wielding scribe, *No hablo inglés*, or just hanging up.

'It concerns the hijacking,' she said.

'This is Bennett. I'm really tired of playing games, Calvin,' I finally answered gruffly. 'Especially with you.'

'Mike,' the reporter said brightly. 'Please let me apologize for that piece I did. You know how crazy it was. My editor was breathing fire down my neck and . . . What am I saying? No excuses. I screwed up, and I'm sorry, and I owe you one. I do. Make that *ten*, okay? I heard about the loss of your wife. My sincerest condolences to you and your children.'

I paused, wondering if the *Times* reporter was just playing up to me. She certainly sounded sincere, but I was wary, and I ought to be. She'd made me and the department look like fools. But then again, having a *Times* reporter owe me a favor could certainly come in handy.

'Accept my apology, Mike,' Calvin tried again. 'I feel like a jerk.'

'Well, at least you're self-aware,' I said.

'I knew we were going to be friends eventually,' Calvin said quickly. 'The reason I called was I'm doing interviews with the celebrity victims. Well, I should say, failing miserably because I can't get past most of their lawyers and agents. But I did speak to the civil rights activist, Reverend Solstice, and do you know what he told me?'

The race-baiting quasipolitician Solstice was famous for basically one thing, I knew. Hating cops.

'I'm holding my breath,' I said.

'He said he thinks the hijackers were cops,' Calvin went on. 'I just wanted to call and let you hear. Also to tell you that I refuse to print such bullshit. Okay? See, I'm not all bad.'

'Okay,' I said. 'I appreciate the call.'

After I hung up, I leaned back in my chair, thinking about Solstice's accusations. Though he was known to court controversy, the man was savvy enough to realize he needed something – however outrageous – to back it up and get some attention. So what did Solstice know? Was it anything important? Was he involved somehow?

I called back Calvin and got the reverend's number. Solstice answered on the first ring.

'Hello, Reverend. This is Detective Michael Bennett of the NYPD. I'm investigating the cathedral hijacking. I hear you have an insight into the case. I'd like to hear it.'

'Ha!' Solstice said forcefully. 'Insight my butt. I know what you're doing. What you're trying to pull. It's starting already.'

'What is it you think I'm starting exactly, Reverend?'

'What you punks are best at. The coverup. Sweeping the truth under the rug. Listen, man, I *know*. I been inside. I know cops. Only pros like you could handle us the way you did. Oh yeah, and then everybody just conveniently gets away. Just missed 'em, I bet. You cops pulled this off, and now you're covering it up. Same as it's always been.'

Could that be true? I sure doubted it.

But Solstice had raised two serious questions: How

did the hijackers know so much about siege tactics? And how did they always seem to know what we were going to try next?

Chapter One Hundred
and Eight

There are actually ten prisons on Rikers Island in the Bronx, housing as many as seventeen thousand inmates. Rikers is almost a small town, with its schools, clinics, athletic fields, chapels *and* mosques, grocers, barbershops, a bus depot, even a car wash.

As I arrived there early the next morning, I was hopeful again. I'd had an idea during the night, and now I had the opportunity to execute it.

At a little past eight, I walked by the Amnesty Box, where prison visitors are allowed to deposit drugs or weapons without fear. I had neither, so I proceeded inside and was escorted to a small meeting room inside Rikers' Central Punitive Segregation Unit, also known as 'the Bing.'

About a quarter of the inmates at Rikers are poor people who can't afford to post bails of five hundred dollars or less, but I was more interested in the hard cases. For the next four hours, I sat in the room and met dozens of inmates.

I played them a tape of excerpts with Jack's voice from the negotiations. Maybe somebody would recognize him from a previous stay at Rikers or one of the other prison facilities around New York.

But not Angelo, a burglar with an exaggerated shoulder curl, like a boxer always ready to fight.

Not Hector, a gang player with two tear tattoos at the corner of his right eye, signifying he'd killed two people so far in his twenty-one years.

Not JT either – a white thug from Westchester with a serious drug habit who was a walking *Merck Manual* on pills and meds.

Or Jesse from 131st Street in Harlem, placid face with one lazy eye, soul patch under his lip, inside Rikers for alleged felonious assault.

In fact, not any of the seventy-nine inmates who came to see me in the cramped meeting room space had anything for me. How depressing was that?

Until my eightieth visitor, Tremaine, a skinny older guy, maybe forty, though he looked fifty, at least that. He said he thought maybe he'd heard that voice before – Jack's voice. 'Don't know for sure, but *maybe.*'

On the way back from Rikers, I called One Police Plaza and told Lonnie to run the prints from the dead hijacker through the city, state, and national law enforcement employee records.

It was an hour later when the fax rang back at my office. The cover sheet told me it was Lonnie with the results.

It seemed like a month before the second sheet hummed out of the machine.

I lifted it up slowly, careful not to smudge the ink.

It wasn't the smiling ID picture of the dead hijacker that I couldn't tear my eyes away from so much as the captioned information underneath it.

Surprise mixed with a sick, guilty feeling that washed through my stomach like battery acid.

Unbelievable, I thought.

I took out my cell and speed-dialed Commander Will Matthews's office. 'This is Bennett,' I said when I had him on the line. 'I think we got 'em.'

Chapter One Hundred and Nine

I t started to snow as we crossed over the city line, racing north on the Saw Mill River Parkway. Myself and an eight-vehicle convoy of FBI sedans and NYPD ESU trucks had already passed over the Harlem River and were now speeding through the Westchester woods, but it wasn't to grandma's house we were going.

We took the exit for Pleasantville and rolled west down toward the Hudson. At the very bottom, alongside the wind-scoured river, we stopped before high, harsh gray concrete walls decorated with razor wire. A barely legible sun-faded sign was bolted to the rock.

SING SING CORRECTIONAL FACILITY, it said.

Nope, not grandma's house, I thought. *The Big House.*

Infamous *Sing Sing.*

Up the River.

There was a distinct chill in the air as I got out and stood next to the prison walls. It was as if cold emanated from the place itself. I felt it get even chillier when an armed guard, in what looked like a miniature airport control tower above the wire, swung his sunglasses in my direction. The barrel of the M16 he carried across his chest seemed the only gleaming object for miles.

All this time we were running around trying to send the hijackers to the slammer, I thought, staring across the gravel parking lot at the maximum-security facility. And wouldn't you know it, they were already here.

The print of the deceased hijacker in the car dealership had belonged to Jose Alvarez, a corrections officer who'd worked at Sing Sing prison until six months ago.

A call to the warden's office revealed that a dozen men on the prison's three-to-eleven tour had staged a sick-out the week of the hijacking.

Suddenly, so many things made sense to me. The tear gas, rubber bullets, and handcuffs, the street lingo mixed with quasimilitary terminology. The answer was right there in front of us, but it had taken Reverend Solstice's suspicions and the memory of a prisoner at Rikers named Tremaine Jefferson, who had previously served time at Sing Sing, to set it free.

Prison guards, as well as cops, were capable of handling crowds and containing people professionally, and capable of being efficiently violent.

'Ready, Mike?' Steve Reno asked as he stepped in front of a dozen ESU SWAT cops.

'I've been ready since the minute I got to St Pat's that morning.'

Our suspects were *inside* the prison, on duty. To arrest them, we were going to have to go in, enter the belly of the beast. Though jail is one of the least favorite places cops like to find themselves, I was looking forward to this. I was especially looking forward to matching Jack's face to his wise mouth. I was psyched, completely fired up.

Though the wind cutting off the choppy water was like a Mach3, I was actually smiling. 'Let's go meet Jack,' I said.

Chapter One Hundred and Ten

We had to cross a footbridge bonneted in razor ribbon just to get to Sing Sing's main gate. Though none of us was too happy about it, because firearms are under no circumstances permitted in maximum-security facilities, the dozen of us cops and Bureau agents had to check our weapons at the window of the arsenal before being buzzed inside.

'The men who staged the sick-out have already been summoned into the lineup room,' Warden Clark said as we arrived in the drab hallway outside his office.

An urgent-sounding squall ripped from Warden Clark's radio as we were coming down a flight of stairs on our way to the muster room. The warden listened closely.

'What is it?' I said.

'A-Block,' the warden said. 'Something's happening.

A lot of screaming and yelling anyway. Probably nothing. Our guests are always complaining about the service.'

'Are you sure all the men from the shift are there?' I said as we arrived at the mesh-windowed door of the muster room.

The warden looked intently through the wired glass at the nervous-looking uniformed corrections officers.

'I think so. Wait. No,' the warden said. 'Sergeant Rhodes and Sergeant Williams. The two shift foremen. They're not here yet. *Where the hell are they?*'

The shift foremen, I thought. Sure sounded like ringleaders to me. I thought about the message the warden had just gotten on his radio.

'Let me guess,' I said. 'The shift foremen are stationed to A-Block?'

Clark nodded. 'Our largest maximum-security building,' he said.

'We have to go in there,' I told him. 'Now.'

Chapter One Hundred
and Eleven

L ike the investigation itself, everything seemed to be moving uphill in Sing Sing. Trailing behind Warden Clark and a half dozen of his most trusted corrections officers, I climbed countless concrete stairs and several graded, paint-chipped corridors before we came to a steel door leading to a barred gate.

The gate buzzed open harshly, and there was a metallic *snap* like the hammer of a gun on an empty chamber. Then the door swung wide.

I could *feel* the sound of the prison knock against my chest as we passed through the enormous chamber of the multitiered cell block. Radios, inmates yelling, the constant hard and booming echo upon echo of steel on steel. It sounded like some form of torture, coming up from a bottomless metal well.

The prisoners in the closest cells rose immediately, screaming obscenities from behind double-thick bars as we passed. All along the double-football-field length of the building, I could see the glint of mirrors held out between the steel forest of cell bars. I hoped to hell we didn't get 'gassed,' a nasty soup of urine and feces hurled down by an inmate.

'Let's check the gym before we go upstairs to the different galleries,' the warden yelled above the racket surrounding us.

We were buzzed through another locked door at the block's opposite end. There was no one at any of the weight-room benches or pull-up stations. No one on the basketball court. No one hiding behind the stands. Where the hell were they? Had Jack and Little John gotten away again? How *did* they stay a step ahead of us?

I was leading our group back out onto the bottom level of A-Block when I was shoved from behind. *I went down!* The weight room's steel door boomed to a close as I skidded my palms and knees against the concrete floor.

I turned to see two of the warden's most trusted corrections officers smiling above me as the warden and Steve Reno and the other cops, sealed in the gym behind, began pounding on the steel door.

I noticed that one CO was gargantuan, the other short and stocky. Way to go, Professor Bennett. They fit the physical description of Jack and Little John. That's because they *were* Jack and Little John.

The one and only Jack had a black riot baton in his hand. He spun it easily between his fingers. He had close-cropped curly brown hair and a permanent sneer. A tough guy for a tough job, right?

'Hey, Mikey,' he said. 'Long time no talk.'

How could I not recognize that voice? No wonder Tremaine Jefferson had.

'So how come you never call anymore?' Jack said. 'I thought we were buddies.'

'Hey, Jack,' I said, feigning courage I wasn't really feeling. 'Funny, you didn't sound like a midget on the phone.'

Jack chuckled at that one. Still a cool customer. If he was worried about whether help was on its way, he was hiding it well.

'You made *another* mistake, Mike,' he said. 'Only this one's kind of fatal. Coming into a man's house uninvited. You thought I wouldn't anticipate you might find us? Shit, even a broken clock is right twice a day. You think that fat bastard Clark is in charge here? This is my prison. My turf, my people.'

'It's over, Jack,' I said.

'I really don't think so, Mike,' Jack said. 'Think about it. We got out of one fortress. We can get out of another.

Especially now that we have *hostages.* Hell, Mike, maybe I'll even let you negotiate your own release. How does that sound?'

'Sounds great,' I said, taking a half step back. My heel struck the flat, hard steel of the door. There was nowhere to run.

The heavy radio I'd been given by the warden was the only thing remotely resembling a weapon. I hefted it as Little John pulled his baton out with a sickening smile. The bastard had a face as repellent as a stinkbug's.

'Why don't we just talk about this for a second?' I said as I reared back, then hurled the radio. The Rocket would have been proud of my pitch. The radio and Little John's nose exploded simultaneously. He screamed; then he and Jack lit into me and I was lifted right off the floor.

'Upsy-daisy, Mike!' Jack yelled in my face. Then they both threw me down on my face.

Chapter One Hundred and Twelve

I thought the prisoners had been loud before, but it turned out they were only warming up. As I attempted to wrestle on the cement with Jack and Little John, the communal screams off the concrete shell of the cell block sounded like a jumbo jet taking off *inside* a hangar.

Then stuff started to rain down from the top tiers: various liquids, wet sheets, magazines, a wad of burning toilet paper. *Had I just been gassed?*

When Jack got in a lick with the riot baton on the back of my head, I went down on one knee. My consciousness was coming in and out like bad radio reception. I was pinned and blacking out as Little John rolled onto my chest.

I screamed and pushed off the floor with all my might.

I thought about my kids. I couldn't leave them now.

I couldn't allow them to have no one. I wouldn't let it happen. I was almost on my knees when Little John rolled off me and started booting me in the ribs.

I dropped back down, my breath gone; then his steel toe kissed my solar plexus. I wondered idly if Jack, pulling back the baton above me, might be the last sight I'd ever see on the earth.

That's when something completely unexpected happened – an arm snaked through the bars behind Jack.

It was so huge, it barely squeezed through, and so covered in tattoos, it looked like its owner wore a paisley sleeve. A massive hand wrapped itself around the back of Jack's uniform shirt collar. It sounded like a gong when Jack's head was slammed back into the bars again and again.

'How you like it, CO?' the convict inquired as he slammed and reslammed Jack's skull into the bars of his cell. 'How you like it, you vicious prick? How you like that one?'

When Little John got off me to help out Jack, I managed, wheezing, to gain my feet. The riot baton Jack had dropped was on the concrete. I stooped, lifted it, brought it to my shoulder.

It had been a while since I'd had a nightstick in my hand, walking my first beat in the Hunt's Point section of the South Bronx. On those long, cold nights I'd kept myself awake practicing with it, swinging it over and over until it whistled in cold air.

The nightstick whistled now, and I guess it was like riding a bike, because Little John's left knee shattered like balsawood with my first two-handed swing.

I had to backpedal immediately as the big man howled and hopped around surprisingly fast on one foot and came toward me. There was rage in his wide, bulging eyes, spit spraying out of his twisted, screaming mouth.

I swung from my toes at his jaw. He ducked, but too little, too late. I broke the baton across his temple. He hit the concrete a half second before the splintered wood.

The inmates were cheering something wicked as I stumbled around the big guard's bleeding, unconscious hulk. Their rage-filled voices met in a violent mantra as I stepped toward the inmate who was choking Jack with both monstrous hands. Jack's face was turning blue.

I picked up the other dropped baton. Got myself ready for this.

'Kill, kill, kill, kill!' the inmates screamed in unison.

I have to admit, the suggestion was tempting. I swung the baton hard.

But I didn't hit Jack.

I hit the tattooed hands that were very close to throttling the life out of him. The inmate yowled and let go of Jack, who slumped unconscious to the floor.

'Hey, like, you're welcome, bro,' said the muscular convict behind the bars in a hurt voice. He was nursing his injured hand.

'Sorry, Charlie,' I said as I started dragging Jack around the barrage of projectiles toward the sealed gym door. 'I can't arrest him if he's dead.'

But I can give him one good kick in the teeth. For old times' sake, Jacko. Because we're such buddies.

And that's what I did – one kick – and the inmates went wild.

Chapter One Hundred and Thirteen

O f course it couldn't be quite that easy.

They found the two actual shift foremen, Rhodes and Williams, handcuffed in one of the cells on A-Block.

It turned out that 'Jack' and 'Little John,' whose real names were Rocco Milton and Kenny Robard, being close to the warden as shift supervisors, had heard we were coming. They'd convinced the warden that they'd had nothing to do with the siege of St Pat's, even though they'd taken part in the sick-out. Then they'd ambushed the two innocent foremen – who'd been in on the sick-out but not the hijacking – and hidden them inside the cell block to shift suspicion and to get us to go into the population so they could make a play. Milton and Robard had many contacts in the inmate population, the warden told us, so who knew what their next move would have been. A riot, more hostages, a mass prison break.

I Miranda-ed Rocco 'Jack' Milton in the parking lot of Sing Sing. For both business and pleasure, I made sure to do it right in front of Steve Reno and his men before opening the rear door of my cruiser and shoving him in.

Reno left in a paddy wagon filled with the rest of the suspected hijackers. Kenny 'Little John' Robard was on the way to the hospital with a fractured skull. I couldn't help hoping the EMTs took the long way.

I stood outside for a moment, figuring out how to play things. Then I retrieved something in the trunk of my cruiser before I climbed behind the wheel to drive Jack to New York City.

Funny as it sounds, a lot of suspects are dying to tell you what they've done. And the more full of themselves, the more they want to give you the dirty details. I had a feeling Jack was pretty fond of himself.

I stayed silent for the first part of our trip back to Manhattan and let his annoyance build. 'Comfy back there?' was about all I asked. 'Temperature okay?'

'Did you know,' Jack finally said, 'that in the summer of 'ninety-five, four guards were taken hostage out on Rikers? Did you know that, Bennett?'

I glanced at him through the mesh behind me.

'Is that right?' I said.

'Only two of us made it out.'

'You and Little John?' I said.

'On the money as usual, Mike,' Jack said. 'You ever think about trying out for *Jeopardy!*? Suffice it to say that nobody gave a crap about a few corrections officers, especially the mayor.'

'So that's why you killed him? Why you stabbed him? Burned him with cigarettes?'

Jack scratched his chin ponderously. 'Between you and me?' he said.

'I wouldn't have it any other way,' I said, smiling back at him.

'You better believe it,' he said. 'The animals who'd gotten their hands on us blinded one of my buddies with a butter knife and put out cigarettes on *our* arms. Wouldn't you know it, Hizzoner decided he was above negotiating with the inmates on that one. Guess some men are created a little more equal than others. You know, it's funny. I didn't see the mayor by my dead buddy's widow at the funeral either. Guess you have to be a smoke eater or a flatfoot like you to get that kind of special treatment.'

I nodded neutrally. I wanted Jack to keep talking, something he liked to do anyway.

'When my post-traumatic-stress disability claim was denied by the city for the third time, I decided, to hell with it, I'm done. I was going to pull off something large, or die trying. The St Pat's idea came to me when I moonlighted as security at the state funeral for the previous cardinal. I thought it was going to be so impenetrable, with the legendary Secret Service and all, but I found out what a joke it was. Like the rest of the security assholes, those guys were soft, all show.'

'What about the other jackers? Your coworkers?' I said. 'How'd you convince them to go along?'

'Convince them?' Jack said. 'I don't know about you New York's Finest, but being a guard chews you up. We're inside the belly of the beast, too, and we didn't do nothing to get there. Put shit pay on top of that, divorce and suicide rates in the stratosphere, and hassle from the bosses, you got a gourmet recipe for disaster. Ever get feces thrown in your face? Not good for a man's general well-being.'

'Sounds heartbreaking,' I said. 'But executing the First Lady, the mayor, a priest, and John Rooney because you were stressed out? That might be a hard sell to a judge.'

Jack didn't seem to have heard me. He was staring off at the side of the road. The setting sun through the leafless trees made a bar code of shadow and light on the curving asphalt.

'We did it for each other,' he said quietly. 'Go ahead

and put us back in jail. Won't matter. I've already been there for the last fifteen years. Guards do life just like prisoners, only we do it in eight-hour shifts.'

'If doing life is what you're worried about, then I got good news,' I told the cop-killer as I clicked off the tape recorder I had running in the pocket of my Windbreaker.

'I'll do everything in my power to see you get the death penalty, Jack.'

Chapter One Hundred and Fourteen

It was eight o'clock and dark when I pulled to the curb down the block from a small house on Delafield Avenue in the posh Riverdale section of the Bronx, just a few blocks from Manhattan College, where I'd learned to reason, analyze, and be a better person.

Five minutes before, we had finalized our plan at a rally point in the parking lot of a Food Emporium two blocks away. Steve Reno and his guys were already set up in the neighborhood. We had the house surrounded and wired for video and sound.

It was time to pick up the final and most putrid bag of garbage.

The inside man. The one Jack called 'the Neat Man.'

According to one of our snipers perched on the backyard wall, our suspect was inside on the ground floor right now, finishing up dinner with his family. Prime rib of beef with the works – brown gravy, mashed potatoes, white asparagus, reported the sniper.

'Car coming from the south,' I said into the radio as a blue Lincoln passed my position. I saw the airport taxi placard in its side window as it slowed before our target's house.

'Looks like our boy's ride is here,' I said. 'Where is he now in the house?'

'Just went upstairs,' said the sniper.

'What's he doing up there?' I said.

'Washing his hands,' the sniper said after a pause. 'Okay. He's finished. Coming downstairs.'

'Heads up, Steve,' I said into my Motorola. 'On me. I'm going in.' I climbed out of my car. This was going to be good. I *hoped*.

'Get another fare,' I told the taxi hack with a flash of my badge as I stopped in front of the neat, narrow brick steps to the house. 'His flight just got cancelled.'

I rang the doorbell and crouched to the side behind a meticulously clipped hedge. There was a small glazed window beside the door, and down the hall I could see a woman and three kids cleaning up the dining-room table with practiced efficiency.

I guess they hadn't been invited to Costa Rica with dear old Dad.

A form passed the window and I drew my Glock. Then the front door opened slowly.

Struggling with a bulky carry-on and a black Tumi suitcase, Paul Martelli had a puzzled expression as he watched the airport limo pull away down the block without him. That's when I stepped out from my spot beside the hedge.

'Paul, how are ya?' I said. 'Funny seeing you here like this. I was just talking to a friend of yours. Jack. He sends his regards.'

I watched a terrible flicker in the FBI negotiator's eyes. A tremor seemed to suddenly affect his right hand holding the suitcase, the one nearest to a still-holstered nine millimeter.

I showed him the Glock I was already holding beside my leg – as three sniper laser dots suddenly danced on his chest like a squadron of angry red bees.

'That would be some very poor decision-making there, Paul,' I told him, 'going for that nine. But I'd like to see you try. Give it a shot, Neat Man.'

Chapter One Hundred
and Fifteen

'I wa-wa-want a lawyer,' Paul Martelli said when he
was handcuffed to the leg of my squad room desk
about half an hour later in Manhattan.

The cool, calm demeanor I remembered from
outside St Pat's seemed to have taken a long bathroom break. The man's hands were shaking, and circles
of sweat had formed beneath the sleeves of his crisp
blue dress shirt. There was an army of Feds out in the
hall, waiting to get their crack at him, but not until I
was done.

There was one thing I needed him to clear up for me.

Jack had already told me most of it. How he and
Martelli had become fast friends after the Rikers Island
hostage situation. How they found that they shared
an undying contempt for the system; how they felt
their pathetic pay was beneath them.

Martelli had been the inside man during the siege.

He was the mastermind working behind the scenes, pushing our buttons. Literally having written the book on the subject, he knew what our reactions would be. Plus, he could influence what we did.

'I don't have to explain to you how the game works, do I, Paul? Cooperation is the only thing that can save any of you losers,' I said. 'Right now, the music's still playing, but I'll give you a little tip. The seats are almost full.'

Martelli sat there blinking and sweating. I could almost see the thoughts shifting through his head. His right knee began to jump suddenly.

'I'll tell you whatever you need to know on one condition,' he said.

'What's that?' I said.

'This place is filthy dirty,' the FBI agent said. 'I need a moist towelette. I'm nervous, Mike.'

'How was the First Lady killed?' I said after I tossed him a lemon-scented one from under the take-out menus inside my desk drawer. Martelli didn't speak again until he was finished meticulously scrubbing his face and hands. He seemed to have calmed down considerably, too.

'Alvarez did her,' he said.

'Jose Alvarez?' I said. 'The hijacker who was killed at the dealership during the escape?'

'Actually, his cousin Julio,' said Martelli. 'We had a pretty tall order,' he went on, staring at the back of my computer monitor. 'In order to get a state funeral going, we needed to kill somebody high-profile and make it look like an accident. For months, I pored over potential targets. When I read about the First Lady's allergy and her and the former president's annual holiday meal at L'Arène, I figured we had it solved. We all put our heads together; then we made our pact. Julio quit his guard job and got a prep-cook job at L'Arène. When the president and First Lady came in, he put peanut oil in her foie gras in the kitchen.'

'So it was all over money?' I asked the FBI agent.

'We can't all be Boy Scouts like you, Mr Mom,' the negotiator said, looking me in the eyes for the first time. 'Of course it was about money. Ring up those rich-and-famous assholes we kidnapped. They'll tell you straight up. If they take your call, that is. Money's what makes this dirty world go round, Mike.'

I looked away from Martelli in disgust. A young FBI agent with a wife and two small kids had been killed during the standoff, and it was obvious Martelli couldn't care less.

But I could see panic start in Martelli's eyes as I motioned at the door and the Feds walked in for him.

'You wouldn't happen to have another Wet-Nap for the road there, Mike?' he said quickly.

I opened the desk drawer for a millisecond, then slammed it shut.

'Wouldn't you know it,' I said. 'I'm fresh out.'

SAINTS

Chapter One Hundred and Sixteen

Though it was freezing cold and windy, the sun was shining as we Bennetts resolutely made our way through the stone-walled entrance to Riverside Park on Saturday morning a week later. Beyond the bare trees, the Hudson River, *our river* as Maeve used to call it, looked like an endless field of molten silver.

It didn't take very long for me to find the orange-taped stake. My darling wife and I had carefully placed it at the edge of a meadow overlooking the water just three months before.

I put down the oak sapling I was carrying on one shoulder and lifted the stake. I glanced at my oldest son. Brian nodded and stabbed the spade he was holding into the earth.

We all took turns. I had to help with Shawna and Chrissy, but Trent insisted on taking his turn by himself. I finally placed the sapling into the hole we'd made. Then I got down on my knees and started pushing the dirt back in with my hands. Pretty soon, I had a lot of help. All of us were down on the ground, hands buried in the fresh dirt.

I stood up finally, staring at the baby tree silently, feeling the cold, moist wind on my mud-covered hands. A tugboat, chugging lazily north on the river, seemed to be making the only sound on the earth.

I remembered watching the sun go down on a late picnic we'd had in summer the year before. Before the cancer, the last time things were really right. The kids catching fireflies as I rested my chin on Maeve's shoulder, the sky turning aqua and gold. I could feel her now as I stood there without her, the weight of Maeve against me, the way an amputee feels a lost limb, a phantom pain in the heart.

'Mommy's present to us,' Chrissy said finally, patting the slender tree trunk gently. 'Right, Daddy?'

'That's right, Chrissy,' I said, scooping up the baby and putting her on my shoulders. 'Ever since you were little, this was Mommy's favorite place in the world to take you guys. She told me that anytime you wanted to think about her or talk to her, she wanted you to be able to come here, or just look out your window at this spot and think of her.'

I held Julia's and Bridget's hands and gathered our

family in a circle around the small tree. I was aware of the single earring I still wore in my left lobe, and would always wear, whatever the fashion, whatever my age.

'Mom brought us all together,' I said, looking at my kids' faces one at a time. 'So as long as we stay together, she'll always be with us.'

I felt more than heard Chrissy start to cry as we were leaving across the grassy meadow. I lifted my daughter down from my shoulders and cradled her in my arms as she cried.

'What is it, honey?' I said.

'Baby Peep misses Mommy Peep,' she said inconsolably. 'So much. So much.'

'I know,' I said, trying and failing to dry her tears and mine at the same time. The wind picked up, drew lines across the still river, painted icicles on our wet cheeks.

'Daddy Peep does too,' I said.

Now you can buy any of these other bestselling books by **James Patterson** from your bookshop *or direct from his publisher.*

FREE P&P AND UK DELIVERY
(Overseas and Ireland £3.50 per book)

Miracle on the 17th Green *(with Peter de Jonge)*	£7.99
Suzanne's Diary for Nicholas	£6.99
The Beach House *(with Peter de Jonge)*	£6.99
The Jester *(with Andrew Gross)*	£6.99
The Lake House	£6.99
Sam's Letters to Jennifer	£6.99
Honeymoon *(with Howard Roughan)*	£6.99
Lifeguard *(with Andrew Gross)*	£6.99
Beach Road *(with Peter de Jonge)*	£6.99
Judge and Jury *(with Andrew Gross)*	£6.99

Alex Cross series

Cat and Mouse	£6.99
Pop Goes the Weasel	£6.99
Roses are Red	£6.99
Violets are Blue	£6.99
Four Blind Mice	£6.99
The Big Bad Wolf	£6.99
London Bridges	£7.99
Mary, Mary	£6.99
Cross	£6.99

Women's Murder Club series

1st to Die	£6.99
2nd Chance *(with Andrew Gross)*	£6.99
3rd Degree *(with Andrew Gross)*	£6.99
4th of July *(with Maxine Paetro)*	£6.99
The 5th Horseman *(with Maxine Paetro)*	£6.99

Maximum Ride series

Maximum Ride: The Angel Experiment	£6.99
Maximum Ride: School's Out Forever	£6.99

TO ORDER SIMPLY CALL THIS NUMBER

01235 400 414

or visit our website: www.headline.co.uk
Prices and availability subject to change without notice.